Enchantment

Enchantment

NEW AND SELECTED STORIES

Thaisa Frank

COUNTERPOINT

BERKELEY

The following stories have been previously published, some in different forms: "Poland," "Dream Envy," "The Cat Lover," "The Terrain of Madame Blavatsky," "The Eye of the Needle," "Milagros," "The Dungeon Master's Mother," "Stairway to the Stars," "In the Middle of the Night," "Silver," "Rossetti's Closet," "The White Coat," "Sleeping in Velvet," "The Mapmaker," "Stories We Began to Tell," "The Mole," "The New Thieves," "Using the Car for Business," "The Second Husband," "Hyperventilation," "Buying a Rug in Esquares," "Postcards," "Soulmates," "A Brief History of Camouflage," "Night Visits."

Library of Congress Cataloging-in-Publication Data is available

ISBN: 978-1-58243-810-8

Cover design by Nina Tara
Interior design by Domini Dragoone

Counterpoint
1919 Fifth Street
Berkeley, CA 94710
www.counterpointpress.com

Distributed by Publishers Group West

Printed in the United States of America

10 9 8 7 6 5 4 3 2 1

FOR KEITH. . . . .

the best of enchanters

Acknowledgements

VERSIONS OF SOME of these stories appeared in Gargoyle, The City Lights Review, The New Review, Fourteen Hills, Able Muse, and The Barnabus Review. Other stories appeared in Sleeping in Velvet and A Brief History of Camouflage, published by Black Sparrow Press. The author is grateful to the editors of all these publications, with particular gratitude to John Martin, publisher of Black Sparrow Press.

Contents

Enchantment

Thread

I HOPE YOU once saw our act. We twined our bodies together and passed through the eye of an enormous needle. It was a splendid twelve-foot needle mounted on a high silver ladder with an eye that was four feet wide. Two threaders, Mariposa and Antoine, stood on opposite ladders to guide us through. But we always had to twist. We studied two-ply thread. Hours with a magnifying glass. We recreated its properties.

During the act we wore soft clothes: velour leotards that made us feel naked. Our faces were white and covered with silver stars. After the act we went to our trailer and ate cantaloupes, prosciutto, bread, cheese, whatever we wanted from the circus kitchen. Igaz read what he called chick magazines—big magazines with glossy covers, horoscopes, and fashion tips. I read Icelandic sagas: They were the only books I'd kept when I quit linguistics.

Later we made love in the built-on bed. Igaz stroked me carefully, one hand on a vertebrae, a finger on my nipple. Again the ignition between our skin. Once more we went through the needle.

WE ALWAYS DELIGHTED audiences. They were tense before we went through, and they clapped and cheered when we came out. But seven nights ago, Carrogen was there. Carrogen is my ex-lover and the owner of the circus. He had just come back from Paris where La Belle Madeleine, who moved like a snake, didn't want to be a contortionist with his circus—or his lover. This put him in a bad mood, and the night he came back he sat in the last tier in the audience, wearing a bright red scarf. When Igaz and I stepped into the silver ring, Carrogen caught my eye, and an arc of light passed between us. Igaz caught the arc.

He looked at you, he hissed.

He didn't look at me at all, I answered.

We climbed up the ladder and couldn't go through the needle. Antoine and Mariposa pulled and pulled and pulled. We remained two stubborn bodies and had to climb down the ladder. Massimo the clown saved the day by punishing us. He lifted us up to the tall Renaissance clock and bumped our heads against the minute hand. Then he threw water on our feet and chased us from the ring.

We blew it, Igaz whispered in my ear.

WE DIDN'T GO to the dressing room but walked back to the trailer in our costumes. I sliced melon for prosciutto and asked Igaz if he wanted to share some brandy.

No, he said, beer's for me. He crouched on the tiny bed and put on a T-shirt. Then he sat at the table and opened a bottle.

So what was it like with you and Carrogen? Igaz said. His face was still covered with stars. When he leaned over to drink, some disappeared in the ridge around his chin.

What do you mean?

You know what I mean.

It was like: Nothing. Not the way it is with us. You know that Carrogen liked men. There used to be two clowns besides Massimo— Hermes Papdoupalous and Claudio Ricatelli. He brought all three of them to bed twice.

Did you like them? said Igaz.

I did for a while and then I didn't. Anyway, it was only twice.

And what was it like without the clowns?

Just okay. I've told you.

Well Carrogen put his eye on you. And you fell out from the act. I saw you fall like a hat from a window. That happened to me once when I was twelve and I got breakaway in soccer. My father was in the crowd. He was the only one wearing a long coat and a hat with a brim. And he caught my eye and I slipped. It was the only time I ever got breakaway.

You told me that.

Well I'm telling you again.

WE HEARD A thud outside our trailer.

Jesus Christ, said Igaz. He went outside and brought in a rattan hamper filled with white-fleshed peaches and a note from Carrogen that said, *Remember that a circus should be a perfect Renaissance clock, with demons appearing on the half hours, sword-eaters, tumblers, clowns, fire-eaters, and ne'er-do-wells on the quarter, and divine interventions at noon and at midnight. Better luck next time.*

Igaz took a peach and ate it with a sucking sound. He doesn't wish me luck, he said. He never wanted me in the act.

His mouth was full of peach when he talked. I didn't look at it.

Don't think about it, I said. Everyone flubs in the circus. But not because someone put his eye on you.

A flub is a flub.

He spent a fortune over these peaches, Igaz said.

He didn't. He got them from the kitchen.

I TOOK ONE. The smell was more pungent than the taste. Then I saw the pearls at the bottom of the hamper. They were draped over some peaches, deep grey with a diamond clasp, glinting like something at the bottom of the sea. I lifted them up and put them on.

What a bastard, said Igaz. He fished around in the hamper and pulled out a dark green wrapper. They're from that Hungarian jeweler with a name like mine. Igezni. The meaning of enchant.

Does every Hungarian name start with an *ig*?

What does it matter? They're popular letters.

I looked in the mirror and saw the pearls around my neck. The grey was the color of the dust Marcus the Circus Master scatters on the ring. I felt beautiful and duplicitous. Igaz went to the corner where he keeps his weights and lifted one.

Look how I lifted this thing. Like a feather!

You look like a statue.

No way! I'm good blood.

I meant, I said, that you look close to the earth.

Igaz kept his body frozen and lifted more weights. I crawled into bed. I could see the cross from his father's grave smack on the wall in front of us. It was tarnished pewter with a wheat shaft stuck behind it.

I wish you wouldn't keep that there, I said. It's creepy.

You were born with a silver spoon in your mouth. You don't need traditions.

What do you mean?

I mean your old man taught history at Yale. I mean your house was like a library.

IGAZ LIFTED MORE weights, then got into bed and stared at the cross until he fell asleep. When he began to snore, I felt the same claustrophobia I'd felt with Carrogen and the clowns when they began to decline to fuck in Latin. Igaz started to talk in his sleep. What is the order of night? He asked. And then, as if answering, he said Hungarian words I'd come to recognize. *Félénk*, shame-faced. *Vétek*, sin. They were lonely words, followed by a string of sentences I couldn't understand.

I went outside and sat on the wide trailer steps. In a few minutes, Rose the Fire Eater came out from the trailer opposite mine. Then Olaf the Interchangeable Man appeared. We all sat on our separate steps, not talking. After about an hour, Olaf pantomimed sleep by clasping his hands to one side and putting his head against them. We all went into our separate trailers.

WHEN I WOKE up, Igaz was eating pudding stuffed with raisins and poppy seeds.

I made it for consoling myself, he said. I couldn't sleep so I went to the kitchen and talked to the baker. He hadn't heard what we couldn't do.

No one heard, I said. No one even remembers. Anyway, we should rehearse.

I got up and splashed cold water on my face. Igaz noticed the pearls.

You wore those all night, he said, leaning over and touching them. You wore them all night. Like those movie stars with diamonds of De Beers.

He touched the pearls and covered them with white pudding shot with black poppy seeds.

Look what you did, I said.

I was just touching of them, said Igaz.

Not *of*, I said. Just touching.

Okay. Be fancy. Igaz watched while I wiped each pearl. I told him we should rehearse. We have to get back on the horse, I said.

OUTSIDE THE AIR melted with summer heat. I tugged at Igaz, and we walked to the big tent where there were stilts and hoops and cables and swords and nets and banners that said *Le Cirque d'Horloge* and the enormous Renaissance clock from which we all take bows.

What if Carrogen rigged that needle up so we can't go through it? said Igaz.

I'd wondered, too, and was already climbing the ladder so I could touch the huge metal eye. But Carrogen hadn't done a thing. I could see the whole tent through it.

Everything's the same, I said.

Not them pearls. They're real.

THERE WAS A red and gold quilt in the sawdust. We sat on it, and I thought we might make love and didn't care if we were caught. Igaz and I had once made love in Carrogen's trailer when Carrogen and I were still living together. One of the clowns spied through the window and asked if we could be a threesome.

I touched Igaz's shoulders.

Our skin knows about the act, I said.

It doesn't, he said. And he brushed me off with a story about his father who had been a soccer player in Hungary and got an injury that fused one hand into kind of a claw. His mother thought this was a sign they should leave and the family came to America where his father became a baker and his mother did bookkeeping.

They were true in themselves, he said. *Igaz* means true in Hungarian.

He'd told me the story before, but I didn't mind, and I didn't tell him the correct phrase was *true to themselves*. Each time I heard the story, I could see his family in a warm, lit kitchen, sitting around a table: The calm breath of his mother. The bitter eyes of his father. The dutiful face of his sister. Igaz in his undershirt pretending to do math but really working the books for a high school casino. The family canned preserves, stuffed sausages, baked bread. Their lives were knit together like a fairy tale.

Let's get Mariposa and Antoine so we can practice, I said.

No, said Igaz. I want to go to church. The confessor can tell me if Carrogen gave you the eye.

What does he know?

Nothing. But he can tell what I imagined.

Wherever we go, Igaz finds churches. In the last city it was a small Ukrainian cathedral with a painted red door, a cerulean dome, brilliant stained glass. Inside women in kerchiefs were praying. I met a big-boned woman in jeans who said to me, Isn't it *awesome?*

Go, I said, if that's how you feel about it.

HE LEFT AND I sat in the sawdust and looked at the clock, which was a duplicate of a famous clock in an Austrian village. The clock was Carrogen's idea. Everybody had to bow on different hours, even the cooks. Igaz and I bowed at six, a number I considered unlucky. The favorite clowns got seven, four, and nine. Olaf the Interchangeable Man bowed at every quarter hour. Rosie the Fire Eater got eight. The Circus Master bowed at noon. Carrogen bowed at midnight. I thought of how he liked to wind things, and wondered if the pearls were artificial, something he'd gotten at the flea market. I wondered if he'd invented the House of Igezni. But when I found its address in the phone book, I asked for a circus car and drove to the heart of the city. I'd been to this city twice before and remembered its wide boulevards and shops with arched windows. I wondered how long I'd stay with the circus and how many times I'd see this city again.

THE HOUSE OF Igezni had a chocolate brown carpet. The jewels were in mahogany cases like bones in a museum. As soon as I walked in, men and women in white shirts and dark slacks gathered around me.

How can we help? They said in slight accents, looking at the pearls.

I said I couldn't work the clasp, and they swarmed around the back of my neck and unclasped the pearls. A bald man with a jeweler's glass came out. He had a shrewd and intelligent face.

There's nothing wrong with the clasp, he said. Do you know what *Igezni* means?

Yes. It means to enchant.

Well we enchant, but we don't deceive. Those came from the Cook Islands.

So they're real.

What do you want me to do? Bite them? You can only do that with gold. This is the House of Igezni. We don't sell anything fake.

WHILE WE TALKED, Carrogen knocked on the window. He was wearing his red scarf, even in the summer heat, and looked amused. I came out, and we walked down the street in step. Our reflections shone in the buildings, and I remembered Carrogen once saying, We are a *natural* couple! As if it were decreed. I was aware of his height and narrow shoulders. I also saw how he put his attention on me, unlike Igaz who gawked at women and garbage pails and shop windows and careened down the street.

Those pearls look good on you, said Carrogen.

I don't know why you bought them.

It was a whim. Like the automatic flues. I want to do those again. He pulled out a green velvet notebook and jotted something down.

We went to a store that sold ices. It was marble and cool inside. I ordered lemon ice; Carrogen had a coffee granita. He threw back his scarf. I noticed his red-gold mustache and his gold watch glittering on his wrist. We talked about adding pneumatic fountains, like the one we'd once seen in Russia that imitated ducks and geese. Carrogen said he was disappointed about his trip to Paris.

I gave that Madeleine a box of soap, but she didn't like them. She's stuffy, even if she's a brilliant cobra. They were hand milled and they came in a wooden box. They smelled like lavender. Maybe I'll get you some.

It's as though we'd slipped into an earlier time and could go back to our trailer and lie on the wrought-iron bed with white pillows. Carrogen took my hand.

About last night, he said. I'm afraid it didn't look very good.

You can't be thread on command.

It was Igaz. He's too big for the act. I saw him the minute he lost it.

I don't think so, Carrogen. I think he saw you look at me. You broke your way inside us.

I always look at you. What does he read, by the way? Those women's magazines.

What do *you* read? A few detective stories. Books about extravaganzas?

I know what he reads, said Carrogen. Those women's magazines. With the horoscopes and the gossip. He must be boring.

You're a meddler. You always were. Are you disappointed about Madeleine? Give these to her. Maybe she'll join the circus.

I took off the pearls and pushed them across the table.

No, said Carrogen, shoving the pearls back like a deck of cards. What Madeleine doesn't want, she doesn't get. Now come with me. The cooks need a new butcher block for the kitchen.

No, I said.

I put the pearls in my purse and left.

WHEN I CAME back, the trailer was lit with candles. Igaz was with Rosie the Fire Eater, who was reading his fortune with Tarot cards. One of his parents' old Hungarian records was playing—gypsy music with fragile violins. When the music got wild, Igaz said it was the soul of Hungary and the violins were like branches waving in the wind. Rose spoke softly and kept notes.

Oh my, she said. There are a lot of knights in this fortune.

What's that? said Igaz.

Serious matters, said Rosie. Or it could be about your father. And possibly good fortune. You can turn anything upside down.

While they talked, I looked around the room. I didn't know how we lived, the two of us, with so much dead time in all that clutter. I took out *Nils Saga* and was pulled into a sense of something old, durable, and repeatable. Rosie left, I asked what the fortune was about, and Igaz said it was bleak, very bleak.

Besides, you were with Carrogen. Massimo told me.

I tried to give him the pearls. He wouldn't take them.

So you have them.

I suppose I do, I said.

I scraped some pudding out of the bowl. Poppy seeds crunched in my mouth.

What do you call this? I asked.

Püding, said Igaz, pronouncing the word in an odd way.

Püding, I said. Is that all?

What? You think everything is with a z or a t? Igaz turned up the music and lifted a weight.

We Hungarians are a sad people, he said. You can hear it of our music. We've never been in charge of our country. The trees are sad. The branches are sad.

I told him he was being sentimental. He said he was going to see the confessor. I said I thought he'd already been.

I went to the diner instead. I had pancakes that laid very heavy on my stomach. I must have known you were with him.

I wanted to find out if the pearls were real. I went to Igezni. I met him by accident. You never dived. You worked on the docks.

I did dive. I dived in the sea. In a life different of this one.

From, I wanted to say. Not different *of*. Different *from*. But I knew he would say: Of. From. What does it matter? I know my life.

AFTER HE LEFT, I ate another peach and looked at Rosie's notes from the fortune: *Arrival, approach, advances, proposition, demeanor, invitation, incitement, trickery, artifice, swindling, fraud*—one good thing melding into something less good and reversing itself. I read more of *Nils Saga* and remembered going to Iceland with another man, riding a jeep over moonscapes, falling asleep past midnight when the sun was out. I wondered idly if I'd ever go again, then decided I wanted to go again. It began to get dark, then darker. I blew out the candles, turned on the light, picked up clothes and a spoon covered with pudding. Every moment I thought I would see Igaz's big face looming in the door. At last I put on my leotard and walked to the makeup tent alone, holding my slippers. As soon as I opened the door, everyone looked at me.

Where's Igaz? asked Sid the makeup artist. He was lifting a handful of golden comets for Olaf in his incarnation as a deity.

Where's Igaz? The makeup artist asked again.

At church.

For what?

For praying.

I painted my face white and pinned on a silver tiara. The makeup artist sprinkled me with silver stars. And all at once people began to ask where Igaz was as if they'd never heard me say he was at church. The trapeze artist asked and the sword swallower asked and even Olaf asked. Soon his name was everywhere—*Igaz, Igaz, Igaz*—like bees swarming at the top of the tent. In the midst of the buzzing, the door opened. It was Carrogen. He walked to my makeup table, and everyone was quiet and pretended to turn away and brush dust from their costumes. Carrogen leaned toward me. His red scarf fell from his dark blue suit and swept over the makeup table.

You'll go through the needle alone, he said.

I looked in the mirror. Carrogen's blue suit was in back of my tiara like night in a starry sky.

You're unfair, I said.

I run a business.

I CAME TO the ring alone and was dazzled by the silver floor. Without Igaz, it was slippery like stones at low tide. I climbed the ladder and saw a thin wire across the middle of the needle's eye. It was cut precisely in half.

You bastard, I thought, sending the thought to Carrogen. *You made it smaller without telling me.* I paused, then felt myself separate and realign.

Antoine eased me into the upper half of the eye. Mariposa held my feet. I twisted and turned and became a piece of two-ply thread, winding around myself as I went through. A current jolted inside of me. The crowd applauded. Massimo did cartwheels.

BACKSTAGE, CARROGEN SAID I was splendid.

I don't want to talk to you, I said. And fuck your clock.

I slipped from his arms and walked off wearing my slippers. I could hear them tearing on the asphalt. I liked the sound of the rip.

In the trailer, I found a note from Igaz.

I just don't think I can do it. I need your attention on me except it's on Carrogen. He's diverting of you. He wants you back. I told you we Hungarians have been confused with the Huns because we always shoot in retreat.

Everything was gone. Igaz's clothes. His weights. The record player. Even the magazines. I looked around the room. It seemed smaller for what it was missing. I put on the pearls and sat on the wide trailer steps. How big the night seemed. How ordinary for the likes of a circus.

Enchantment

S HE WAS ABLE to open the box as soon as the shipping company left because the children were still in school. He was encased in bubble-wrap like a mummy, and when the wrappings came off, he looked just like the catalog had promised: dark velvet britches, a green jerkin, and a blouse with billowing sleeves. His blond hair fell across his face, and he was handsome in spite of an overbite. He was surrounded in a nimbus of light.

She saw a cream-colored note pinned to his jerkin: *Hello*, it said, *my name is Lars and I come from an undisclosed castle in England. If you follow the instructions, I am yours forever:*

Mist me twice a day.

Do not probe, fondle, or startle me.

Keep me in low light.

Never kiss me anywhere.

Keep me hidden from your family.

The note was signed *courtesy of The Wondrous Traveler*, the online site where she'd ordered the enchanted man. In the doorway, she waved at a mother who was guiding her two-year-old on a lavender-colored bike and stuffed the note in a pocket of her jeans. Then she shut the front door and dragged Lars and his box to her studio. It was next to the living room and a hodge-podge of computers, digital cameras, tripods, old cameras, and developing trays. The box was so long she was afraid it would look like a casket and was relieved when it looked just like a shipping crate on the floor. She tacked up old blackout curtains and looked at Lars.

Marsh light came from his body and cast the room in a haze so objects went in and out of focus. She saw phosphorescent papers, an illuminated wastebasket. The light from his body was the same light that people poured into the world every day—lavishly unthinkingly, as they went about their lives—so by the time they went to sleep it was all used up. But, as The Wondrous Traveler explained so carefully, enchanted people accrued this light because they hadn't done anything for at least one hundred years.

This had all been explained when she placed her order over the phone. A real voice had answered. And was kind. What color hair did she want? She chose blond. What country would she like? She chose England.

AT DINNER HER husband, whose name was Bradford, said:

You got something from The Wondrous Traveler again, didn't you? Is it one of those garden hoes with fake rust? Or a banyan-tree birdhouse from Guatemala?

He was drinking wine from a wineglass with a long bowl that made it easier for him to sniff the nose. Their children, Justin and Philomena, were picking at their food. Philomena was fourteen, had a ring through her left eyebrow and an orange streak through her hair.

Justin was sixteen and stared like psychic teenagers in movies who disassemble factories with their third eye.

How do you know I got anything? she asked.

Bradford said she'd left wrapping paper on the porch, and she said she'd gotten a new table for her photography studio. They looked at each other irritably because they each had different ideas about spending money. Philomena and Justin knew the look and made eyes at each other. Then Justin said:

Do you know how chickens are raised?

It's not a discussion for the table, she said.

Especially when we're eating one, said Philomena. •

Well they cut off their beaks, said Justin. And when an egg-laying chicken is born a male, they just put it in a bag and grind it up for compost.

Gross, said Philomena. She pushed away her plate, siding with Justin.

They don't even call them chickens anymore, Justin said. They're so genetically altered the breeds get numbers.

That's an urban legend, said Bradford.

Urban legend my ass, whispered Philomena

You are so not with it, said Justin.

She looked at Philomena's orange hair and smoke-colored eyeliner and at Justin's mangy beard and demonic stare. She could see nothing of what her children had once been.

Bradford lifted his nose from the wineglass.

Did it occur to you that your mother and I actually worked to pay for this chicken? he asked.

Philomena shrugged. Justin said:

The chicken worked harder.

After dinner, she sat in the living room and read the brochure that came with the package. It had a section called *Frequently Asked Questions about Enchantment.* She hid it in a copy of *People* magazine and began to read:

Q. *What is enchantment?*

A. Enchantment is a state of such prolonged sleep the enchanted person isn't part of the world. This is why—in the unlikely event they wake up—enchanted people are always the same age they were when they were first enchanted.

Q. What causes enchantment?

A. A powerful ill-willed glance from one pair of eyes to another. This glance shocks the victim who travels to other realms. It can never come from incantations or spells.

Q. *Who is able to enchant?*

A. Anyone who is miserable and/or vengeful. In the seventeenth century book *The Anatomy of Melancholy,* Robert Burton says that evil tutors are notorious for casting spells on their students.

Q. Can enchantment happen to me?

A. No. The last recorded case was in 1867. Radio waves, satellite waves, and cell phones all interfere with the power of evil eyes.

This would have made Bradford happy because he was launching a project to supply people all over the world with cellular phones. The tag line was *Only connect,* which he'd taken from E. M. Forester. She'd recently said, thoughtlessly, that no person in Uzbekistan would understand what that meant, but Bradford said of course they'd understand: Connection was always happening in the air.

She looked at him now, deep in Mahjong. At one point he'd taught college English, but he got tired of not making money and now said Mahjong was his only way of relaxing. He looked back at her, and she smothered herself in *People* magazine. Enchanted women were rare, according to the brochure. They were never put on the market and were allowed to stay in their castles.

After she finished reading, she went to her studio. It looked like her old darkroom because of the blackout curtains except it was brimming with light, night skies, and opulence. Paperweights were stars, grocery lists diamonds. She wondered if Lars really had achieved a state of wanting and needing nothing. If this were true, it wouldn't matter if she talked to him. She leaned close to him and said:

Lars. You're safe with me. I'm here to take care of you.

Lars stirred. The light stirred with him, flickering over her hands. She leaned closer and said:

I love you.

More light. More flickering. She noticed he wore a codpiece and wondered what scullery maids he'd found in the hay, what princesses in curtained beds. She ran her lips a few inches over his mouth.

There was a knock on the door. It was Philomena saying she was sorry about the chicken, she knew they had to eat. And then Justin said the same thing. Sometimes, without warning, they acted kind. She almost wished they wouldn't so she could dislike them permanently and give up any hope that they'd be nice again. She spoke to them through the door.

THE FOURTH TIME she came upstairs to bed, Bradford asked if she'd drunk a gallon of water because she kept going to the bathroom. No, she said, she just couldn't sleep. He pulled her to him and said she felt like an armored car because she was wearing her sweater and jeans.

Let me help you take them off.

No, she said. I'm tense and cold.

Are you pissed because I asked about the table you ordered?

No. But the wedding I'm doing is depressing.

Bradford sighed. It was an old subject. They'd never gotten married because their previous weddings—two for her and one for him—had ended in divorce and another had seemed like a bad omen. It was a decision they'd both made, but from time to time—never at the same time—one of them had regrets. It was Bradford's turn.

Let's get married, he said.

I don't see how we could. Everyone thinks we are.

We'll tell them we're really not.

Philomena and Justin would get upset.

Just the two of us then. At City Hall.

That doesn't sound festive.

But would you *like* to get married?

Probably, she said.

What do you mean *probably*?

She couldn't bring herself to say she would like to anymore than she could bring herself to bring up persistent grievances that scratched at the back of her mind. She wished she could distract him by telling him about the decline of enchantment because of so many waves in the air. Airwaves helped his business. The news would please him. But suppose he asked for references? She said nothing and let him stroke her hair.

LARS BEGAN TO talk on the third day, after she had tasted the light above his lips for the sixth, or maybe the seventh, time. The light was fluid, ephemeral. It certainly wasn't a kiss. But she must have tasted one time too many because Lars sat up and said in a loud, clear voice:

I am real and ready in my heart.

What?

Real and ready in my heart.

Then he lay down again.

She tried to get him to repeat what he had said, but he closed his eyes and seemed to be in such a remote state she could call it neither sleep nor enchantment. She put a blanket over her worktable to block his light and developed pictures she'd taken of a recent wedding, one in which the bride's mother insisted she not take digital pictures for old time's sake. The bride rose from transparencies, and then the bridesmaids with large unfortunate bows and three sets of parents with strained smiles. When she was finished, she came out of the blanket and saw Lars sitting up, gesturing toward her bookcase.

What is that? he said.

A bookcase, she answered.

And that?

A lamp.

He looked confused.

Something like a candle.

All through that day, Lars pointed at things in the studio and asked what they were. She brought him a piece of paper. She brought him coins, an onion, a book, and herbs from the garden. At one point she noticed a pocket watch in his jerkin and asked him if he knew what it was. He looked worried and said he didn't know. She said *watch*, and he shook his head.

AT DINNER PHILOMENA and Justin talked about free-range chickens. Justin said they weren't really free, and Philomena said you had to log onto a special web site to find out which eggs were okay to buy.

Thank God we're not having egg salad for dinner, said Bradford.

He was drinking Sangiovese from his special wine glass and was unhappy because a country that committed to cellular phones didn't exist anymore.

How come? said Justin.

It split into different countries, said Bradford.

But doesn't each country want phones? said Justin.

Now they're part of some other country that already has them.

That's because the world is fucked up, said Philomena.

That's not a word for the table, she said.

Jeeze, said Philomena, it doesn't mean what it used to.

Then what *does* it mean? Bradford said.

Like totally out there and bad, said Justin.

DINNER TURNED INTO a fight about the phrase *fucked up*, and no one noticed when she went back to her studio. Lars was fast asleep, coursing in unknown realms. Light from his face played over carpet, the blinds. When she sat beside him, he opened his eyes and said:

What are those?

She was wearing black suede flats. She took one off and handed it to him.

Shoes, she said.

Shoes, said Lars.

And then she saw Bradford in the door and realized she'd forgotten to lock it.

Jesus Christ, he said. So this is what you're hiding.

Who is that? said Lars.

My husband, in a way.

What is a husband? said Lars.

That's what I'd like to know, said Bradford.

A partner, she said. Someone to live with.

And hide things from, said Bradford.

It's not what you think, she said.

Then what is it?

An enchanted man. He lived more than a hundred years ago.

Enchanted, my ass. He can talk.

Just a few words. And only now and then.

So it's come to this. You're in love with someone who's not even real.

Maybe none of us are real, she said.

Listen, Margaret, I don't want to get into any metaphysical crap with you. Every day I go into the world and pitch these phones. And what am I really pitching? Connection. That's what I'm pitching. And now and then some CEO breaks down and tells me how lonely they are and how they have to go home to frozen dinners by themselves. I believe in my product so much people trust me. And you bought yourself a sex doll.

Please, Brad. He's not a *doll*.

What is he then?

Under a spell.

As if to illustrate her point, Lars lay down in his box and closed his eyes. He looked less like an enchanted man than a dog that knows he's been banished.

You have to get rid of him, said Bradford.

It's not that easy.

Why not?

He doesn't know how to cope. He's from a different century.

Then I'm leaving.

You can't.

Then get rid of him.

But he can't take care of himself,

That's it. I'm packing.

What about the kids?

They can't take care of themselves either.

SHE FOLLOWED BRADFORD upstairs, where he pulled a weather-beaten suitcase from the closet and began to pack at random, throwing in one of their pillows. When he was finished, he sat on the bed and put his head in his hands.

Jesus, he said. I thought you loved me.

She wanted to say she did, but things were in the way, things she couldn't remember, followed by things she could—like Bradford not including her in his stock options because they weren't married or bugging Philomena and Justin to play a team sport when one liked running and the other aikido. More things occurred to her, and she didn't notice Bradford had locked the suitcase until he slammed it on the floor.

Why won't you get rid of him? he asked.

I told you: He can't cope.

Why did you get him in the first place?

I could make up a thousand reasons, but I don't know.

BRADFORD DROVE OFF in his old Mustang, leaving her the better car. She went back to Lars and talked to him, telling him she didn't want him to be upset. His eyes were closed, and he didn't answer. She sat with him through the night and came out of her studio to make breakfast for Justin and Philomena.

Is Dad really gone? said Justin.

Only for a while. We have some things to work out.

Like the guy in your studio?

There's no one in my studio.

But we saw him during that blowout, said Philomena. We thought you had a boyfriend.

Well I don't.

BRADFORD CAME BACK a few hours later with unkempt hair. He called in sick and lay on the living room sofa in a sleeping bag. He had a headache. She brought him an ice pack.

I've never called in sick before, he said. I've never called in sick a day in my life.

Brad, listen. We'll work it out.

How?

I don't know.

You don't *know?* And that's working it out?

I mean we'll find a way.

What's *a way?* What the fuck do you mean?

Soft sounds came from the studio. Lars opened the door,

My God, he can walk, said Bradford.

I've never seen him do that. I swear.

What do you think I am? said Bradford. A moron?

No. Not at all.

Well you act like you do.

He got up slowly and walked over to Lars, who looked fragile standing up, like wheat waving in the wind.

And what do *you* think? he said to him. Or are you a moron, too?

Lars looked at Bradford as though he were watching something far away. Finally he said:

I'm sorry I made you sad.

Sorry? said Bradford. You let them ship you in a box and you're sorry?

He sat on the floor and began to weep. Lars took the watch from his pocket and pressed it. She heard a buzzing sound.

What are you doing? she asked.

Calling The Wondrous Traveler.

But why?

I have to tell them I made someone sad.

But Lars, she said. Everyone gets sad. It's a part of life. You didn't do anything. You don't have to call.

I made a promise, said Lars.

She pleaded, but Lars shook his head and lay down in his box where the space above his head throbbed with light. She said his name many times, but he was either enchanted or pretending to be, and soon she got a phone call from a man speaking on behalf of The Wondrous Traveler. He said they understood she was having problems with one of their products and were concerned. She said she wasn't having any problems at all.

I think we should see the product ourselves. And it would be better if he were alone tonight, and you left the window open.

She spoke softly so Bradford wouldn't hear, and said she didn't want to leave the window open because Lars would get cold. But the voice went on with such authority she took down the blackout drapes and opened the window. Then she helped Bradford upstairs.

Margaret, he kept saying, this is our undoing.

It's not. We've gotten through worse things.

I can't think of anything worse.

I can.

She was going to list all the things, but Bradford said he wasn't able to hear them. She put the pillow he'd packed on his side of the bed and brought him a pot of tea.

THAT NIGHT SHE slept on the couch in the sleeping bag. She wanted to go to Lars, kiss him, hold him, and tell him she was sorry she'd woken him, but she was afraid that she would excite him or that one of the Wondrous Travelers would choose just that moment to appear in the window. All night she listened for sounds and heard nothing except the house settling into its foundations. But at dawn, Lars and his box were gone. All that remained were a few pieces of bubble-wrap, the instructions, and a note that said: *We are sorry this product was not completely satisfactory. You can expect a full refund according to our policy of return within thirty days. Sincerely, The Wondrous Traveler.*

She threw everything away, except for the sentence that said Lars would be hers forever. This she cut out carefully and taped on the wall. Later she might burn it or leave it in a corner of her studio until it was strangely lost, the way things disappear when they haven't gone away.

The Loneliness of the Midwestern Vampire

TONIGHT HE WILL fly for human blood. The clock in the hall is poised to start ticking. The empty coffins are raising their lids. And the orange moon is low, grazing above the prairie. He checks his hens to make sure they have grain. He brings hay to his cattle. They look at him obsequiously, happy to bare their necks. Not tonight, he says to them.

He's about to take leave when there's a knock on the door. It's Patsy Hardy who needs eggs for the bake-off. He goes to the straw-scented coop and brings her a basket. When her truck rumbles off, he soars into the air.

It's a hot summer night. The wheat below him looks like fire under the orange moon. He flies over the white church where Reverend Peak gives sermons. He flies over the creek where the children swim. And the town bar, glittering with yellow lights.

Most of his neighbors farm, so they have houses set far apart. In winter he sees smoke from the chimneys. In summer there are lights in the windows. Reverend and Mrs. Peak are already asleep—Mrs. Peak so large she nearly fills the bed, Reverend Peak clasping her, like a child holding a globe. Their daughter, Lorna Peak, is under the elm tree on a blanket with the Olmsted boy. Judge Greavey and his wife are watching television. His wife is eating a bowl of popcorn. The Judge is resting his squat neck against a pillow.

And now he sees Patsy Hardy get out of her truck and go back to her farmhouse. The moment she disappears, he swoops by the bedroom of their eldest daughter—the startlingly beautiful Alison, and one of the few neighbors he hasn't bitten in the last twenty years. Alison is wearing shorts and reading a book about veterinary medicine. Her long red hair as fiery as the harvest moon. He brushes by the willow near her window and the branches shake. Alison looks up. He sees her clear green eyes and restrains himself from coming too close to her. Tania, his bride, disappeared years ago, and when Alison was a wild teenager, hanging around town smoking, he fell in love with her. Now Alison is studying veterinary medicine and just comes home during the summer. He helps her father harvest tomatoes just so he can see her.

He flies past her window one more time, and then he passes over his own town where nothing is lit up except the town bar. And now he's over dark wide fields of wheat and corn.

Every few miles there's a farmhouse. In one he hears a man and a woman arguing and listens with his radar hearing. Something about their daughter. Something about her being too good for the boy down the road. It makes him think of how Alison is an untouchable mortal and how there's no loneliness greater than his. It blows through him like a cold wind on the prairie.

He flies over more fields until he gets to a heap of mirrors and doors in the middle of a field. There are numerous places like this on the prairie—forgotten places with abandoned objects, places that seem like secret lovers because they're known only to him. There's a roofless attic with trunks and china, and a collection of boots by the side of the road. There are four empty bookcases on their backs in the middle of a field.

These places are landmarks on his flight to the city. When he passes the roofless attic, he's knows that he's halfway there. When he passes the bookcases, he knows he's a third of the way there. And when he passes the boots, he knows it's nearly time to land.

HE SLOWS DOWN at the outskirts of the city. There's a granary and a lit-up Ferris wheel, and he treads the air so he can see the spinning circle. He flies over dark warehouses, movie marquees, and a crowded street where people are listening to a band on a dais. He's looking for a certain bookstore where he can pretend to browse and choose his victim slowly, noticing her face, her hair, and what sort of book she's reading. He'll bite her when she leaves, turn her into a vampire, and she'll fly with him for a few hours. But only a few. Midwesterners somehow possess an immune system that restores them to human life. They're always happy to fly for a while, awed to be closer to the moon. But by dawn they notice fields that need plowing, a roof that needs mending or—in the case of a city person—people sweeping the steps and leaving for work. Then they fly back down, regain their humanity. For this reason he has no company.

THE BOOKSTORE HAS a whole section devoted to vampires. Most books aren't accurate: For example, vampires don't mind sunlight. And most don't come from Eastern Europe but from back in the cave days when it was a relief to be bitten and saved from floods, fires, and mastodons. The errors in these books annoy him. And other books fill him with envy because the vampires are teenagers and have relatively normal lives. Like him, these vampires resist the urge to bite. Unlike him, they're understood by their friends and forgiven when they succumb. Because they're under age, they drink Cokes whenever they're in bars, but once they go back to their mansions they have huge glasses of brandy. He thinks they have the best of both eternity and mortality.

He avoids the vampire section and immerses himself in a children's book about a land where everything happens at night. Kids go to school at night and libraries are open and people shop in hardware stores where tools are illuminated by an invisible light source. While he reads, he looks up to scan people browsing. He considers a blond with a long braid—a braid like Tania's—but ends up choosing a tall redhead like Alison Hardy. She's reading *Letters of a Portuguese Nun* and looks amused in a way that makes him think she would be good company for a few hours. She doesn't leave but keeps reading, leaning against a shelf with her amused expression. Eventually someone announces that it's closing time, and he waits for her near a flower stand where a woman in a gardener's apron is closing for the night.

When he was a barrister in eighteenth century London, streets were full of flower girls. Most had red noses and chapped hands. But this is the twenty-first century, and the woman has a glow of well-being and a taut, contained way of bending and lifting that he finds enchanting. She snaps the sides of the flower booth shut and wheels it into a narrow shop. Then she starts to bring in flowers—so many vases the shop starts to look like a garden. She is beautiful in spite of her imperfections—or perhaps because of them, he thinks, with large eyes and a clever pointed chin. He would like to talk to her, but time is of the essence so he hides in the shadows, thinking past the flower girls to medieval France when he was a troubadour. And then thinking further back, far back, to the cave days. Yet it only takes the click of high heels for him to snap into this century. The redhead has left the store with a bag of books. She's wearing a burnt-orange scarf, hiding her vulnerable neck. His incisors extend. He leaps.

The redhead screams. And before he can pierce through the scarf with his incisors, two policemen surround her, and the woman at the flower stand rushes toward her. He has no alternative but to fly off, gripping half the scarf with his teeth.

His heart is beating while he flies. Nothing feels worse than a failed attempt because he only bites when he feels unbearably lonely and wants a few hours of company. Eventually he's comforted by the harvest moon and then by some of his landmarks—the trunks in the roofless attic, the heap of mirrors and doors.

Close to home, he flies by Alison's window and treads the air for as long as he can. She's looking at translucent models of mammals that she's brought from veterinary school. There's a cow, a dog, and a horse attached to electrical cords so one can see their hearts pulsing light and their arteries and veins coursing blood. These animals seem as though they're going to spring to life, the opposite of being undead. He envies them being in Alison's room.

Alison's white freckled legs hold up the book in a way that seems artfully folded. He looks at her legs and wonders would he would do if she called out to him and said she knew he flew by her window. Would he talk to her? Confess he's a vampire? Or would he hide in the willow tree?

But he mustn't allow himself too many thoughts about mortals and the way they love. He mustn't feed his loneliness. He hurries home and doesn't—as he usually does—pause to look at Lorna Peak and the Olmsted boy, tangled in each other's arms, no longer wearing clothes. At home he visits the cattle, also blessed with immunity. They're always glad to see him, grateful not to be slaughtered. They offer him their necks. Before he bites, he realizes he's still holding half of the scarf in his mouth.

HE WASN'T ALWAYS lonely because he came to the Midwest with Tania over a hundred years ago. They wanted to escape the decadence of Europe. They wanted to found a community of vampires. They bit indiscriminately—confused, frightened people who joined them for a night, morphed into humans the next day, and never mentioned being bitten. *Best left unsaid* is the motto of the heartlands.

At first he and Tania had nothing but contempt for these people, whom they regarded as ants, living small mortal-minded lives. Then Patsy Hardy's great-grandmother gave them her old featherbed, and it was so comfortable they violated the vampire code and stopped sleeping in their coffins. Soon they began to go to sleep earlier and earlier. With each bright day, the friendly neighbors drew them in.

He went to barn raisings, winnowed wheat, and helped dig out people who were snowbound. Tania went to quilting bees and made pies and casseroles for the harvester picnics. She started to chide him for drinking human blood and pestered him to build a chicken coop so they could start an egg farm.

If only we had a child, she would say.

One night there was a great crash, and Vladimir the Ur-Vampire with his great black wings and gnarled third eye flew over the bed. He shouted that they'd disgraced the undead everywhere by violating the code, mingling with humans and sleeping in a bed. He took Tania in his arms and carried her across the ocean.

Tonight he dreams about Tania. He dreams they are at the court of a Renaissance king, where she's possessed with great powers and can spin straw into gold. In truth, she was the scullery maid in the home of a French doctor, and one night he bit her and spirited her away. He has a vivid sense of Tania in the dream, with her blond braid and blue eyes and creamy skin. He wakes up and goes to Tania's closet, which he's never emptied. An old calico dress is hanging on a hook. He touches it, the last threads break, and the dress falls to the floor. He puts his head in its folds and weeps.

HE DREADS THE next day because Judge Greavey has summoned for him without telling him why. Judge Greavey schedules appointments precisely—Wednesday at 11:50, Thursday at 4:10. He's used to thinking in decades. Minutes make him nervous.

Judge Greavey has a squat head, long narrow lips, and looks a little like a toad. His office smells of leather and reminds of the days when he was a barrister in London and there was plenty of human blood. Sometimes he and Tania went to the moors, loving the heather and the villages where inhabitants walked freely at night. There were vampires everywhere. He was never lonely.

Judge Greavey clears his throat and begins to broach his subject— namely, that of becoming a U.S. citizen. Because of their wide and generous nature people of the heartlands have ignored rules and never bothered with the census. And everyone knows him for as long as they can remember and is always ready to vouch for him. But now the government is cracking down, and it's time to throw in the towel and claim his existence here.

LAST YEAR HE flew by Judge Greavey's house and saw him in front of a bedroom mirror in his underwear. The Judge had hooked up a device to hold up his neck and was trying to stretch himself. He felt sorry for Judge Greavey when he saw him rigged up. Sorry that he looked like a toad and sorry that it bothered him. The memory comes unbidden, and he realizes it's dangerous. As long as he's a good neighbor, it doesn't bother Judge Greavey that he's a vampire or even that he bit him once.

There are night classes in Dusty Falls, the Judge says. Five minutes away by truck.

The Judge says *truck* delicately because he knows he can fly. He nods to the Judge in a non-committal way.

You know what I mean, says the Judge. Life isn't so free anymore. There could be trouble.

Those Slotsky people, he continues, never bothered to become citizens and now they're under investigation. One of their ancestors was a Russian count, and that doesn't go over well with the U.S. of A.

He happens to know that the Slotskys, formerly Russian Orthodox, now believe in the Radiance, and he wonders if that could be a problem.

The Judge shakes his flat head.

Of course we like a plainer way of worship, he says. But what the Slotskys believe isn't the point. The point is the government doesn't like their family tree. Tell me: Is there any chance of getting a wife?

For a moment he thinks of Alison Hardy. About how it would be to live with her, bury his face in her hair, share a bed. But only for a moment.

I had a wife once, he says to the Judge. She was lovely. I'm not sure I can marry somebody else.

For a moment the Judge looks at him with a tinge of envy because his own wife is a harridan. Then he composes himself and says:

You'd get automatic citizenship. It would take care of everything.

Everything? he wonders. She'd get old and he'd stay young. People would start to talk.

I'll think about it, he says to the Judge.

THAT NIGHT, HE flies to the town of Dusty Falls and looks in on the U.S. citizenship class. All the Slotskys are there. So is Asuncia, the lovely dark-haired woman from Guatemala who helps Reverend Peak's wife with church events. The beetle-browed teacher is handing out papers. He says it's a pop quiz, and everyone must guess what state the capitol cities listed on the paper belong to. There's much pencil chewing and erasing. Only one person gets everything right. This is the oldest Mrs. Slotsky. She turns her babushka'd head toward the class and smiles the condescending smile of someone whose ancestors surely were Russian counts. He can't bear the thought of being trapped in a room with her or people like her and decides that in spite of his loyalty to Tania, he should find out how Alison would feel about marrying him. Nothing direct. He'll just knock on the door and ask her advice about better feed for his chickens. Then he'll raise the subtle question about where she wants to live and if she wants a family. He flies home for his truck so he can drive over like a proper farmer.

But when he knocks, Tom Hardy says Alison's gone to help birth a calf.

He's lent her his truck, in fact, and would love to go to the bar for a drink. Could he use one, too?

He doesn't want a drink but says yes. He drives Tom to the smoky town bar; they get beers and talk about a new fence for his chickens. Suddenly Alison walks in—beautiful even in overalls and startling her father who says he still can't believe it's legal for her to be in bars and what does she do after hours at veterinary school anyway?

Stop acting like a dad, she says. I just birthed a calf and I want a drink.

She sits next to them and orders a rum coke.

What about a rumba coke? says the bartender doing a little dance and filling him with envy for his youth and ease with the culture.

Rum is fine, says Alison.

ALISON DRIVES HER father home and doesn't offer him a ride because she assumes he has other means of transportation and doesn't want to embarrass him.

I brought my truck, he says pointedly.

That's good, she says laughing.

He really did, says Tom.

There's an awkward moment in which they almost come to the edge of acknowledging his unspeakable state. Alison has never seemed more unattainable or more beautiful, and he's torn between the urge to bite her repeatedly in hopes that she'll become a vampire and the desire to want her to agree to be bitten. He has momentary thoughts about living with her—she'd go off to birth calves, he would take care of the chickens, and at night they would fly and he'd show her his landmarks. They're wild thoughts, making him want to bite her again and again. He's relieved when they say goodnight and leave in their truck.

After that night he doesn't fly near Alison's window anymore. Now and then Judge Greavey asks him about citizenship and he says, with no sincerity at all, that he's still thinking about it.

But in late August, Alison goes back to veterinary school, and he dares to fly past her window again. It's partially open, and on an impulse he climbs inside. She's left clothes she hasn't taken on the floor—a blue halter and purple flip-flops. There's also a lipstick tube on her desk and an open case of green eye shadow, both of which surprise him because it never occurred to him that Alison did anything to look beautiful. He also sees a bookcase with old Barbie dolls, most of which display their misshapen feet. Suddenly he's saddened by the sheer normalcy of Alison's life, the ache of distance between them. Before he leaves, he puts the tattered half of the orange scarf under her pillow. It happens to be in the pocket of his jeans, and in some way he doesn't understand, it's a way of saying good-bye to her.

WHEN HE COMES home the chickens are clucking, and every light in his farmhouse is on. He's afraid it's Tom Hardy coming to chastise him about Alison and hopes it's an intruder so he can bite him and numb him and fly him to the side of the road.

It's neither Tom nor an intruder. It's Tania. She's sitting on his faux-leather couch holding the other half of the orange scarf. Triangles of anger sparkle in her eyes. They coalesce, disappear, and now she is crying. Of course she was the woman who sold flowers. He should have recognized the round eyes and clever chin, the beauty that's alive in imperfection. And he should have recognized the sense of enchantment he felt when he saw her. Now she is before him, beautiful, miserable, too enraged for him to hold. She asks him how he could give the other half of the scarf to Alison. She says the scarf has been her keepsake until she could come to him.

So you knew it was me that night, he says.

Yes . . . But I needed to get my bearings first.

Your bearings?

It was a terrible time in that castle, an awful journey over the sea. I had to take time to be at one with this life. And now you're in love with a mortal.

I'm not. I just missed you.

Then why did you go into her room?

I wanted to leave her something, he says. I'm sure I knew you were coming.

Did you love her once?

I told you: I just missed you.

HE'S ON THE verge of telling her how often he woke at night and wept, buried in her clothes. Yet he feels awkward, as though all he's ever been is a Midwestern farmer in a checkered shirt and blue jeans with nothing to talk about but the price of eggs. He goes to his winter garden, a small patch on the side of the farmhouse, and weeds the moist, rich earth. He can smell the fragrance of an old tomato vine, feel earthworms in their tunnels. The door to the farmhouse opens, and Tania kneels next to him, stroking his back, telling him she loves him. Soon he's carrying her to the featherbed and everything is the way it used to be—light dissolved into more light, centuries disappearing. He thinks about Vladimir's gnarled third eye and his thin reptilian body and asks Tanya how she survived his rages. She says that his twelve brides lived on hope, tapping code on their coffins to plot his murder. It took sixty years to find a stake in Vladimir's cellar and drive it through his heart. The end was terrifying, gruesome.

He holds Tania close until she starts to breathe calmly. Not all of the undead breathe. But he and Tania took their first breath on the prairie more than one hundred years ago. He thinks of his neighbors—the Peaks, the Greaveys, the Hardys. He thinks of all of them in bed, sleeping and breathing. And for a moment, he takes comfort in the thought that he and Tania are no different.

THE NEXT DAY they walk through town, and no one remembers Tania except the oldest Mrs. Slotsky, who's angry about some eggs she says Tania never delivered sixty years ago. She's about to go into a tirade when Patsy Hardy comes up and welcomes her, and soon everyone is crowding around Tania, laughing, delighted that she's back even though they never met her, and there's a tacit understanding she knew their great grandparents as children.

Reverend Peak's wife goes to the dry goods store and buys transparent silver ribbons. She weaves them into a bow for Tania's blond braid.

To a lovely homecoming, she says.

To a lovely couple, says someone else.

IT'S AS THOUGH people were waiting for you, he says when they get to the farm.

Maybe it's an ancestral memory, says Tania.

She leans toward him, and the sun illuminates her blond braid, the silver ribbon, her green eyes. He's wants to carry her to bed again, but here's a knock at the door. He opens it to see Judge Greavey's wife with a casserole, and behind them Patsy Hardy balancing three pies. The Peaks are holding baskets of bread and potato salad. Judge Greavey has a case of beer. More neighbors arrive, bringing ham and corn and apple pie and ice cream. Judge Greavey raises his beer glass.

To the lovely Tania, he says.

Everyone clinks steins—even children who are drinking root beer. Someone lights sparklers—little earth-twins to the stars. Reverend Peak's wife lights candles. Children catch fireflies in the dusk.

Everyone's in a soft blur—he, Tania, all the neighbors, enclosed in dusk and twinkling lights. And then the orange moon appears, casting light on the candles and sparklers and fireflies, so he sees all his neighbors made out of one piece, whole and bound together by finite lives. Only he and Tania are apart, condemned to live beyond them and to know what came before them. Once more, he feels unspeakable loneliness, like wind blowing through the prairie.

The Olmsted boy and Reverend Peak's daughter sneak off without a trace. People start to say goodnight, taking plates and cups and spoons. Judge Greavey's wife balances a casserole dish. The Peaks go off with empty bowls. Jim Hardy takes pie tins. Patsy Hardy scoops up the tablecloth and trails it behind her like a veil.

One by one, they get into their trucks and rumble off into a night that will cradle them in sleep. Then he and Tania are alone, except for Lorna and the Olmsted boy near the barn moving under a blanket.

Whose kids are those? says Tania.

He starts to explain in detail, then stops. Lorna and the Olmsted boy could be so many people during so many centuries it doesn't matter.

Just some lovers, he says.

It was nice to see everyone again, says Tania.

He smiles because almost no one was born when she was last here. Still, he knows she means everyone who's dead, alive, and yet-to-be born on the prairie, all of them bound by finite time—the kind of time they'll never understand.

Sometimes I wish I wasn't a vampire, says Tania. Then we could have kids and be like everybody else.

Yet even as she speaks, the clock in the hall begins to tick, the two empty coffins raise their lids, and the moon glows outside the window. He remembers the mirrors and doors, the roofless attic, the bright Ferris wheel outside of town. He remembers the slow flight over the lake, the church, the fields. And the way Tania's shawl used to flutter in the wind.

Come, he says, taking her hand. There are things I want to show you on the prairie.

Schrödinger
in Exile

Words didn't work properly at the time. He was stern on the coarse street. When people bumped into him, he covered them with his own black coat and explained that they were moving according to the laws of Brownian motion: Each street behaved like a cigarette, emitting puffs of pedestrians, sometimes in rings, often in clouds. Pedestrians couldn't feel the exhale or inhale of the street and didn't know they were being sucked in and released at intervals. This ignorance, combined with fuzzy notions of free will, gave them the idea they could behave like trucks. They entered the streets honking and screeching, and there was much rearrangement of bodies as they shifted gears, accelerated, and worked clutches. They enjoyed the illusory sense of speed and didn't care when they arrived too early or too late because sometimes it took an hour to walk a city block and five minutes to walk two miles. Schrödinger hoped his words had authority in the coat's wooly darkness, but as soon as he finished lecturing, people blasted out, popping buttons.

TRAFFIC CONGESTION WAS complicated by the fact that visible things (5 percent of the universe) were jockeying for position with dark energy and dark matter (95 percent of the universe). Schrödinger alone understood this: At night he woke up with a pounding heart and reached for one of his two wives who slept on either side of the narrow bed in the dreadful furnished room they'd been forced to rent. Whenever he reached for one, the other also woke up, and he was surrounded by annoyance at being woken and hearing the same thing about dark matter again and again when there were more important things to worry about like getting out of the dreadful room and going back to their country. They always turned on the light and made tea on the Bunsen burner, which they laced with scotch. He rejected the tea. He left and walked through the streets, which were as crowded at night as they were in the day. At night he didn't try to lecture the honking, button-popping, careening pedestrians. Instead he leapt over inhales and exhales of the street looking for the space in between the fall and rise of the breath even though he knew that he, too, was caught in the breathing. Eventually he returned to the fourth-floor walk-up where his two wives were still drinking tea. He wished that he could assign dark matter to one and light matter to the other, but he knew that everybody in the world was similarly permeated. Sometimes this elated him, and he embraced them both on their rickety chairs, toppling them to the floor, holding them close, when they said *Edwin, it's time to sleep,* and pulling them back to the narrow bed where he was comforted by the beating of their hearts.

BUT AT OTHER times these thoughts about the permeation of dark matter depressed him when he came home. And although this, too, went against the laws of physics, he had visions of dark matter suffocating everybody. He sat on the floor with his head in his hands, and his wives put down their cups and sat beside him. One rubbed his back, the other rubbed his shoulders, both telling him: *Edwin, we understand the way you see things, but even so we get by.* When they began to talk, he said that the furnished room was depressing, and one of them always said that his exile wouldn't be forever and they would return to their house with its books and clocks and comforting beds. They knew he would counter by saying everything was temporary, and they always invoked carefully worked-out systems of space and time. They talked about how the sub-atomic related to the atomic, and how the atomic related to the world of couches and cars and clocks. They talked about velocity, planets, and galaxies. They talked until he fell asleep on the floor.

WHEN HIS BLACK coat got holes and his wives had to buy him a used one, Schrödinger grew more distraught. He started to lecture children, as well as his wives, who began to take circuitous routes to shop for groceries. When he went out at night, he stopped leaping between the inhale and the exhale of the street and arrested pedestrians. Soon he began to ignore his own principles, which he'd not worked out completely because his own brain was also a random particle. One evening he was forced to arrest himself for speeding. It was warm inside his coat, and sound was muffled. From an opening in the flap he could see pedestrians expanding and retracting in the milky light—thinking they were walking, not knowing they were only particles of smoke. In the distance he saw his two wives. They each had baskets of food and were aloft on circuitous routes. The breath of the street was a labor of love, the act of walking an act of faith. Schrödinger said a few words and let himself out. *After all,* he thought, *I'm not very far from home.*

Poland

HER HUSBAND DIED suddenly of a heart attack right in the middle of writing a poem. He was only thirty-eight, at the height of his powers—and people felt he had a great deal more to give, not just through his poetry but through the way he lived his life. His second wife, who was nearly ten years younger, found the poem half-finished, moments after he died, and put it in her pocket for safekeeping. She'd never liked his poetry, nor did she like the poem, but she read it again and again, as if it would explain something. The poem was about Poland. It was about how her husband kept seeing Poland in the rearview mirror of his car, and how the country kept following him wherever he went. It was about fugitives hiding in barns, people eating ice for bread. Her husband had never been to Poland. His parents had come from Germany, just before World War II, and she had no sense that Poland meant anything to him. This made the poem more elusive, and its elusiveness made her sure that it contained something important.

Whenever she read the poem, she breathed Poland's air, walked through its fields, worried about people hiding in barns. And whenever she read it she felt remorse—the kind you feel when someone has died and you realize that you've never paid enough attention to him. She thought of the times she'd listened to her husband with half an ear and of the times he asked where he put his glasses and car-keys and she hadn't helped him look. After awhile, she began to have similar feelings about Poland—a country she'd never paid attention to. She studied its maps, went to Polish movies, bought a book of Polish folk songs. Poland stayed on her mind like a small, subliminal itch.

One day when she was driving on a backcountry road, she looked in her rearview mirror and saw Poland behind her. It was snowy and dark, the Poland of her husband's poem. She made turns, went down other roads, and still it was there, a country she could walk to. It was all she could do to keep from going there, and when she came home, she mailed the poem to her husband's first wife, explaining it was the last thing he'd ever written and maybe she'd like to have it. It was a risky thing to do—neither liked the other—and in a matter of days she got a call from the woman who said:

Why are you doing this to me, Ellen? Why in God's name don't you let me leave him behind?

There was static on the line, a great subterranean undertow, and soon both women were pulled there, walking in the country of Poland. He was there, too, always in the distance, and the first wife, sensing this, said:

Well, as far as I'm concerned, he can just go to hell.

She said this almost pleasantly—it wasn't an expression of malice—and the second wife answered:

I agree. Completely. It's the only way.

The Silk
Velvet Blouse

WHEN SHE WAS wheeled into the emergency ward everyone noticed her blouse. It was velvet, nearly black purple, with billowing sleeves and black lace-trimmed cuffs. Her arms trailed over the gurney and the blouse shimmered, as though it were in water.

Previously the staff noticed her when she waited in the emergency waiting area for an emergency-room psychiatrist, whom she dated. She'd sat with the patients, reading a book, her long legs stretched out in designer jeans. She'd looked calm, mysterious, and a little distant. And here she was—in front of them.

That blouse is silk velvet, said the emergency room doctor on call.

The nurse was surprised that she knew.

My dad worked in retail, said the doctor. He was always bringing stuff home. Silk velvet is expensive.

They wheeled the woman into a cubicle and she sat up, shaking her long auburn hair. She'd complained of a pain in her elbow and the doctor touched it carefully, relieved to discover it wasn't broken and they wouldn't have to cut the blouse to ease it off. The woman said nothing while they removed the blouse. But as the nurse was folding it, she said:

I've just killed someone. I've just killed another person.

It wasn't your fault, said the doctor. He was going off the edge.

Are you crazy? I just killed a man.

They were talking about a priest named Father Kane. For six months he'd been walking around town in a state of distraction, giving away reprints of all his scholarly articles to whoever would take them. Until then, he'd had his own church. But when he began to slide, the local parish sent another priest to his church and took him in. Tonight was a dark rainy night, and he'd walked in front of her car.

Like a bird, said the woman. He fell against the windshield like a bird.

You mustn't think like that, said the nurse. He stopped being himself a long time ago.

He fell against my windshield like a bird, the woman repeated. That's what I thought it was.

She'd been surprised, then frightened, by the weight against her car. When she got out, she saw him lying on the street, surrounded by sheaves of paper.

I couldn't remember where phones were, she said. I thought maybe they were in trees. Then I remembered my cell phone and called the police.

The doctor touched a wedge-shaped wound on the woman's forehead.

How did you get that?

From those telephone poles they used for posters, she said. I thought maybe I could find a phone in one of those, and I put my head against it and there were these staples. My God. I killed someone.

It was an accident waiting to happen, said the doctor. Ever since he started giving tracts away. You know—just stopping people on the street. Just like that saint. What was his name? Oh: St. John the Bookseller.

How do you know that? said the nurse.

I was raised Catholic, said the doctor. And I had to memorize all of the Johns. There were so many of them and they each had to think of something strange to do as if the last one hadn't done something strange enough.

Once he came here, said the nurse. Do you remember? It was around the holidays and everyone was having accidents in their kitchens. Kids were running into stoves and someone severed a finger in a blender.

Sure I remember, said the doctor. First he came into the waiting room and waved a pamphlet in front of everybody and couldn't believe no one wanted to read it. We had to call the parish to take him home.

INDEED IT HAD been one of the most uncomfortable moments that had ever happened in that emergency room. People had looked at their feet, or their hands, or reached for a magazine. A mother pulled a five-year-old boy onto her lap. A few had known Father Kane when he'd been their priest and were frightened by his transformation into a crazed eccentric, spouting theories and stopping people on the street and in grocery stores to explain Saint Augustine. The parish had taken him in and replaced him with another priest. They had considered confining him, but his rants were so intrusive they let him come and go as he pleased.

I hate to admit it, said the nurse. But after that night, if anyone on the staff saw him we went to a different store or crossed to the other side of the street.

You felt sorry for him, but you couldn't feel sorry forever, said the doctor.

She looked again at the triangular cut in the center of the woman's forehead and decided that she needed stitches. She motioned to the nurse for alcohol.

Who cares if he was crazy? said the woman. Have either of you ever killed someone?

The doctor and the nurse didn't answer. They hadn't killed anyone. But the doctor had failed to make a call for Code Blue and had once ordered morphine for someone who had a fatal allergy. And the nurse had miscalculated the number of ccs in a transfusion and once ignored a man who'd been hit in the eye and died right on the floor of the waiting area. There were board reviews and explanations. Until the voice that said *I killed someone* morphed into a voice that said *I accidentally did something that hastened the end of someone's life,* and then became a voice that said *I did the best I could.*

Just as the doctor was about to put in stitches there were loud footsteps in the hall, and Luca Varriano, the psychiatrist who was the woman's boyfriend, parted the curtain and came inside. He still wore his motorcycle jacket, and when he came to sit on the gurney, the flashing red light on its back raced from the woman's face to the white walls and settled on a cabinet of instruments.

The hospital had a rule that only people who'd accompanied a patient to the emergency room could come into cubicles. It was some notion that had been concocted long ago as a way of testing love and loyalty. And no one except a doctor or a nurse could sit on a gurney. Luca wasn't on the staff that night and hadn't come with the woman to the hospital. But instead of telling him to leave the doctor and nurse looked at the opposite wall as though nothing could interest them more than red light flashing on silver instruments.

The woman began to cry, and Luca put his arm around her.

I killed a man, she said. There was a thud against the windshield. Like a bird. I could see he was dead, and I put my coat over him. The police still have it.

I'll get your coat, he said. And I'll come back with the car. I'll take you to my place and we'll do a hot tub.

A hot tub? Are you crazy? I just killed someone.

You killed someone who didn't know where he was going, he said. You killed someone who was very upset.

I killed a holy man, said the woman. He gave away all his possessions.

Her voice was rising. The doctor raised her eyebrows.

Believe me, he had plenty of possessions, said Luca.

How do you know? said the woman.

He paused, wrestling with the issue of confidence. Finally he said:

Last year the parish called and asked if I'd take a look at his room because they were thinking of sending him to managed care. He was out. They let me in with a key. You wouldn't believe that room. Hundreds of manuscripts and two hand-operated printing presses. His own woodcuts of the crucifixion. But his bed was made, and there was a lamp and a cup of tea on a nightstand. So I told the parish he could take care of himself and they didn't need to send him away.

And then I finished him off, said the woman.

That's absurd, said the doctor.

Except all of you are absurd, the way you're talking. He's probably in the morgue right now, and you're telling me not to worry and take a hot tub.

Her rising voice attracted attention. An anesthesiologist parted the curtain. She looked concerned and said she remembered the priest.

I met him, she said. In a vegetable store, actually. I know, I know—he told me about Augustine. But he was special in a messed-up way.

For God's sake, said Luca, this isn't what she needs to hear right now.

How do you know what I need to hear? said the woman. I killed someone. Two hours ago he was alive and I killed someone. And you're telling me to take a hot tub. Get the fuck out now. I mean it.

Luca stood up and handed the woman a twenty-dollar bill.

Call a cab, he said. I'll wait for you at my place. You shouldn't be alone tonight.

I don't want your fucking money. She threw the bill to the floor. The nurse gave it back to him.

WHEN HE LEFT, the doctor followed him down the hall.

Try not to get too logical with her, said the doctor. No matter what anyone says, she needs time to get over it.

Don't we all? Luca said.

He saw the look on the doctor's face and added: You're right. I should be more understanding.

For a moment he reminded the doctor of her own husband, hiding beneath a show of honesty.

You ought to be, she said. She seems like a caring person.

In a way it's part of her job, he said. Did you know she's a shrink?

He didn't say how they'd met, and the doctor, in an unbidden vision, saw the two of them in a book-lined room, the woman leaning forward, a box of Kleenex on a table between them. It wasn't clear who was the therapist, but she suspected it was the woman because Luca had gone into a depression after he and his wife split up. Now he reached into his pocket and pulled out the twenty-dollar bill.

Tell her to take a cab, he said.

The doctor nodded, and Luca left in a blaze of red light. When she came back to the cubicle, the woman was crying.

What a jerk, she said. What a total asshole.

Shh . . . , said the doctor. Everything feels like too much right now.

Why shouldn't it?

The doctor motioned to the nurse for more alcohol.

All I need to do is take two stitches, she said. Then you can leave. I'm using black catgut because you can take them out in three days.

SHE STITCHED, THE woman winced, and when it was over she asked for a hand-mirror. She looked at herself for a long time.

I look just like Raggedy Anne, she said.

You don't look like Raggedy Anne at all, said the doctor. And it will heal without a trace.

But what's going to happen to him? she said, meaning the priest.

I heard they called the parish, said the nurse. Someone there said he was very loved. Strange, maybe, but loved.

Like a saint is loved, said the woman.

I doubt that he's a saint, said the doctor. But I think he'd forgive you.

She stepped back to look at the stitches and nodded.

You definitely won't get a scar, she said. And you're okay to go. We'll give you some pills for the pain and call a cab.

I'm not riding in any cars tonight, said the woman.

She got off the gurney, smoothed out her designer jeans, put a white flannel blanket around her shoulders, and left. The nurse ran after her, holding the silk velvet blouse. The woman waved it away.

I won't ever wear that again, she said. It was the first thing that touched him after he died.

You'll feel differently in a couple of days.

I won't. And I'll never forget the way that blouse felt against the wheel when I tried to swerve.

The nurse said it wasn't possible for her to leave with the blanket because it belonged to the hospital. Besides, she needed sleeping medication and had to sign a discharge form. But the woman ran through the glass doors and disappeared down the street, the white blanket billowing into the night.

BACK IN THE cubicle, the doctor was sitting on a chair with her head in her hands.

Luca can never keep his mouth shut, she said.

At least we got to see him in his motorcycle jacket, said the nurse.

They both laughed. The nurse showed the doctor the blouse.

We'll have to store it, said the doctor. And then—seeing the nurse frown—added:

Unless you want to risk taking it.

Me? said the nurse. I've got shoulders like a football player. But it would fit you.

You know we can't take things.

The nurse shoved the blouse at the doctor who disappeared behind a curtain, put it on, and took off her hair clip. When she came out her hair was loose around her shoulders, cascading over the shimmering black purple.

Aubergine's your color, said the nurse.

But the doctor looked at herself in the mirror and shook her head.

You can't do anything these days, she said, pulling her hair back and jabbing in a barrette. You can't even leave your house without worrying you'll hurt someone.

The Girl with
Feet That
Could See

EVERY YEAR WHEN the Traveling Mystery Circus came to a defunct coal town in upstate New York, Malinka's mother dragged her to the freak show. They passed the feral child, the snake lady, the fat man, the dwarf, the human torso, and the monster until they found the empty booth donated by her mother's church. Then Malinka's mother blindfolded her with a kerchief and Malinka took off her shoes and socks and lay down with her feet toward the audience. The crowd held up dimes and watches and sticks of gum and pearl necklaces and stuffed animals and miniature cars and spare tires and computer parts and violins and accordions and watch gears. Malinka wriggled her toes and told them what they were holding. She was the girl with feet that could see.

They'd come from Belgrade when Malinka was seven. Her mother still ate radishes for breakfast and sweetened tea by holding sugar between her teeth. Her older sister was useless—smoking by ten, in trouble with the police at twelve. So one daughter who made money was a blessing.

It wasn't a blessing for Malinka. She didn't like being associated with freaks, exposing her bare feet, and giving all the money to her mother. And she always worried that someone from her school would turn up. No one ever did, and Malinka was relieved because kids teased her about her size—she was only four foot nine—as well as her accent. Every year when the circus was about to come to town, she lay in bed, dreading the freak show. Her sister was in the upper bunk, clouding the room with cigarette smoke, and her mother was in the next room crying. Since her father left, her mother's tears could wash the floor.

When Malinka was sixteen, she took a bus to where the circus was setting up. It was dusk. And when the great tent puffed up, it looked like an extension of the sky. Malinka wandered into the costume room, looking at leotards, clown noses, collections of masks, until she found the Circus Master. He was a tall man in jeans and a black shirt, smoking a cigarette, and handsome in an angular-dangerous-older-man sort of way. He leaned down to look at her.

Who are you? he said.

I'm the girl who comes to the freak show, said Malinka. The one with the feet that can see.

That's too bad, he said, because we've decided to end the freak show after this year.

Malinka smiled, and the Circus Master said:

Why are you smiling? People always came to see you.

It's not as good as being in a real circus.

But what can you do besides gawk with your feet?

Almost anything, said Malinka.

Almost anything? said the Circus Master. We'll see. Then he took Malinka to the tent she'd just seen raised. It smelled of fresh sawdust and was filled with the clang of hammers. He handed Malinka a pair of pink slippers, pointed to a forty-foot ladder with razor-sharp stars, and told her to climb it. She climbed the ladder, and the Circus Master told her to climb it again and then again. On her third descent, he shouted an order, and the air was filled with the aroma of lilacs. It caught her breath and reminded her of a long-ago summer in Belgrade when she'd taken a walk with her father. Only two days later he boarded a train to Latvia, slept on a coal car, and saw the bright enduring stars. He wrote her a postcard about it and never came home.

The lights went on, and the Circus Master asked her to take off her slippers. When he saw there wasn't one rip in them, he knelt beside her and said:

Your feet have a thousand eyes. And I'm going to give you your own act. But you're only sixteen. So bring your mother here tomorrow.

Malinka couldn't comprehend what the Circus Master was saying. But when her mother came and started to bargain, everything was clear. Her mother's voice rose when she talked about the income she would lose, and Malinka sat in the sawdust, reminded of open markets in Belgrade. Finally her mother struck a bargain and shoved a check in her worn black purse.

WITHIN DAYS SHE began to perform an act that the Circus Master called From the Stars to the Garden. She sped up and down the star-studded ladder until she made a final descent, and the air was filled with the aroma of lilacs. The audience gasped at her speed.

A few stars always fell from the trembling wire. They were sharp, encrusted with rhinestones, and the troupe began to wonder why her slippers never ripped. Malinka didn't want to say she'd been part of a freak show and never told them her feet could see the stars and knew how to step around them. Her silence generated theory after theory: The slippers were made of special fabric; the stars weren't all that sharp. Malinka never said a word, and her willingness to entice and emanate mystery pleased the Circus Master who often said the job of the circus was to illuminate illusion rather than explain it.

After the show, the audience always clamored for Malinka's autograph. Punk boys and girls with nose rings, fathers with babies on their shoulders, tall, elegant men and women. Malinka was so small that from the top of the tent, all one could see of her was a dip in the middle of a circle. The autographs exhausted her, and when the crowd dispersed she went back to her trailer. It was a relief to be away from her sister's cigarette smoke, a relief not to hear her mother cry. She tried not to think about her father.

ONE EVENING SHE saw a tall blond man walking with a backpack and mistook him for someone from an online dating site: People often booked their dates before coming to a particular town.

Can I help you? she asked.

He said that his name was Flaminio, that he'd just flown in from Turin, and that he was the new Fire Eater. Soon he was drinking wine at her Formica table and then he was in the bunk bed. Malinka kissed him and said she'd never felt anything like that before—not with Profiterole or the Circus Master or—

Shhh—said Flaminio. I don't want to know about any of them.

Malinka dried her eyes. They had been filled with tears, and he hadn't noticed.

You seem sad, he said.

It was just that they were all so different. I could imagine I was living different lives. But now . . . I don't know. I might not imagine things like that anymore.

When she said this, Flaminio knew he had permission to move from his makeshift tent into her trailer. And without question, Malinka let him. Her mother had been sad, her sister angry, and her father had vanished. But Flaminio was so infused with a sense of adventure, she forgot all of them. Whenever he laughed, he threw back his head and spun her around, and soon she was laughing, too.

Your color is better, said the Circus Master. But don't tell him the secret of your feet.

MALINKA DID HER own laundry because she didn't trust the washers and dryers with her delicate costumes—white tutus with flounces that glittered when she climbed the ladder, tights with silver sequins. She strung her wet clothes around the door of the trailer, and when Flaminio bumped his head on it he said:

This is just like Italy.

Then the two of them laughed and climbed the ladder to bed. Soon the troupe joked that their trailer was just like Italy and came over late to drink red wine. Even the Circus Master showed up—a good way to mingle with the troupe while maintaining the proper distance.

FOR SOME REASON—and no one can understand this—it was impossible to pinpoint the date when the circus fell on hard times. Was it when Profiterole, the head clown, began to develop a late-onset fear of other clowns, officially diagnosed as Coulrophobia? Or was it when the trapeze-catchers stopped catching their partners, who flopped on the nets, trying to look graceful?

Or was it when the bloggers—those faceless creatures in cyberspace—began to write that the Traveling Mystery Circus created illusions with lanterns and dry ice that that any child could create? According to these blogs, illusions were fine for earlier centuries, but not for this one, when it was nearly impossible to know what was true.

The house was still packed, but a pall fell over the troupe. The Circus Master said they shouldn't read the blogs, that everything would return to normal, but every day people shared computers in the dining tent—the only place connected to cyberspace.

One evening at dinner, Flaminio told the Circus Master that maybe the bloggers had some points that could be addressed with simple explanations. The Circus Master grew furious and said the less attention they got the sooner they would stop.

Entertainment is our only obligation, he said. And the job of the circus is to illuminate mystery not to explain it.

ONE NIGHT, AFTER the audience crowded around Malinka for her autograph, they laid out sleeping bags. Flaminio and Malinka could hear whispering all night, soft little scratches of sound. In the morning they walked around sleeping bags and saw people drinking coffee. During the day, the air was filled with the smell of frying onions. That evening a new audience arrived, and the same thing happened. Indeed it began to happen night after night, and soon the grounds were clotted with people of all ages and quite a few parents with children. There was no end to what they'd brought: hand-held blenders, hats, soft pillows, razors, shaving cream, towels, books, board games, dolls. And computers where they wrote things about the circus, using words like *mystification*.

The children were well behaved. Some were handed over the fence in the morning so they could go to school, and then handed back in the evening. Profiterole found this touching and wanted to take pictures, but the Circus Master confiscated his camera and said it would be bad publicity for the circus. At all costs, he said, he didn't want to call the police.

One night Profiterole knocked on the door of the trailer, and he and Malinka and Flaminio sat at the Formica table drinking stale wine.

That idiot isn't paying attention, said Profiterole, referring to the Circus Master.

He never does, said Flaminio.

You're the only person he cares about, said Profiterole to Malinka. The way he bargained with your mother. He wanted to save you.

He only wanted my feet, said Malinka.

All three drank wine and were silent, uncomfortable about the distrust they felt toward the Circus Master. Did he really think he could replace them? Find another girl with feet that could see? Or a clown like Profiterole who was the funniest? And what would happen when it was time to go on to the next town? There was a rumor that the Circus Master had once been a spy and traveled incognito. He might incite violence. Or call the police.

On the tenth evening, a news anchor found his way in to the tent. And when Malinka was about to sign autographs, the Circus Master appeared on a stepladder with a bullhorn.

I've been patient with all of you to a fault, he said. But no more!

The crowd grew quiet. Their pens—poised to give Malinka for autographs—became still, like small swords.

I haven't called the police, said the Circus Master, because I've trusted you to settle this in a law-abiding way. But since you can't, I'm going to call them if you don't leave now. It will only take them a minute to get here. And another minute to throw you in jail.

The crowd began to chant an indistinct syllable—swaying, holding their pens in the air. It was a primitive sound from a time when there were very few words. It reverberated, thrummed, beat inside people's hearts. Malinka was surrounded by swaying bodies and looked for a way to escape: The crowd was seamless.

The swaying bodies began to push her back and forth, crowding her against rough sweaters and jeans, making it impossible to breathe. She didn't know what to do and remembered times in Belgrade when kids sat on top of her—saying, again and again, *She's vanished!*

At last she saw a loose pocket and used it as a lever to climb up arms and shoulders until she was standing on someone's head. Malinka was so short she rarely reached past a chin. Now she was on the head of a man wearing a baseball cap and looking at a sea of heads—some with radiant hair, some bald. She walked over the heads until she reached the Circus Master, who had no other choice than to bow and kiss her hand. The chanting stopped, and the audience applauded. Then someone in the crowd said:

We want to know how you did that.

We never explain, said the Circus Master, who was about to go into a polemic about illusion.

But Malinka leaned down and whispered in someone's ear:

I have feet that can see. They see every jewel on the ladder. They see every razor-sharp edge on the stars. They know exactly where to climb.

Soon everyone was passing the whisper. When it reached the outermost edges, the crowd applauded again and praised the ladder climber who'd been willing to talk about magic. Without further whispering, they gathered their paraphernalia and left.

When the grounds were empty, the troupe went to the main dining room. For days they'd been too nervous to eat. Now they devoured cold chicken and bison grass vodka.

We are well out of it, said the Circus Master. And they all left, just like I said they would.

He ate another piece of chicken and wiped his hands.

All the same, he continued, I think we should have our own blogger. Someone who can reveal a secret or two a month.

A few nodded. Most poured more vodka. But Malinka looked at her feet and said:

You know, they're going to come back. Whatever you saw was just a shiver of what's to come.

Dream Envy

FOR MONTHS SHE'D been envying her husband's dreams. It might have started around her fourth week of pregnancy, after he'd moved out and then moved back again. Or maybe it began around the twentieth week, when he wanted to name the baby after himself, and she said no. The truth is, she didn't remember because the condition of envy had become a chronic background noise. Her husband always had baroque and complex dreams, and she'd never minded. Now her envy enclosed them like a hot electric fence.

She could see her husband clearly. He was blond, bearded, surrounded by the haze of his dream. He woke up, propped himself up on one elbow, and looked slightly disoriented. She didn't ask to hear the dream. He told her.

This morning his dream was about time travel. He'd visited a country where people still thought the earth was flat and never traveled far because they were afraid they were going to fall off. Since he knew the earth was round, he convinced them otherwise, but when they started to disappear over the horizon, it seemed he had made a mistake. She leaned forward, looking encouraged—maybe this was a dream of failed adventure, after all. But no. It turned out that when everyone disappeared, they were really flying. Her husband could fly, too: As he flew, he saw the entire country below him. Thatched roofs. Children with hoops. Quaint little streets.

A fairyland, he said, just like Disney.

He often had flying dreams. They were giddy, hallucinatory, perilous. She lay in bed listening, trying to look happy.

What's wrong? he asked.

Nothing, she answered.

Nothing? he persisted.

No. Nothing.

She smiled, concealing her envy, but he caught it.

Just life, she reassured him.

In a sense, she was telling the truth. Their faucets leaked. Their washing machine overflowed. Yesterday they'd bought two-dozen minuscule T-shirts that turned out to be for nine-month-olds, not newborns. They were investigating breast pumps that looked like devices from the regime of Torquemada. Lists of names for the baby lined their kitchen wall, and they couldn't agree on any of them.

But in another sense, the truth was only her envy—not just any kind of envy, but dream envy, an affliction of trolls, gremlins, bats, sad, dreamless beings relegated to caves. A dangerous omen. An unhappy and violent passion. Her midwife had advised her of this, pressing into her hands herbs, amulets, arcane books, a dream pillow filled with lavender and sage. Dreams are essential, she'd said. You must work to get yours back.

Her husband leaned over and touched her belly.

Whatever happened to the good old days? he asked. It was something he'd been asking for a while, a compelling, urgent question.

Nothing, she said. They're here right now.

The baby chose this moment to shift inside of her. An obscure dolphin. A rumbling miniature subway. He was always, without a doubt, the most important person in the room, an unruly character, waiting for the chance to speak. On ultrasound he was the size of a kitten, his transparent heart no bigger than a dime. After they saw him, her husband drew a heart on her stomach and kissed it. *See. I'm being good now.*

TODAY HE TURNED to her, not unkindly.

You resent my dreams, he said. You begrudge me this little corner of my mind.

Of course I don't.

But you do. You begrudge me. I know it.

She said nothing. Under her large white pillow, she could feel the velvet dream pillow the midwife had given her. It was prickly, filled with sage and lavender. The sage had come from the Bolivian mountains. The midwife found it last summer at the witch's market in La Paz.

I'm being exemplary these days, he continued. I've found a crib. I went with you to buy those ridiculous T-shirts, and today I'm going to help you return them. I've even gone to those damn birthing classes with what's-her-name.

Laurel Moonflower, she supplied. Laurel Moonflower was the midwife. Her husband didn't like her. He said she was a New Age parody.

Laurel Moonflower, he agreed. I've gone there and I've sat there and I've admired her models of the pelvis. I've chanted atonal chants. I've offered prayers. I've rubbed your back. And you begrudge me my dreams.

I don't begrudge you; I blame you. She didn't say this, but thought it. The day after he'd moved out, to a lawyer friend's place on a street with the improbable name of Taurus, she'd woken from a dream about being trapped in the city of Dresden during the Second World War. She was in a house, standing by a cabinet full of fragile china, when a bomb fell. Cup after cup after cup shattered in slow motion. A miniature china shepherdess was severed from her sheep. Plates decorated with flowers crashed. This had been her last dream. Her nights had become a blank canvas.

What are you thinking? he asked.

Nothing.

Are you hungry?

Just for grapes. Grapes are all I have room for. It's like someone put a grand piano in there.

He went to the kitchen and came back with grapes for her and a huge hunk of toasted French bread for himself. He climbed into bed, and they started to eat. It was a custom they used to enjoy.

How are the grapes?

Fine.

In fact, they were too soft.

SINCE HE'D MOVED back, traits that she'd previously found charming had become irritating beyond belief. One surfaced now. The way he crunched his toast. Once it was boyish enthusiasm. Now it was greed.

Do you have to eat so loud? she asked.

What do you mean?

I mean you're taking very big bites.

His hand slammed against the white comforter.

I'll eat the way I want to.

She waited. The words arrived.

You pig, she said.

It was a dangerous thing to say. She looked a lot more like a pig than he did. *You're a pig.* He could say that. But he didn't. He threw his toast on the floor.

Oh my, she said. A food fight.

Spare me your irony.

He went into the kitchen for a sponge and soon was picking butter from the fringes of the woven rug.

IT WASN'T A wanted pregnancy. That's how she thought of it now. It wasn't a wanted pregnancy, and it was a miracle that he stayed. A lot of them don't, you know. A lot of them just leave. But when they finally see these wonderful little beings, they always love them. If they stay. . . .

Laurel Moonflower, the midwife, had told her this last part. She'd also said she should be more generous with her husband. *Allowing* was the word she used: For heaven's sake, be more allowing.

In truth, she thought Laurel Moonflower had problems of her own: Last summer, in La Paz, she claimed to have fallen in love with an enormous black-and-white bull that lived near the hacienda where she stayed. She didn't call it falling in love. She called it a soul connection:

I have a soul connection with that animal. And it has cured me of my bitterness concerning males of every species.

Not that the love would ever lead to anything. But it was real.

Sometimes the midwife wrote the bull, care of the owner, in Spanish. The bull's name was *Flacadillo.* Little lazy one. The owner said he had a deep heart and promised her he'd never be slaughtered.

HER HUSBAND CONTINUED to clean the rug, muttering damn under his breath. Even as he muttered, she reached for a book of dreams Laurel Moonflower had given her. The book was old, with a serious black cover, filled with symbols and incantations. In the back there was a chart that listed angels in charge of dreams for every hour of the night and day. The angels were always rotating: This morning, Sunday at 8:30 AM, the archangel Michael resided. He would soon be replaced by Haniel, who would be followed by Raphael. The angels must be exhausted, juggling their heavenly schedules. Maybe they forgot. Or maybe no one was in charge. She lay back in bed and tried to imagine Michael, angel of ice, with fiery wings that never melted. She was interrupted by the sound of a knife scraping against toast, followed by rebellious bites, her husband eating in the kitchen. Soon he came into the bedroom and sat beside her on the bed. He was filled with a lot of toast and very little forgiveness.

So, he said. What's on the agenda for today?

He asked as if he didn't want to know.

Laurel's coming this morning.

Why?

I already told you. She likes to make house calls. To check out the vibes.

I wish we weren't using her. She gets on my nerves.

Laurel's okay. And we can't do it alone. No one can.

In that case, I'll dress.

He went to the closet and pulled out a brown-and-white striped djellabah that made him look like a prophet. He put it on, adding sunglasses.

How do I look? Will Laurel like it?

Give me a break. You look awful.

IN A FIT of nest-building she'd put up lace curtains, which made the bare trees outside seem covered with snow, the landscape done in petit point. He didn't like the curtains. Every morning he pulled them back, making the stretch-rods slip. She got out of bed and recovered the windows, transforming the landscape back to winter. She wondered if she should try to dream: Michael was on for another twenty minutes, and then the intimidating Haniel, guardian of gates for the west wind, would arrive. What would happen, she wondered, if you were having a dream during a change of shifts? Would the dream evaporate? Would angels fight to claim it? Not that she believed in them. She believed in accidents, lucky breaks, forces of nature. No wonder the dream pillow didn't work. One had to be sincere. One had, as the midwife said, to *believe.*

She went back into bed and began to read an old copy of *People* magazine she'd snuck from the dentist's months ago. Two of the stars whose weddings had been featured were already divorced, and a prominent socialite had died. She liked reading old copies of *People* magazine: It was a curious form of time-travel. Her husband opened the door, and she snuck it under the covers. He was still wearing the djellabah.

Laurel's here, he announced.

She wasn't supposed to come until eleven, she said, making no move to get out of bed.

Well, she's here. In all her glory

THERE WERE TWO taps on the door, and Laurel Moonflower walked inside. A medley of crescent earrings, silver bracelets, floral scents, woven shawls, velvet paisleys. Laurel Moonflower was large, and her flowing hair was the color of moonbeams. She wore two lockets and carried a carpetbag.

My, she said softly. What a wonderful room!

Her husband scrunched over in a straight-backed chair. Welcome to our humble birthing hut, he said in a peasant accent.

Oh, but it's wonderful, said Laurel, missing the irony. All you need is a picture. Something to look at while the baby is being born.

She floated around the room, pressing the mattress, touching the curtains. Everything seemed whiter in her presence, the trees outside dusted with real snow. She sat in the rocker, saying that a rocker was a blessing with a baby. Laurel should know. She'd had three children, each by a different man.

How are you doing? she asked them both.

Fine, they lied.

Really? Somehow the vibes feel . . . Laurel groped, Not exactly . . . mellow. I mean, if something's wrong, I'd like to know.

He leaned forward, adjusting his sunglasses.

I'll tell you the truth, he said, still using the accent. Things are not so fine with us in our little hut. No. As we near the hour of the birth, things are not so fine.

Really? Laurel looked at him warily. In sunglasses, with his hairy legs sticking out of the djellabah, he looked like a strange celebrity from *People*. Like what? she asked.

Like her begrudging me my dreams, he said, dropping the accent. Like her hating me when I happen to have a pleasant night.

Really? Laurel looked upset. What do you mean?

He paused, plunged on.

She envies me my dreams. Not that she'll admit it. But she begrudges me. Talk about vibes! *These* are vibes!

OVER THE PAST months, they'd tried out various names for the baby, some of which persisted in the form of errant greetings. From her aunt, a check accompanied by a card, saying, *Galen, be sure your mom and dad have a teddy bear waiting for you when you arrive.* From two friends overseas, a note: *Love to the future Christopher—our favorite warm fuzzy.* These were on the bedside table, reminders of near-hits, possible errors, compromise. She swept them off, along with the grapes.

I despise you, she said to her husband. You don't stop at anything!

A silence entered the room. An expectant silence. Laurel opened her carpetbag, and the air was perfumed with herbs and flowers. She pulled out sage, dried lavender, rose petals, kept rummaging through the bag. Laurel was looking for something, or pretending to. An amulet? The essence of an angel? She found a small, dark blue book the size of a postcard and carried it over to the bed.

Not another New Age tome, said her husband. Really, we have plenty.

Laurel turned to him.

You leave, she said fiercely. You leave right now.

He left. Laurel handed her the book. It was the size of a child's storybook. All the pages were blank.

What's this?

A book of dreams. Your dreams. Nobody else's. You write down whatever you want to dream, and eventually you'll dream it. Really. It works.

Laurel looked at her sternly. Dream envy is a terrible thing, she continued. Dreams belong to everyone. Even men.

She paused and looked sad. Be grateful, she said, that you share karma with your husband. I only have karma with an animal.

IT WAS QUIET when Laurel left. The smell of lavender was everywhere. She lay back in bed, wondering what Laurel's bull would dream about in his meadow of flowers: cows, perhaps—large, compassionate, forgiving. Or Laurel. With her crescent earrings, staring at him across the fence. Laurel once said that every night in Bolivia, she went to the barn where Flacadillo slept and sat opposite his stall in the straw. They looked at each other for hours.

She shifted. The baby shifted, too, and the space inside her seemed vast, boundless. She got up quietly and took everything Laurel had given her from the bedside table: the dream books, the book of blank pages, the amulets, the dream pillow.

The hell with dreams, she thought, stuffing everything in a drawer. *I'll envy him as much as I want.*

Her husband came in. He'd found clean laundry in the dryer and changed into jeans.

Let's return those T-shirts, he said.

THAT NIGHT, IN the hour of Gabriel's ascendance, she had a dream. Again, she was in Dresden during the war. It was night, and she was escaping in a car driven by a stranger. She could sense every part of the fragile city: its statues, its stonework, its houses about to be bombed. At some point the car was stopped and flashlights shone in her face. It was the police. She reached for false identity papers. The SS nodded and the car drove on.

The dream made sense, the way an echo affirms sound. She didn't tell it to her husband. But he guessed that she had dreamt.

You've been traveling, he said when she woke up. I see it in your eyes.

FOUR WEEKS AGO to this day their baby was born. She wore long purple socks, recommended by Laurel, because purple is the color of healing, and a Renaissance angel in fiery robes watched from a picture on the wall. When he saw the baby, her husband cried. *You see,* Laurel said to her with her eyes, *When they see these wonderful little guys they always melt. . . .*

Their baby still doesn't have a name, although they're coming close to finding one. At night he sleeps between the two of them, in a sense unknown, but no longer obscure. And her husband still dreams. He dreams of crusades and first ascents and trips to Nepal. He's a juggler, a spy, a magician, a tosspot, a double agent, a clown. But she no longer envies his dreams, and this has less to do with her dream of Dresden than with the baby, whom she pushed out by herself, straight into the world. In the morning, when her husband wakes up, he still stretches, smiles, pats her on the belly.

Whatever happened to the good old days? he asks.

The Cat Lover

WHEN A DOOR opens and you can't see who's coming, it's almost always a cat who would like to be your lover. All cats are small, so the opening door looks like an accident. It's not an accident, though. These cats take great care until one paw hooks and the door swings open.

When the door opens, the cat sits at a distance. This is the distance of masked balls, eighteenth-century calling cards—once known by humans, never forgotten by cats. You see its slanted eyes. You see its elegant face. The cat stares at you in all its wildness and comes to rest upon your heart.

Last night my cat lover woke me from a dream where I'd been looking for someone who wouldn't come to find me. This was someone I'd known years ago, and I was searching the narrow streets of an unfamiliar city. When the cat woke me, I realized the entire family had gone to bed in chaos: My son was asleep in front of the television, my husband on the living room couch, my daughter in my son's room, and me in my study wearing all my clothes—soft velvet clothes, something I do when I hope there will be no night. It was three AM, and there was an unplanned feeling to the house, as though all of us, in order to sleep, had entered different zones, and the house itself hadn't been allowed to dream. The cat purred on my chest, but I shook him off and went downstairs to cover my son. Then I wandered to the kitchen and ate lemon ice that reminded me of a place in France where summers were so hot, ices dissolved as soon as they hit the street. I had to stay in the store to eat them. I never knew what they looked like.

While I ate, it occurred to me that nothing has skin—neither me, my children, nor my husband. Falling into his body was just something I did over fourteen years ago because light bound us together like gold. I finished the ice and my cat lover visited again: the approach, the encounter, the looming, and then he rested against my body. His fur and my soft velvet dress felt the same—dark, pillowy textures, things to love and dream in. I felt his small wild heart beat against my chest.

The Terrain
of Madame
Blavatsky

H E DIDN'T WANT his kids to know that he was going to see a woman who channeled angels, so he took them to school early and went home to put on clothes that would disguise him, since—in a small way—he was known around town. He decided to keep it simple: a long coat he didn't usually wear, a scarf he could put over his face. When he got home, his housekeeper, Asuncia Martinez, had arrived from her apartment in the Mission. She was sitting in the kitchen staring at a garden she had helped him plant two years ago. It was winter. The verbenas were scraggly stumps. The beanpoles were empty.

Mrs. Martinez, would you like some breakfast? he asked. It was a question he'd begun to ask every morning.

No, no, por favor, said Mrs. Martinez. She was a small, plain woman with luminous eyes. She wore a black shawl and a cross around her neck, and she often held a rosary. Since she'd discovered her sister and daughter were missing in Colombia, she spent most of her time staring at the garden and crying. Sometimes she worked her rosary. Occasionally she lit candles. He did all the cooking and cleaning.

We should plant the garden soon, he said, gesturing toward the beanpole.

Si. Yes. We should. Mrs. Martinez often spoke in subtitles, and he'd learned a lot of Spanish that way, allowing him more fluency as a talk-show host.

He spooned the rest of the morning's oatmeal into a bowl and brought it to Mrs. Martinez. Try some anyway, he said. She shook her head.

Why don't you just let her go? his friend Charlie had asked him. Charlie of the vodka, the cocaine, and the crazy ways. *Why don't you just let her go?* Charlie didn't have kids. Charlie didn't understand.

You don't buy love, he'd said to him.

After he put the oatmeal on the table, he went upstairs to find the coat—a long coat, purchased years ago, when he and his wife were into vintage stores. He stared in the mirror and wondered if he looked anonymous, or merely strange. A year earlier he would have asked Mrs. Martinez, and she would tell him, *Un poco* too strange. Or, Strange, but in a very nice way. He stuffed the scarf in his pocket and gave Mrs. Martinez money in case she wanted to buy food or candles, although he doubted she would. Then he left the house, carrying his coat, and sorry he hadn't taken his denim jacket after all. It was a cold day.

HE AND CHARLIE were talk-show hosts for the same radio station, and it was because of Charlie he'd discovered the woman who channeled angels. Charlie left her pamphlet in the station's reception room; the instant he read it, he thought of Mrs. Martinez.

Have you ever prayed to angels or wished you could? Do you get solace from a belief in the miraculously divine? Are you aware of guiding forces? If you have answered yes to any of these questions, you will welcome my help! I am an experienced angel channeler and can direct you to higher powers, which will give you solutions to your most personal, heart-wrenching needs. Special rates for house visits, and angel purification ceremonies. Call Roxanne, 861-ANGE, to make an appointment.

Roxanne, the angel channeler, was photographed in blurry light. She had starlit hair, diamond earrings—a parody of a cameo. He assumed Charlie had interviewed her, but Charlie said, No. I left it there as a joke. People are nervous before they come on and I wanted to lighten them up.

What if they believe in angels?

Then they'd feel all good and mushy inside, said Charlie, who noticed he'd stuffed the pamphlet in his pocket. You don't believe in all that crap, do you? he asked.

No. I'm doing research.

HE STUCK THE pamphlet under a pile of mail at home and Seth, his eleven-year-old son, found it: Dad, he said, there's this crazy pamphlet here. Some nut says she can talk to angels.

Give that to me, he said. Now.

Sylvie, who was nine, grabbed the pamphlet from her brother. She sat cross-legged on the floor, touched the pink pearl clasp on her ponytail and read out loud. Call Roxanne, 861-ANGE, to make an appointment, she concluded. He wanted to fall through the floor.

Seth looked at him carefully. No one can talk to angels, he said. That's garbage.

Yes, they can, said Joel. He was four and making an elaborate Ferris wheel out of Legos.

People have different thoughts about these things, he said, speaking quietly because Mrs. Martinez was in the next room. People can believe whatever they want.

Seth sat in a lotus position and closed his eyes. Beware! he intoned in an all-purpose foreign accent. Heavenly beings are on their way.

Sylvie pulled at his sleeve. Don't insult Mrs. Martinez. She's Catholic.

Well I believe in angels, said Joel. And I can get them to ride on this Ferris wheel.

You believe in everything, said Seth. You're *gullible.* He smiled cruelly.

Stop, he said to all of them. Stop arguing. This minute.

He ushered them towards a violent cartoon. He gave them bowls of ice cream covered with gummy bears. Then he brought Mrs. Martinez some lasagna he'd made for dinner.

Mrs. Martinez. Do you believe that people can talk to angels? he asked.

Mrs. Martinez looked at the lasagna like it was some forgotten part of the garden. It all depends, she said. Sometimes they can. Sometimes not. Nothing is for certain.

Could they help you with your daughter?

Oh, not to find her. Not with that. I've never believed in witchcraft. She looked offended.

Then how could they help?

Maybe they could talk to her, tell me how she is.

Would that make you feel better?

Mrs. Martinez paused, as though she was listening to something. *Si.* Yes. Probably.

He remembered there were people in the Mission who claimed to be sorcerers. Would you ever think of going to someone who does that? he asked. You know, someone who sells milagros and answers questions?

Mrs. Martinez waved her hands. No! They don't understand. They sell the wrong candles. She pushed the lasagna away and began to cry.

ROXANNE, THE ANGEL channeler, lived in the fog-belt of San Francisco. Her house, a small grey Victorian with one turret, was next to other tiny houses, all surrounded by mist. There was a knocker on her door in the shape of wings, and he held it in the middle, where an angel's spine would be.

Hello! said a thin voice when he knocked. Can you give me five minutes? The last one had a lot to say.

Sure, he said. But I don't have all day.

What do you do? the thin voice asked.

I happen to be an English teacher.

Cool. That was my favorite subject.

He waited on her steps reading a school bulletin, something about parent's night, something about a raffle. He was always getting bulletins from the school and never had time to go. He jotted down dates in his appointment book, just in case. Soon the door opened and there was Roxanne, not looking at all like her picture. Her hair was short with green streaks. One eyebrow had a silver ring. Each ear was dotted with silver stars. She wore a black T-shirt with cuffs rolled up and a long rust-colored velour skirt with a big slit up the left side. She was short, thin, pale, maybe twenty-three. She reached out a small white hand.

I'm sorry to be late. But if I don't pause properly, I might get the wrong angel.

She's a nut, he thought, following her down a peach-colored corridor. *Mrs. Martinez knew what she was talking about.* They got to a small parlor with climbing-rose wallpaper, Roxanne waved to an overstuffed chair, and he sat down. Roxanne sat opposite him. He'd been prepared for dreamy, opium-eyes. Hers were small and sharp.

What are you thinking? she asked.

That you don't look like your picture.

That's right. Angels don't care for Victorian stuff. People just think they do. She gestured toward the room—its silk pillows, its piebald velvet furniture. She leaned forward, reminding him of Sylvie when she wanted something from the mall.

Pretty soon I'm going to get rid of this stuff and do everything over in black and chrome, she said. You see, I got that funky photograph because I thought I should ride the crest. Then my face went punk and my body started to follow.

What's the crest?

You know. The crest. Whatever people believe in these days. Ideas that fly by at a hundred miles an hour.

You mean the zeitgeist?

The *what*-geist? I'd rather call it the crest. Anyway, she took a sip of Coke from a nearby table, how come you're here?

It's about my housekeeper. She's unhappy and I thought you could help her.

You mean it's not about *you*? Roxanne looked concerned, even angry. You mean you came to talk about someone *else*?

Well in a sense it really is about me. What I mean, he paused. What I mean is that my wife left me about three years ago and this woman has taken care of my kids ever since. Now her sister and daughter have disappeared in Colombia and she can't cook, or eat, or even sleep. All she can do is cry. He was close to tears himself.

Roxanne looked at the ceiling as though invoking invisible spirits.

Mr. Rose, she said in a tone that made him regret that he hadn't told her his real name. Mr. Rose, let me be honest: In all my years as an angel-channeler—and I've had a few—I have found that people who want to hook *other* people up with angels are always concerned with *themselves*. To be blunt—she took another sip of Coke—these people need an excuse to find their own personal angel and they hide behind some other person's problems. I'm really sorry to say this, Mr. Rose, but that's been my experience.

He looked at the velvet plush couch, lamps with pink silk fringes, crystals dangling from lace-curtained windows and a filigreed lamp that was creepily arcane. The only book in sight was a large black book called *The Terrain of Madame Blavatsky*. He could tell it was old: The gold of the title was peeling.

I'm sorry, he said, but it really *is* about my housekeeper. I don't mind doing the cleaning, or cooking. It's just terrible having my kids watch her suffer. They love her; they care about her. And all she does is cry.

Then why don't you get someone else?

Someone else? *Get someone else?*

Yeah. Just put an ad in the paper and get someone else.

Roxanne, how old are you?

Twenty-two and a half.

Have you ever had kids?

No.

Then you don't understand: Mrs. Martinez is all my children know. They'd be heartbroken if she left. Besides. We love her.

For a moment Roxanne's face softened, as if lit by interior light. Why didn't you just send her then?

I'm sorry, I feel protective. I needed to check you out.

Check me out? Listen to that: He needed to check me out. She looked at another invisible presence on the ceiling. Needed to check me out, she repeated.

So you won't help?

Roxanne didn't answer. She closed her eyes. Mr. Rose, please be quiet. Your personal angel has arrived.

The room was hot. He thought he smelled incense and was starting to sweat. He felt trapped in mud, brick, lime—whatever was in the walls of the tiny, run-down house.

Mr. Rose, please. Don't move around so much. I'm starting to channel. Roxanne fluttered her eyelids. A tremor appeared in her hands. *I should go,* he thought. *I should get out of here this minute.* He shifted in his chair, a first step in starting to get up. Don't leave! Roxanne commanded. Don't leave or your personal angel will be upset.

She was still trembling. Her eyelid moved like butterflies. Oh my, she said in a quiet voice. Your angel is giving me some information that we're going to have to clear up right away. He's telling me that you're traveling under an alias. He's telling me that you really aren't Mr. Rose, that your last name starts with an *S* and you're pretending to be some else because you feel weird about seeing me. She opened her eyes and looked at him. Is that right?

Yes, he said. The word flew out, unbidden.

Good. That's what your angel says, and I'm relieved you agree. You don't have to tell me your real name. You just have to tell me the truth. If you don't want to tell me the truth, don't say anything. Okay?

Okay.

Good. Thank you. Your angel understands. Roxanne frowned. Are you cynical?

I'd prefer to say I was skeptical.

Skeptical, she repeated, closing her eyes. That's probably why you used an alias.

What?

It doesn't matter. Your angel just told me not to get into this sort of thing with you. He says he wouldn't be helpful.

Roxanne's head was against the back of the chair. There were beads of sweat around her mouth. Even if she were a quack, he could see she was exerting tremendous effort. Mr. S, she continued, this is what your angel is telling me: Your problem isn't your housekeeper. It's you.

I should leave, he thought. *I should just get up and leave.* He looked around the room for signs of his angel, thinking he'd take anything: An odd quality of light on the rug. Rustlings from the big black book. The only luminous object was a small TV in the corner; Roxanne had covered most of it with blue velvet cloth.

I'm sorry to disappoint you, he said, but it's her I've come about. Nothing between the lines. My kids need her and I thought you could help. It's just that simple. And now I'm leaving. You know? Like I'm going to get up.

Mr. S! Roxanne opened her eyes. Nothing is that simple. Why have you been alone all these years? Why haven't you gotten married?

That's a personal question.

I didn't ask it. Your angel did.

Wives don't grow on trees.

Have you ever looked?

He didn't answer. Roxanne's eyebrows fluttered, and he watched while the silver ring went up and down. Mr. S, she said softly, angels only know the truth. That's why they can talk to you. Angels are *beyond.* They're beyond the crest of this current age.

He no longer remembered whether he was supposed to be answering a question or asking one, and Roxanne leaned way back in her chair, clearly listening to someone else. He closed his eyes, too, and they sat together in silence. There was a floating feeling in the room. It made him think of his wife floating out of the house, enclosed in a nimbus of alcohol. It was almost like a levitation, the way she left, early one Sunday morning, carrying a small white bag, wearing an angora dress that seemed airborne. She floated out. Mrs. Martinez floated in. Where's Mom? Seth had asked. She left for a while, he said. Everything will be okay.

Is something occurring to you, Mr. S?

No. And you can call me John.

All right, John. Is anything coming to mind?

No. Nothing.

Well I'm hearing something. Do you want me to tell you?

If you like.

Well . . . It's a letter your wife left. A letter that said something like: *We have children, a house, friends. And we're caught up in this ridiculous net that people like to think is called the world. I want to go outside. I want to go back to where the stars burn underwater.* Yes. That's what I've been hearing. . . .

He remembered the letter. He kept it in the trunk and found it every Halloween when he kept costumes for the kids.

Does that sound right to you? Roxanne asked.

Listen, I didn't come here to get my mind read, and I think I'm going to leave.

That's fine. You can leave whenever you want to. But please don't call me a mind-reader. I'm not and neither is your angel. He's simply lived your life. He's lived it from the day you were born.

How come he hasn't bothered to tell me then?

Because. You haven't asked him. Roxanne took a deep breath. Anyway, he's told me not to quibble. And I happen to have something difficult to tell you, which is that Mrs. Martinez wants to go back to Colombia. Even if she gets killed there, she wants to go back, and she's only staying with you because she's worried about your kids, and she also worries you'll be sad without her.

That's not what she says at all. She says she wants to stay.

It doesn't matter what she says. I'm telling you what she wants.

You mean there's nothing I can do?

Oh, there's a lot you could do if you wanted to. Roxanne frowned. The lines between her brows became dense. I'm sorry, Mr. S., she said. Your personal angel has to leave. He's needed elsewhere. He sends his blessings. She leaned back, breathed deeply. The frown relaxed. She opened her eyes. He saw she was even paler. Her lips were slightly blue.

Who is my personal angel, anyway? he asked.

I can't tell you his name because you didn't tell him yours—at least not your full one.

What if I tell it to you now?

I'm sorry, but he's gone. If he ever comes back, you can negotiate.

I don't understand.

I don't either, except angels calculate everything on a basis of exchange.

Like money?

Like truth.

Oh Lord. What do I owe you?

Nothing. Your personal angel doesn't want you to pay me. It seems you were a special case.

How come?

He asked me not to explain.

But why?

Something about your rational mind, Mr. S. The way the circuitry is all hooked up. He'll tell you when he wants to.

He stood up, feeling disembodied. He looked over at *The Terrain of Madame Blavatsky*, and it occurred to him that maybe the book was a country and he could travel there tomorrow. Roxanne stood up, too. She looked smaller, more waif-like.

How long have you been in this business? he asked.

Seven years.

What got you into it?

I'm not sure. Maybe if I knew I wouldn't be doing it. Roxanne looked around the room and fingered a fringe on the lampshade. As soon as I get my act together, I'm getting out of this creepy house. That's why I'm sorry he wouldn't let you pay me.

I'm glad to pay you. Really.

I never go against orders.

He left her house and stood outside, holding his coat and listening to the radio, which Roxanne had turned on the moment he left. He could hear someone talking about Zimbabwe, someone talking very fast. Someone riding the crest at a hundred miles an hour.

The Eye of
the Needle

BECAUSE SHE LOVED him and because she was lonely, she'd come all the way from Iowa to visit him in Los Angeles and listen to him talk about his sexual-identity crisis. This crisis was giving him insomnia, inhibiting the flow of his writing, and reducing his diet to kiwi fruit and bread.

I don't know if I like men or women, he said, I don't know if I'm supposed to make love with gadgets or do it straight. I don't know anything.

Caroline was five years older than Jonathan, almost thirty-one, and knew, or believed she knew, what it felt like to be another person. She imagined that being Jonathan was difficult, like having a brain made of hot, electric wires or a body that wanted to leave its own skin. She felt a sense of compassion mixed with pity and forgave the fact that his eyes looked right past her.

Jonathan, she said, Sex is slippery.

Slippery, said Jonathan. He laughed.

They were at his kitchen table—a green Formica table, filled with Jonathan's rewrites of a dog food commercial. She saw stage directions for the dog: *Enter stage left! Exit stage right! Bark twice!!!* She leaned and patted Jonathan's hand. He removed it and peeled a kiwi fruit.

How about that commercial? she said. How many times will you have to rewrite that?

I don't know. Until I get it right.

Well maybe sex is the same way.

Jonathan looked at Caroline as if she'd said something poisonous. *If only he'd sleep with me again,* she thought. *If only he'd sleep with me, then I could show him.* But what? How to distract himself when he lost his erection? Obsessed about the merit of wearing nightgowns to bed? She only saw them in the dark, close together. She navigated by compassion, didn't think things through. That was what her mother always said.

Jonathan, she said, patting his arm again.

They'd become lovers after meeting at a rave five years ago, and for a while she was convinced they would get married. In Jonathan's presence she could remember small, extraordinary things: the time she'd seen a man's fur coat lying on the snowy streets of Prague, or when her mother made a cake in the shape of a swan. Jonathan listened, and then, one day, began to tell her his secrets. The secrets were nothing he'd done, just things he couldn't stop thinking about doing, and eventually they interfered with their lovemaking. She left L.A. and went to film school in Iowa. Now, whenever she visited, Jonathan did most of the talking, and she did most of the listening.

This time was exactly like the last: Jonathan took her to bars and stayed up all night talking about people there who'd turned him on.

I see why you're confused, she'd said this morning. Everyone in L.A. is beautiful.

Really? I don't think so.

It was nearly dawn and they were lying on his black futon. She stroked Jonathan's cheekbones and his green-spiked hair. It was clumped, solid, like leftover food.

JONATHAN HAD A clock that told time all over the world. She stared at the clock and tried to imagine what people were doing in Sweden, Tokyo, Spain. She looked at her flowered dress, and thought *I must go shopping.* In Iowa she wore whatever she wanted, usually uncool baggy blue jeans and T-shirts. Here everyone wore black and looked like they modeled for unisex stores. No wonder Jonathan was in a crisis. Maybe he should leave L.A. and come to Iowa. She was wondering what would happen if she suggested this, when he said,

Caroline. I want us to be lovers.

You mean you want to sleep with me again?

Yes. But I have to prepare. I want to get an ampallang.

Jonathan said *ampallang* slowly, as though it were a foreign word. He also said it carefully, as though Caroline might not know what it meant.

Caroline knew: Last winter in Iowa she'd slept with someone who had an ampallang—a soft-spoken student in economics with a deep concern for third-world countries. His touch was so light, her whole body felt like lace. She'd eventually stopped seeing him because of Jonathan. She almost told him about Corey now, then reminded herself that being Jonathan was hard enough to begin with; it would better if he thought he were the first.

What are you thinking about? Jonathan asked.

About whether I should dye my hair orange, she said. What do you think?

Try Kool-Aid first.

THEY WENT TO the piercing parlor on a rainy afternoon. It was the kind of rain that enclosed the city in mist and created a sense of isolation from the rest of the world. The wind whipped around the car and Caroline had the sense of living in an earlier time—a time when what Jonathan was about to do would be discussed in a book called *Perverse and Unusual Practices*. She'd seen a book with that title in the rare-book room at Iowa when she was researching the history of film. It had daguerreotypes of seedy Paris dives where stern madams wore nothing but pearls and British lords begged for canings.

Are you scared? she asked Jonathan.

No. Not at all.

Caroline looked at herself in the rearview mirror. She liked the orange blaze she'd put in her hair.

Do you like it? My hair? she asked.

I don't know. I guess so. But it smells like Kool-Aid.

The piercing parlor was called The Eye of the Needle and was furnished in retro-Victorian funk. They entered with reluctance and sat on purple velvet chairs that concealed broken springs. A child of about ten sat opposite them reading *Cricket* magazine. Caroline hoped she wasn't there to get a piercing.

Once you do it, she said to Jonathan, you're going to live with it forever.

I know, he said. That's how I want it to be.

She patted his arm, he took it away, and then he held himself in by both elbows. She thought he looked terse and secret, like a desert plant.

Soon a man wearing leather chaps came out, told Jonathan they were ready, and asked if she wanted to come along to see. She said she didn't, not really, unless she had to, and Jonathan said she didn't. When they disappeared, she picked up a copy of *Pierce!* magazine and looked at all the pictures. She was looking for an ampallang and found it on page five. It floated above all the other gadgets like a prehistoric painting: smooth, totemic, an artifact from the Iron Age.

COREY, THE GRADUATE student in economics, had discovered Caroline in a closet on New Year's Eve when he came to get his coat. The closet was a walk-in, there were piles of coats on the floor, and Caroline was buried beneath them crying because Jonathan wasn't answering her calls.

My God, a real person, said Corey when he found her.

Hardly, she said, sitting up.

While the party raged and the professor of film history imitated Garbo, she and Corey turned the coats into a cave and crawled inside. Corey undressed her carefully—it had been a long time since Jonathan had done that—and when he took off his clothes, he told her to touch a shiny metal cylinder that went sideways through his penis.

The cylinder was fastened by two round knobs. Caroline liked the way they felt, and she asked Corey if he'd take the knobs off, but Corey said no, it probably wasn't a good idea, since once he'd done that and they'd gotten lost and he was crawling all over the bedroom like he was looking for a contact lens. When they made love, her body felt as fragile as the snow that fell outside the tiny window, and she realized she didn't care that Jonathan hadn't called. She was surprised she'd said he could visit the following month and was more surprised to be with him in Los Angeles now. Two months ago, Corey had said he'd decided to stop using the ampallang and wondered if she'd like to make love anyway. Jonathan was back on the scene, and she'd said she wasn't interested.

EACH TIME THE door opened, Caroline and the child looked up. A tall man with a nostril ring appeared, and soon a woman with flowing copper hair ushered the child to the street. Finally Jonathan came out, looking pale. The man in leather chaps was holding him up.

I'm afraid he didn't handle it well, he said. I'm afraid he didn't handle it very well at all.

A lot of people faint, said Jonathan. It has to do with feelings about body parts.

That's true, said the man. But very few of our customers . . . ah . . . throw up. He said this gently. Jonathan looked abashed.

Do you want something? Caroline asked. A Coke to settle your stomach?

Nothing. Let's just go home.

He's in no condition to understand the care he needs, the man whispered to her. Almost none of them are. They think it's like getting an earring, but an ear is very different from a penis.

The man spoke sternly, with wisdom and compassion. She wondered where his own piercing was. He handed her a list with things she must buy for Jonathan's care: Cotton swabs, Q-tips, alcohol. She shuddered.

Don't worry about it, the man said. In a day he'll be perfectly able to do it himself, and in a two weeks he can have a normal sex life.

What's that?

Whatever he does, said the man. We'd rather not know about preferences.

CAROLINE DROVE QUICKLY, not stopping for things on the list. When they got home, Jonathan took off everything but his briefs and stood very still, holding his crotch. Caroline very much wanted to look at the ampallang yet felt she couldn't ask.

I feel like a mutant, he said.

I think you ought to go to lie down. It's just one of those times when you should rest.

She helped him to the futon. Jonathan cradled his crotch, and it was clear she couldn't touch it.

Could you make me some tea? he asked.

SHE LIT THE fire under the kettle, then went to Jonathan's closet and put on a pair of his black jeans and one of his black T-shirts. Back in the kitchen, she looked at the world clock: In Tokyo, women were taking down laundry. In Greece, people were driving to work. In Sweden, farmers were milking cows. And in Los Angeles, a man had just gotten an ampallang. Caroline strained chamomile tea in a blue willow cup, aware of her black clothes. She felt anonymous, androgynous, oddly replaceable.

Suddenly Jonathan called out: Caroline! I've made a dreadful mistake! I didn't want to do it in the first place! And I think I'm terribly maimed! No, really! I think I'm maimed!

She came into the room with the tea. Why do you think you're maimed?

I can't explain. I can't explain. I just feel like I've got a dog bone in my prick.

She came in and wrapped one leg around his waist. She tried to avoid the affected area.

Well . . . you experimented, that's all. That's what people do. They try one thing and if they don't like it, they try something else. Even people with ampallangs can change their minds.

But you said I'd have this for forever. Jonathan was almost crying.

Well see? I changed my about that mind, too.

Talk to me, Caroline. Please.

About what?

Anything. That coat in Prague. Or the cake your mom made that looked like a swan. Just talk to me, Caroline. Tell me anything.

Anything?

Yes. Anything.

Caroline began to talk. She talked about the coat in Prague and the cake in the shape of a swan. She talked about the black clothes in Los Angeles and the professor of film imitating Garbo. Jonathan fell asleep, one hand around his crotch, and Caroline went back to the mirror. Then she began to look through her purse. Corey's number was somewhere, alive in that tangled darkness.

Milagros

ARTHUR CAME HOME from his bookstore at six o'clock, stood on the steps, and whistled. The dark night. The porch. The familiar smells of home. Inside he could see Emily, Annie, Marc, Eduardo, all bent in unison over the table with the black cat Primus below them. Emily was spooning soup. Annie and Marc were looking. Eduardo was staring in the distance. *This,* he thought, *is my home. This is what I have come to.*

He stood on the steps and whistled again.

And then he was gone.

EDUARDO SITS IN the kitchen. He leafs through copies of *The New York Times* and *People* magazine, which his stepmother reads somewhat guiltily. The small river has been dragged. The police have arrived and asked questions. The swollen body of his stepfather has been found. It's very bloated, Ma'am, the police say. You wouldn't even want to see his clothes. But Annie brought the clothes home in a bag and set everything out to dry on the line as if Arthur was about to come back.

He whistled! she kept saying to the policeman. He whistled and I heard him. Just like he always does.

His stepbrother and stepsister said that, too.

He whistled! He really whistled!

They said this like it would lead them back to Arthur's warm, living body. They said this like this was a clue. They'd been born in this house, knew Arthur since they had been babies. They had seen his head over their cribs. They had felt his arms around them when they cried. He had taught them how to play ball and read to them from the funny papers.

EDUARDO, HOWEVER, COULD believe exactly what happened, although he didn't say so. In fact, he feigned surprise only because he knew people expected it. He could believe it because his mother had died and his grandmother had died and his uncle also had died, and Eduardo knew death had a way of making itself known. Before the person departs, the air opens around them, and whenever one happens to look out a window with them the view is large. Eduardo's uncle Oliviero had killed himself rather than be taken by the police, and the day before, Eduardo could read the space around his uncle's body as though it were a map. Not everybody who looked could see what was on the map. But his grandmother could.

Look at uncle Olivero's back, she said. But don't look too closely. You don't want to follow.

Eduardo didn't. Death was everywhere.

DURING THOSE DAYS in the sharp California summer, the air around Arthur was large, spacious. He also moved slowly, as though his body were inside glass. And his eyes looked straight ahead, stopping at a fixed point, as though there were nowhere beyond that point they needed to look.

At night, Arthur sat in his study and drank strong cups of coffee. Eduardo knew he was fighting sleep because in sleep, he would disappear. Once, Eduardo went downstairs to get a glass of Ovaltine, which he was allowed any time because since coming from El Salvador he was always hungry. Arthur was sitting at the kitchen table drinking milk, surrounded in wild, friable air. Eduardo's grandmother had told him to look inside the air, as though he were parting curtains, so he could get a good last look at his uncle. He parted the air now, to look at Arthur, and Arthur was very much himself, except he was one notch back from the world and waiting.

What are you doing? he said to Eduardo.

Getting Ovaltine, said Eduardo.

ANNIE HAD WANTED to adopt another child. To Eduardo's way of thinking, it meant that she wanted two of him. She wanted an Eduardo in the third grade and an Eduardo who was in kindergarten. She wanted an Eduardo who wore his own new clothes (she was careful not to use the other children's hand-me-downs) and a smaller Eduardo who wore the real Eduardo's hand-me-downs. Annie and Arthur had tense discussions about the second Eduardo, while he, the first one, crouched by the door. Sometimes their voices grew so loud, he wondered if Arthur were intending to leave and was tempted to ask. In fact, he did something close to that. He leaned toward Arthur and asked in Spanish. Are you sorry that you got me?

No, said Arthur, carefully. I'm not sorry at all. How come?

I just wondered. Eduardo drank his Ovaltine. Arthur drank his milk.

Suddenly Arthur asked, Do you believe in milagros?

No, said Eduardo, even though he did.

I do, said Arthur. And then he took one out of his pocket—a bent right arm, the kind that people get when they hurt themselves on a construction site. Here, he said.

There's nothing wrong with my arm.

No. Not literally. This is for strength. For muscle. For purpose.

I don't need that, Eduardo said, not wanting a gift from someone who was going to die.

LATER THAT NIGHT, Eduardo heard the discussion again.

I can't take in every kid who walks those railroad tracks, said Arthur in a low calm voice.

I'm not asking you to do that. You know I'm not.

I think you are, said Arthur. Eduardo's a good kid, but you treat him like a cause. He's himself. Himself alone.

Eduardo did not listen the way he had listened back home, where voices were threaded around him while he slept. These had been soft, laughing voices, talking of amulets, witches' markets, neighbors, and later, in lower voices, about the *junta*. *Shhh! Eduardo is sleeping!* the voices said. Here it was different. He had to shift, move, press his ears against the wall, the way his grandmother made him listen to crops grow.

He shifted now, and the floor creaked.

Eduardo is up, said Arthur. That kid knows everything.

He has to, said Annie. How do you think he walked those railroad tracks? She said this loudly, throwing her voice in Eduardo's direction. She was trying to reassure him. Eduardo wanted to run out and tell her *Arthur is thinking of dying.*

ARTHUR ALWAYS WHISTLED, Annie was saying for God knows how many times. He whistled every night he came home. That's why we suspect foul play. He worked so hard. He had such a good business. Everyone in town trusted him. Everyone went to the bookstore.

She was talking to a neighbor and Eduardo was listening. This neighbor was a woman from the east, a psychologist named Claire.

Arthur was unhappy, said Claire with authority.

How do you know? Annie pressed her hands on the table.

I just know.

Were you two having an affair, then? After Arthur died, Annie was given to sudden outbursts.

No, said Claire calmly. Arthur and I weren't lovers. I didn't even know him well. It's just when I came into the store one day, he recommended some books about suicide. It was clear he'd been reading them.

Claire looked triumphant. Didn't you know?

What were the books? Annie was trembling.

They were, Claire closed her eyes, they were *When Life is Not Enough, The Ethics of Leaving Others Behind, Six Questions to Ask When You are Contemplating Death,* and *Meditations on a Funeral.* There were also several biographies of St. John of the Cross. Or San Juan de la Cruz, as he really should be called. And except for *When Life is Not Enough,* none of them were self-help books. They were books that Arthur had ordered for himself because there was only one of each in stock. He had read them and wanted to get rid of them. He *gave* them to me. Do you want them back?

No.

Claire was not an unattractive woman, yet she had the marks of a spinster: Sensible clothes. Pulled-back hair. There was a bite to the word *gave.* Annie flinched and reconsidered. Were any passages underlined?

That happens to be why I came. Except for that first book, which was crap, the others are good and I've ordered them. But I thought you should have these. She pulled them out of her briefcase and set them on the table.

Did you read the books? Annie asked.

Of course. That's why I ordered them. Nothing was underlined, by the way—there weren't any notes. But it's clear he read them. You can tell when a book has been read. She didn't say how, and Eduardo stayed still, the way he was supposed to. He spoke more English than people knew, which meant they acted as if he weren't there.

There was one other thing, too, said Claire. Arthur was collecting milagros.

Milagros? said Annie. You must be kidding. He hated that kind of thing.

Maybe. He was a very rational man. Even so, he was collecting them. I saw them in the back of the store. Haven't you been there since . . . ?

Of course I've been.

The night Arthur drowned, Annie had put up a notice that the store would be closed. She hadn't stayed long, of course. On the other hand, she hadn't run. She'd stood in the darkness, waiting, she hoped, for Arthur's murderer. She didn't care if he came out right now and killed her. At least she'd know.

You should go back, Claire said. Look in Arthur's office. That's where he kept the milagros. If they're gone, maybe it was foul play. Maybe even the books were a cover-up. I don't think so.

She stood up and looked at Eduardo. You've seen a lot of death, she said. It was a statement, not a sentiment.

LATER THAT DAY, Annie tapped Eduardo on the shoulder. He was looking out the window, at the vista that had been large the week before Arthur died. It was now an ordinary landscape, consisting of a flat green pasture circled by hills. The week before, it had been enormous, suggesting fields beyond fields, hills that went to the sky. He'd only seen this when he and Arthur were looking together, the way, when people are dying, they look at something for the last time.

Let's go to the store, Annie said in Spanish. I want to see the milagros. Do you mind?

No, said Eduardo. He was used to the haunts of the dead. On the Day of the Dead they had picnics by his grandfather's grave near his mother's favorite park, where his uncle used to played bocce. It was the living who were ghosts, prying human secrets.

You don't mind, do you? Annie said in Spanish. Like Claire's pronouncement about death, it was just a statement.

THE BOOKSTORE HADN'T been opened since Annie put up the sign, and they tripped over a pile of envelopes under the drop-in mail slot. Some of them were condolence letters, and there were also business letters and catalogues from publishers. Annie stepped over them as though they were snow, leaves, or some other inconvenience of the weather. Eduardo put them on a shelf. He felt this mail belonged to Arthur, who hadn't been dead for very long. They walked to Arthur's office in the back of the store, which had a couch, a desk, and Javanese puppets. There was a round box on the desk with an open lid. It was full of milagros.

My God, said Annie. We used to use that for pot.

She turned the box upside-down and they all fell out. There were more arms, some legs, eyes, and several books. Eduardo was sorry that Arthur hadn't offered him a book. He took one of the milagros that was shaped like one.

Put it back for now, said Annie. We'll get to the bottom of this.

She spoke briskly, as though something would lead to the unspeakable. And then she sat on the couch and cried. What was he doing with the milagros? she asked, no longer acting as though Eduardo didn't understand English. What in the world was he doing with them?

Eduardo didn't answer even though he thought he knew. He thought he knew because he saw a metal child among them, and this was a signal that Arthur was having trouble making himself strong against Annie's will about having another child. His grandmother had told him that. Milagros come to people whether they want them or not.

What are you thinking? Annie said.

I wasn't thinking anything.

There was a book on Arthur's desk. *El Secreto de los Milagros*.

Can you read this? Annie asked.

I don't know.

Well, try. Read it to me here. The book was about eighty pages long.

Can't we take it home?

No. I don't want the other kids to see it.

THE BOOK TOOK them four days to read because Eduardo read slowly, and Annie always went back at six to feed the kids. Every evening they locked up the shop and left everything just as they'd found it. And in the afternoons when they came back, Annie walked across the mail and Eduardo put it on a shelf. Eduardo read carefully, omitting certain passages. He didn't want to stumble on anything that referred to fate. It was his grandmother's theory: She believed that if certain things were read, they would happen, and he cared about Annie. Fortunately, the book was so scholarly there was almost nothing he had to leave out. The totemic nature of Spanish Catholicism, Eduardo translated, is often linked to Indian worship.

My God, Annie said, how could he read all this?

Eduardo wanted to say that maybe he hadn't. Maybe he'd just gotten the book. But he didn't because he knew—just as Claire knew—that every page had been read. He could tell by the way they were worn, the way some were bent back. He could also feel Arthur's eyes, a concentration that belied a kind of tired excitement. Eventually he came to the part he didn't want to read: Some people believe that when a milagro comes their way it isn't an accident. The witches of La Paz think that if you don't want another child, but get a cow or a ram or a goat or anything else that symbolizes fertility, you are out of luck. Husbands of women in La Paz destroy milagros of babies in the corn-fields. Especially when they already have sons and are very poor.

When he came to this passage, he stopped and read right on. There was a sense of a beat skipped, a page being turned.

Annie grabbed his wrist. You've forgotten something.

No, said Eduardo, I haven't. This was the truth. He'd been scrupulous about the omission. But Annie made him read the passage anyway. When he was through, she was quiet.

Is there a milagro like that in there? she asked.

No, said Eduardo.

Yes, said Annie. There is.

She walked to the box, and her hands went right for the child.

This is it, she said. Isn't it?

My family didn't believe in crap like that, said Eduardo. We weren't peasants who couldn't wipe our asses. We went to the university. We knew a thing or two.

Annie slapped him.

A good family, really? she said. Then why were you hungry all the time when you got here? Why do you have Ovaltine whenever you want it?

Because there wasn't any food there. You know that. He stuck out his tongue at Annie, and she slapped him again. I'm not reading any more of that book, he said. I'm not being your little Spanish translator. He grabbed the book he really wanted—the milagro—and left the store.

WHEN HE GOT home, all the kids were gathered around the table. It was seven o'clock. Annie had forgotten dinner.

Listen, I'll make tortillas, okay?

It was what Eduardo had done when his mother had died, his uncle had died, and when his grandmother who told him about death had died.

Emily and Marc thought tortillas were a cool idea. They could say that, even though their father had killed himself.

A cool idea, Marc repeated before running to the corner store for a tin of refried beans.

A cool idea, said Emily, taking tortillas from the freezer and thawing them by holding them lightly over the gas flame, the way Eduardo showed her. They were delighted when they found sour cream and tomatoes, scallions and avocado in the vegetable bin. Eduardo made rice. He showed Emily and Marc how to make canned refried beans taste fresh by adding lemon. And all the while he cooked, he thought of how he would cross the border and walk the railroad tracks to Mexico. He also thought he would stop by the river to see if he could get a glimpse of Arthur. *Mourn. Drown. Home.* He chanted the words that had brought him there.

When Annie came back and saw Eduardo making tortillas, she had no idea that later, much later, he would put on old clothes and leave one more empty space around the kitchen table. She was only thinking of the metal child and a piece of paper she'd found in the book Eduardo was reading. It was yellow paper, probably used as a bookmark, and had something scribbled in Arthur's writing: *All good things will come to you.*

The Dungeon Master's Mother

S HE COULDN'T REMEMBER when she began to feel like a time-traveler in her very own house. Maybe one morning when she looked at a plate of her son's half-finished ragged-edged eggs and thought, *This was a human custom at the time. They started their eggs and never finished them,* Or maybe one evening, when she looked at her daughter's homework, noticed she'd quoted an entire poem by Millet and thought, *At the end of that particular century, they quoted poems and filled a lot of space on the page.*

The voice that spoke was not her own. It was quiet, deep, guarded. One evening she put her husband's shoes in his closet and stood there for a moment, looking at his shirts, ties, business suits, T-shirts, blue jeans. She looked more closely at the clothes, and the voice spoke again: *Almost every day, at the end of that century, people dressed one way in the morning and another way at night. It was the custom.*

HER NINE-YEAR-OLD SON was the Dungeon Master at P.S. 59. He was the youngest person at P.S. 59 ever to have the job, and the dining table was littered with *Dungeons & Dragons* literature. One night she paused, looking at pictures of animals, witches, shape-changers. She watched him fill out important-looking charts, wondering how he could keep the entire cast of characters in his head: elves, griffins, black magicians, club-footed dwarves, dragons, unicorns, wizards who bent time. She looked over his shoulder and saw a report he'd done for school. It was wedged into the *D&D* book, accompanied by a pie-shaped graph. It was called Cody's Interview of Fears:

> burning to death was the most popular choice 8/10 of the class chose it. the next most popular choice was getting sucked into a black hole 4/18 of the class chose that. next was a tie between pain and falling to death each got 2/18 last is another tie between just plain dyeing and getting blown up

MOM, SAID HER son. That's *private*.

Sorry, she said, going into the living room to ask her husband what he thought about this *Dungeons & Dragons* stuff. He was absorbed in the newspaper and didn't answer. The voice, however, volunteered: *At that particular time, children pored over books filled with runes, magic, and alchemical formulas. They also thought about various forms of annihilation. It was simply how things were done, and no one could ever guess the century these particular children were living in.*

She made her living as a psychotherapist, so it was easy to check the voice for signs of delusion and grandeur. Was it telling her to do strange things? No. Definitely not. Did it have a distinct personality? No, not that either. *Sometimes,* the diagnostic manual read, *people think thoughts that are slightly foreign to them, and these thoughts appear in the form of detached voices. While it may be beneficial to examine the meaning of such thoughts, it is not always necessary to seek professional help.*

Good, she thought, realizing that she'd grown to feel protective of the voice.

FOR MANY MONTHS the voice was silent. It stopped commenting at home and never spoke at all in her therapy office—although maybe that was because she had no qualities there, but was pale, transparent, a vessel for other people. True, when a client once looked at the cream-colored walls and said, rather angrily, This place feels like one of those panoramic Easter eggs, she felt offended. But this was only for a moment, and then she felt neutral again. And so she was surprised when the voice spoke one evening after one of her favorite clients, a middle-management executive in his early thirties, looked at her directly and said, You know, I hate to say it, but something in here feels tilted.

Tilted?

Yes. Tilted. As though, if you stayed here long enough, you would start to think about things in a different way.

Things are *tilted,* said the voice. *That is the way it is in offices these days. Animals don't have offices. But watch them explore your home! Indeed, they may be aware of more than you know.*

After her client left, she watched him disappear down the street, wheeling his bike as though it were a fragile part of him. Then she lay on the floor and looked at a small crack in the ceiling. It was quiet and restful, and she liked the feeling of the plush white rug against her hair. In a few moments there was a knock on the door. It was her client again, bike and all.

I got worried about you, he said. You shouldn't be in your office with your door open. Last week a woman was killed because of that. I read about it in the paper.

She wondered if he'd known she'd been lying on her office floor and supposed that he did because, in spite of secrecy, everyone knew everything.

I'm fine, she told him, really fine. But thank you.

You did the right thing, said the voice. *It is nobody's business but yours that you sometimes use your office for private, unusual purposes.*

After this episode, the voice didn't speak again for many months. She looked at uneaten eggs, poetry reports, *Dungeons & Dragons* books, clothes in closets. She argued with her best friend about whether or not Laundromats promoted a deeper sense of community, and she gave a presentation on her paper called The Paradox of Psychotherapy, in which she maintained that learning how to be a client involved learning the same peculiar steps needed to function in modern society.

For this reason, she concluded, psychotherapy may be a questionable and perverse form of socialization. We shouldn't overlook other solutions. Several people walked out.

IT WAS AFTER two Jehovah's Witnesses came that the voice spoke again: *Don't condemn them,* it said after she had turned away two women in clean white suits. *They are just innocent human beings trying to make sense of things. Doomsday is just one of many options.*

While the voice spoke, her son was making copious notes about a unicorn. The notes stated that the unicorn had an IQ of 800 and the strength potential of twenty men.

How do you figure it out? she asked.

You just roll some dice, he answered as though she were extremely stupid.

And then?

And then you create a character.

And what does the character do?

It plays with other characters. What else?

Nothing. I just wondered. Listen: Could you make me a character?

Well, not really. . . .

Why not?

You're a grown-up. Grown-ups aren't characters.

Why not?

They don't change.

Oh, but they do, said the voice. *They just use other options. Try page seventy-nine in that book called Dungeons & Dragons Part III.*

That night, when her son was asleep, she snuck into the dining room and looked at page 79 in *D&D Part III.* She saw a picture of a woman who was half beast and half woman, crouched on all fours like a dog and covered with fur. The caption explained: *Women who grow fur are sometimes feral and live in caves. At other times they stay at home like contented pets. Because of their familiarity with human life—as well as their unpredictability—they are* never *suitable characters for D&D adventures.*

She shut the book, but not before looking at some runes her son had drawn. One was shaped like a woman, another like a mouse. From the bedroom, her husband called her: Alice! Alice! For a moment the name sounded strange and foreign.

Her husband was asleep again. He slept on his back, the way he always slept, as if ready to greet the world. She went to the bathroom, looked in the mirror, and then bent close to her arms, listening to her skin.

IT WAS AN incredible act of will, this growing of fur. She grew it at night, concentrating on one subcutaneous layer at a time and thinking of each pore as a single strand. In a week, two black hairs curled from behind her ears; two weeks later, three black hairs curled around her ankles. In a month she had soft, curly strands in patches on her back. She began to wear baggy clothes to sleep.

Are you planning to sleepwalk downtown? her husband asked one night when she got into bed wearing tights, a sweatshirt, and socks.

Maybe, she said. I might have plans.

What do you mean maybe? He pulled her to him, and she pulled back so he couldn't feel her ears. What's going on with you? he asked.

Nothing. I just get cold.

Seriously. What's wrong? At dinner you look into space. And the other day I went to your office to take you out to lunch and you didn't even answer. I know you were in there. I heard you.

I was with a client. You heard us talking.

What about the Jehovah's Witness pamphlets, then? Why do you keep them now?

Because you never know.

Know what?

What will help. What will give you information.

What kind of information do you want? He let her go and leaned back against the pillow.

I don't know. Maybe I don't want any. She felt fur behind her ears and touched it cautiously. There was comfort in its softness. Like touching someone else.

She was relieved that the fur didn't appear on her face. She continued to see clients and was glad when the middle-management executive said he was thinking of leaving.

What can therapy do for you, anyway? he asked.

Give you back to the world, she offered.

Her client coughed his nervous little cough then patted his bike, which he brought inside because he was afraid it might be stolen.

My bike is my only joy, he said. I haven't met my one-and-only yet.

You're lucky you have something that brings you joy, she answered. A lot of people would envy you.

WHAT ARE YOU thinking about, Mom? asked her daughter one night at dinner.

Oh, nothing, sweetie. Just stuff.

What stuff, Mom? her daughter asked.

Just stuff honey. I don't know. Did you finish that report? There was a piece of rice on the table, and she wanted to lick it with her tongue. She also saw a chicken bone on the floor. She wanted to scramble down and eat that, too.

Sure, Mom, ages ago. You read it.

Her husband looked at her evenly. Are you all right?

Yes. I'm fine.

BY LATE WINTER, fur began to grow around her neck, and she couldn't risk sleeping with her husband.

I'm sorry, but you're snoring a lot, she said one night. I think I'll sleep in the extra bedroom.

Are you sure?

Yes, I'm sure. Just for a few nights.

The bedroom was near her son's room, and as she went to sleep, she heard his toads bleat from their separate rocks in the glass aquarium. They seemed lonely, bewildered, caught in a matrix that didn't suit them. She was glad she wouldn't be a reptile.

It was lonely sleeping by herself. Sometimes she dreamt she was a four-tongued beast with three heads, many claws, and fire-breathing eyes. Once she was a dragon on a dangerous, time-bending mission. When she woke, she sat up in bed, rocking back and forth. Sometimes she remembered her favorite client, the one with the bike. What would happen if he wanted to come back to see her? Would he try to track her down? Think how things were tilted? She leaned close to herself in the dark, listening to her skin. She heard something growing, the way farmers talk about hearing corn.

GROWING FUR WAS such a supreme act of will that she didn't notice the day she became an animal. It took the shriek of a neighbor to let her know that something had changed, the cry of the mail carrier to send her running back to the house on all fours. She sat in the hall, panting on the braided rug, then bounded to the mirror. She saw long black hair, topaz eyes, an enormous black nose, floppy ears. *I have become a dog*, she thought. *But I don't even know what breed I am.*

Dogs are simply dogs, said the voice. *They never bother to think about what breed they are.*

Now her husband pets her gently, not able to explain to anyone, not even to himself, that in some innate sense, he knows the four-legged animal is his wife. He's hired a housekeeper who's efficient, humorous, kind, and has never talked to their children about what really happened to their mother. In truth, when she was growing fur, she never thought about her children. She never thought she wouldn't be able to help them with their homework, or that she'd have to let them give her baths and watch her slurp food from plastic bowls. She'd only thought of a life uncharted by maps, a life more suited to cliffs and caves. Yet now that she's a dog, all she wants to do is lick them.

No one seems upset. Her children still do homework and go to parties. Her husband continues work as a paleontologist. And since the housekeeper won't answer the door for the Jehovah's Witnesses, they slip their doomsday pamphlets through the mail slot, and she can carry them to the kitchen in her mouth. Right now it's a late spring evening, and rain is falling outside. She sees their house reflected through the window, hears the howl of another dog on another block. She also smells gradations of dirt and earth beyond anything her family could understand. Her husband scratches her head, her son strokes her ears, her daughter says good dog, and all the while they're doing human things, small, meticulous things, essential to continuing human life. Her fur is long, black, luxuriant, and her children put their soft blond heads against it.

Good dog, says her daughter again.

Everybody holds her close.

Stairway to the Stars

WHEN THEY WERE in central Mexico, they saw a sign by some stairs that said: *Escalier aux Etoiles.* The stairs were wrought iron black and spiraled upwards to a small apartment. The sign was blue on white enamel.

What does it mean? She was slumping over her enormous belly, exhausted from the heat.

It means *stairway to the stars*, he told her. Don't you know? *Escalier.* Stairs. *Etoiles.* Stars.

She shrugged. She should have known. He was always translating for her.

How odd, she said, that the sign's in French, not Spanish. How odd that the stairs have a name.

Let's go up, he said. See what they're all about. Maybe they're even some stars up there.

Oh no. It's a private house. We can't go there.

Why not?

Because. It's private.

They always had the same argument. He wanted to camp in a cornfield; she said they might get shot. He helped himself to a dozen Meyer lemons; she said, Oh my God no, they don't belong to us.

The world is my home. He often said that, speaking in the comfortable, easy manner of the privileged, assuming the imperious friendliness of someone who has grown up with maids, chauffeurs, cooks. When anyone served him, he always asked their names, and then he would use them. Sally, I'd like some more salt for this omelet. Marv, I'd like you to check the oil level on the car.

At last they agreed that he would go up, and she would wait below. It was always how they settled these arguments. After he went up, she looked carefully at some flowers in pots along the sides of the building. There were roses in terra cotta and dark wooden containers with small blue flowers that looked like alyssum. He'd once told her the name of the blue flowers, and she had forgotten. She pretended to be interested in the flowers. In a moment she heard a curse and a man yelling in Spanish,

Get out of here, balls first! You heard me. Follow your dick or I'll cut it off.

She heard running and the sound of a shot. Then he was in front of her, sweating, panting, saying, Oh my God, there's a maniac upstairs, a guy who says he's living in heaven.

He grabbed her hand, and they ran down the cobblestone street, she with her enormous belly.

Come on! Come on! he kept saying. The guy's a nut. The guy's a nut. He thinks he's an Aztec god.

LATER, IN A café, where they ordered mattes, he told her the man wore a silver mask.

One of those sun-god things with rays all around it. He was standing right there on his patio waiting for me. And then, when I came up, he said his house was heaven.

Maybe he meant haven, she said.

No. Heaven. I understand Spanish.

Well maybe he *is* an Aztec god. Besides, you disturbed his domicile. She was surprised she had used the word *domicile*. It sounded odd, strangely legal. For a moment her belly felt enormous, as though holding the man's vengeance, her hair electrified in the form of a silver headdress.

Believe me, that was no God, just some beer-bellied guy with an attitude.

He had a tic that came on, unbidden. It happened now: His left eye began to twitch.

Recently she'd begun to slump, forming a cradle for the baby. She took a sip of her matte and sat up straight. I think he was someone you knew, she said.

What do you mean?

I don't know, she said, not knowing what she meant but knowing she was on to something. Someone you've met on one of your forays.

Forays. What the hell do you mean by that? He stared at her through hooded lids—there was some way he knew how to pull in his eyes. The tic stopped. He looked smart and dumb, like an owl.

Oh you know: Forays into fields. Forays into lemon groves. The kind you take. Domains that don't belong to you.

Domains. Domicile. She couldn't believe her language. The sun had melted a dangerous place inside her. She wanted to walk through town, letting the women pat her belly and hearing them say *Encendido! Encendido!* as though she were ignited, burning, and they could see it.

THAT NIGHT, IN their pension, he kept looking out the window. He'd already disappeared twice today, ducking around corners. When he looked outside, he seemed to blend with the dusk itself, as if he could float over the red-tiled roofs until he found what he wanted. Finally he asked:

What do you mean by forays?

I told you. Those times you just barge onto someone's property and take whatever you want. The times you picked those flowers—the blue ones—what are their names?

This is Mexico. I'm here to see things.

You do it everywhere.

The world is my home.

I know. You always say that I don't agree..

He turned around, no longer blending with the shadows, picked up a copy of *La Prensa,* and suddenly was enclosed in perfect air—air that was sent to him, whenever he needed it. The conversation had taken a wrong turn, bringing them to something old, unspeakable. She knew he wanted her to pursue it so he could figure out what she knew. *I'm living behind glass,* she thought. *And the notion of forays includes territories I haven't dreamt of.* She decided to ask him nothing.

After he fell asleep, she poked around his pockets, looking for clues. It wasn't the first time she'd picked her way through his pockets in cheap hotel rooms. Sometimes she discovered things, registered them, and then forgot. Tonight all she found were a few pages of *La Prensa* containing uninteresting news: Vanilla was being recalled by the Mexican government because it contained impurities that could bring on allergies; a recent survey showed a 5 percent decrease in the use of environmental face masks to protect people from the dust in Mexico City. She had no idea why he'd saved these pages. Nor did she have any idea why she could read Spanish so easily. *Defecto. Vehemente.* The words danced in front of her eyes.

While she was reading, she heard three distinct knocks on the door. They weren't hurried knocks. They belonged to someone who knew how to take his time.

Who is it? she called.

The man who chased your husband. The man your husband said imagined he was an Aztec god, said a voice in perfect English.

She opened the door and saw an ordinary man. He was tall, dark, about her age. He wore jeans and a perfectly pressed white shirt. His only claim to being extraordinary was his eyes: They were blue and piercingly beautiful.

How do you know he thinks this? she asked.

Because. I heard him from my landing.

She let herself into the hall, shutting the door. There were fourteen doors in this particular corridor. Anyone could step outside and see them talking. She realized she was wearing nothing but a large white shirt, reaching to her knees. She bent her knees, and the shirt grew longer.

Why did you come here? she asked.

To answer your questions, he answered.

I don't have any.

Well, you ought to.

What about?

Your husband's improprieties.

The man spoke calmly, without malice.

How did you know we lived here?

I followed you on your walk.

Why?

Because you're beautiful.

She sensed a shift in the atmosphere. The air, previously thick, became thin, without horizons. There were no points of convergence, yet collisions might happen anywhere. She looked at the man: The hairs on his eyebrows seemed alive.

I have to ask you to leave, she said.

Why? Are you afraid I'll wake him?

Because, she said in careful Spanish, I'm married. And I'm pregnant. She pointed to her stomach. There's a baby in there.

So you don't want to know?

I know enough. You don't travel with someone for as long as I have without knowing everything about them.

Your choice, he said. And maybe your mistake. I happen to have something that might help him.

He bowed and made no sign of leaving. She went inside and closed the door. The clarity of air vanished. She saw mounds of clothes, indistinct photographs. The pages of *La Prensa* were where she'd left them, but now she couldn't understand a word. Maybe her fluency in Spanish never happened. Maybe it was a freak of hormones. She looked more closely and saw several telephone numbers scribbled in the margins of the newspaper. Two were in Mexico City. Three in California. She walked to the door and pressed against it.

I'm coming out to meet you, she said softly.

The man mumbled something like Good. She went to the closet and pulled on tights, sandals, and found a shawl. As soon as she opened the door, the air resumed its powers of convergence. It propelled them past all fourteen doors and pushed them into the lemon-scented night. It took them over cobblestone streets and brought them to his house, where they climbed the stairway to the stars. It was long, curved, and she could see the whole village through the banisters. Before she entered the lantern-lit hall, she decided she would tell this man that her husband was a drug addict. She decided to tell him he visited apple orchards and lemon groves to shoot up. No doubt the man already knew. She wanted to tell him anyway. She also wanted to tell him that whenever they traveled he looked for messages, codes, signs on houses—anything that might lead to a deal.

He held her arm carefully, as though he knew what she was going to say. He opened a door and led her to a room with adobe walls and leather furniture. A terrace was close to the room. Outside, stars were everywhere, pressed against the sky like flowers. She sat in a cowhide chair and looked at them. They were large, close, preternaturally bright.

He walked to a kitchen and poured her a glass of water from a bottle.

You aren't used to the water here, are you?

No, I'm not. She sipped for a while, considered what she wanted to say, and realized she'd changed her mind. Really, I should get back, she told him.

To him? he asked. And to what he does?

It can't be worse than what you do, she said, looking at the pictures, the statues, the leather furniture. There's no way you'd know, unless you were part of it.

The man didn't disagree. He rose and held out his arm. No information passed between them. He hadn't even kissed her. They walked back on cobblestone streets, still warm from the afternoon. At the door of the pension, he pressed a package in her hand. The package was wrapped carefully in rough white cloth. The pressure of the man's hand conveyed a confidence, a secret.

You'll give this to your husband, won't you?

You came all the way for *this*?

Of course. I know when someone is in trouble.

She didn't ask who was in trouble, and he didn't say. He bowed and walked slowly down the street. Tomorrow she and her husband would go on other walks. Tomorrow they would visit other houses. She walked upstairs, and he was waiting for her by the window.

Where have you been? he asked.

Getting you what you need, she answered.

In the Middle of the Night

HE CALLED AND asked her to come over because he thought he was going to throw up and he might be dying. It was the middle of the night, past twelve, and the call didn't wake her because ever since he'd left, well over a year ago, she couldn't sleep. She wasn't surprised that he called. In the past, when they still lived together, he'd often said, If I were dying I would come to you because there's something about you that would make dying bearable. He said this sincerely, and she understood: There was something about her that contained the grief of other people.

Please explain more, she said to him. Her tooth was slightly infected, and she could feel a swelling in her mouth like a gumdrop. She worked her tongue around it while they talked.

I told you, he said, I think I'm going to throw up.

Are you sure?

Yes. I can't believe it.

For Yoav, throwing up was the same as dying, and much worse than being put into an iron maiden, or impaled by hundreds of swords, although those things had never happened to him. He was so afraid of throwing up that he'd gone through great feats to avoid it, even in Costa Rica where both of them had eaten a bad lobster dinner.

How do you not do it? she'd asked from her bed in their tiny, depressing room.

I use the power of my will, he said.

He had last thrown up was when he was eight. He'd been at his cousin's in Long Island and eaten far too many éclairs. Now, after twenty-five years of evasion, the game was up.

Get over here quickly, he said. Please.

She didn't say yes right away. They had broken up almost a year ago, and the leave-taking wasn't pleasant: an abortion she hadn't wanted. His sweet, gawky new girlfriend named Sylvie who played the cello without a shirt. And a terrible scene on the street in which she ran into him and Sylvie by accident, and she'd managed to drop half the contents of her purse in front of them. Sylvie had gentle eyes, wore a short black skater's coat, and her cello case hung from her arms like a friendly dog. Yoav's picture had still been in her purse. She'd bent down to pick everything up, and Sylvie had looked at her with pity.

Please, he said again.

All right, I'll come.

While she got dressed, she looked through the apartment to see what she could bring. He'd never moved his things out in any official way, and occasionally he came back to find whatever occurred to him. Just last month he'd spilled a drawer full of papers on the floor, and the month before that, she found seven odd keys scattered on the dressers. She decided not to bring him anything she cherished. She also decided not to bring him anything spiteful because she took her mission to squire him through throwing up seriously. At last she decided on something neutral: Yoav was a vibraphonist and used a lot of mallets. Their padded ends were soft, like stuffed animals, and, in his haste to leave, he'd forgotten most of them. She was always tripping over them, and a guy who had a crush on her once asked if the mallets were sex toys. No! she'd said, and thrown him out of the house.

For tonight, she chose three light-blue mallets, even though a set made four. Then she put on a long Cambridge scarf from another boy-friend, a man that Yoav hadn't liked. He's *mishuginah*, Yoav always said, whenever she wore the scarf.

SHE TOOK A cab to his new apartment, and Yoav met her at the door. His face was pale, making his black hair look darker.

Well, I did it, he said. I just did it in the sink.

Congratulations.

Spare me. It was a dreadful, dreadful event. Much worse than I ever thought it was going to be.

Yoav was wearing a dark kimono, and the bottom of his black mustache was wet in a way that made her recoil.

Maybe you should drink some water, she said. It helps get rid of the taste.

I did drink water. It didn't help.

Yoav looked forlorn, and his black eyes, which were often fierce, seemed terrified. She knew he wanted her to say something comforting. Something like: *For most people it isn't pleasant but for you this is the equivalent of Auschwitz.* She didn't.

Maybe you should drink some more water, anyway. Really, it often helps.

I can't stand your impersonal kindness, Yoav said. It's like you're tak-ing care of Arnold Anybody. Yoav had complained about this before—her distant, measured compassion.

Well I've never been to Arnold Anybody's house. Not since he walked out on me.

Please, Yoav said, Be kind.

She saw he was trembling. The back of his silk kimono was embroidered with an enormous yin-yang sign that was heaving back and forth like two fish.

All right. Truce, she said, and walked into an apartment she'd never visited. The apartment was spotless and smelled of lemon wax. She took off her scarf and put it on a birch chair where Yoav could see it. He noticed and seemed uncomfortable. This made her happy.

Why would drinking more water help? he asked, like a child wanting to be told a fairy tale.

She didn't want to talk. She was far too busy looking around the apartment. Absently, she said, Well, first of all it gets rid of the bad taste. Second of all you're probably dehydrated.

She hated herself for spelling it out. Yoav nodded obediently and went to get water. Again she saw the yin-yang pattern on his kimono. His back looked bearish, elegant, awkward.

Would you like some water, too?

No, not really. She was deathly afraid of throwing up herself and didn't like the idea of drinking from a glass that he had touched.

Are you sure? he said, looking at her with reproachful eyes. It's great water. It's from this special spring in Fiji.

Okay. Just a little bit.

He served her water from a blue container in an octagonal-shaped glass that was interesting to hold. She walked around the apartment, pretending to drink it.

Except for his vibraphone, everything was new. There were black chrome bookcases, low birch tables with smooth, weathered surfaces, and a beanbag chair covered with cloth colored like the inside of a musk melon.

It's clean, she said, dropping into an enormous beige couch, which puffed and billowed around her, like a person scooping her up. For a moment she lay back, feeling comforted.

Do you like it?

What?

The couch.

Everything but the color. It's a little drab. Listen, do you have a maid?

Well, a housekeeper. She comes every week.

Hattie?

No. Someone else.

AT THEIR OLD apartment, Hattie Dunsley, who called herself a maid, not a cleaning person, had been sent by Yoav's mother from Long Island. She hadn't liked the idea of a maid, and after Hattie left on Fridays she usually messed the place up.

Hattie's not doing a good job, Yoav sometimes said.

She's tired, she would answer. Later, usually in the mornings while Yoav was still asleep, she scrubbed, swept, and puffed pillows. It was part of her furtive domesticity.

I think I'm going to again, said Yoav.

What?

Throw up.

Well it's the best thing to do, it you have to. Really. It ends up making you feel better.

Will you come with me? Hold my head?

In a minute. I mean there's a lot to absorb here. Her words released something, and he disappeared. Sounds were heard. Sounds she didn't like. There were postcards on the desk and some checks that belonged to a woman named Eve Sommers, a name she'd never heard. The checks were bronze-colored, and *Eve Sommers* was written in cursive script. The checks had Yoav's address on them.

Who's your maid? she asked, when he came back, looking shaken. That friend Hattie was always talking about? That woman with the seven kids?

How can you ask me something like that now?

I don't know. I guess I can't be compassionate on command. Anyway, who is it? Sylvie?

No, not Sylvie. Sylvie's out of the picture. He cleared his throat and looked around. Noah sent someone over. Noah was his music manager. He was always sending someone over.

She wondered who Eve Sommers was. Again she remembered meeting Sylvie on the street, her warm eyes and dog-like cello.

What about Eve? Does she help clean, too?

No. Eve runs a health-food store. She stays busy. You always said I'd find a macrobiotic cutie.

She never remembered saying anything like that. She wondered where Eve was now. Had she fled when Yoav thought he was going to throw up? Was she not good with the infirm or dying?

I didn't know Eve moved in, she said.

She hasn't. Those checks are a cover-up. She needs an address.

Poor Eve.

Spare me. He sat on the beige couch. She looked at it closely and noticed it was covered with special carelessness, falling in sculpted folds.

Is that supposed to be unveiled? she asked.

No. It's shabby-chic. The latest.

And what else is the latest?

These forks. Yoav got up from the couch, went to the kitchen, and brought over forks with black, wrought iron handles. She didn't like them but wished she owned them anyway.

He sat opposite her. His new bronze clock ticked away. It was one fifteen in the morning.

It's been a long time, he said.

Yes, it has. She reached into her pockets and brought out two of the three mallets. Here. I found these.

Oh God. I'm sorry. I should come back and pack. He took the mallets and used them to tap a chair.

I thought you did come: I thought you came back last month and emptied a whole bureau drawer.

I was looking for my passport.

Well next time let me know. I mean how could you do that? How could break in like this was some sort of pied-à-terre for your past?

Look, I let you have the apartment. The least you can do is let me get my stuff.

She didn't concede. He'd left with his passport and a dozen silver spoons that belonged to his maternal grandmother—and also, by accident, the receipt for a blouse she'd meant to return.

So, she said. Your gigs. How are they?

Yoav didn't answer but stared into space. The space he stared at wasn't ordinary space. It never had been. It was filled with things only he could see. Singers with tufted pink hair, rings in their noses, opaque eyes. Concert halls in Prague where kids in leather jackets reached to touch him. Also musical notes. Yoav said he could see them, just like a visual artist can see perspective. As he stared, he belched.

Oh God, it's going to happen again! Please come hold my head this time.

I don't think I can.

Please.

Soon she was in his bathroom, holding Yoav's head. She held it the way she might have held a child's head, one hand on his forehead, the other cradling his hair. She looked in the other direction so she wouldn't get sick. Everything in the bathroom was dark teal, except for touches of maroon. She saw three maroon toothbrushes in a holder near the sink. One of them was small. When they left the bathroom, she asked,

Who has the small toothbrush?

Edmund. He's Eve's kid. He's three.

I thought they didn't live here.

They visit. Edmund's cute.

Wow. There's your forks, the beanbag chair, and Edmund's toothbrush. What else is new?

Yoav didn't flinch. A flush came over his face, a look of pleasure and excitement. Actually, something's very new. I did my book over.

He was talking about a book he had written for the vibraphone. It had been lost, buried in the old apartment.

Where is it? he often asked.

I have no idea, she answered.

Once his father had called. Yoav wrote a valuable book, he said. It's not exactly the answer to the stock market, but it has good stuff in it. Maybe you could look for it.

I've looked, she told him, not mentioning the socks, pencils, mallets that cascaded at every turn.

Just look one more time, said his father. It means everything to him.

NOW YOAV SAT next to her on the couch and handed her a manuscript full of musical notes. It was called *Exercises for the Vibraphone*. Yoav's notations were unusually neat, not like anything else about him. *The scales*, he had written, *are an ecosystem of sorts, and exercises must take this into account.* . . . She saw the date: It was one year after he'd left her.

So. You wrote it over.

Yes. He looked at her evenly, and she looked at the forks, thinking she found them attractive. They belonged to an age of craftsmanship, when people took their time and cared. She began to like the couch as well. It looked the way a couch would look if it had a secret life as an animal. She eased into it more deeply and found that it held her up. The lack of shape was all in the covering.

The clock kept ticking. It was almost three in the morning.

It's been a long time, he said again.

She nodded, reached into her pocket and brought the other mallet out.

Surprise!

I get it, he said, taking it. I should come back and pack.

We've been through this. Maybe I should go.

No. Stay. I still might have to throw up.

What about Eve?

She won't be here. She's with Edmund.

Ah, yes, Edmund. You have a kid now. After all.

Let's not get into that.

THEY'D ALWAYS SLEPT together. In the middle of the most brutal fights, in the throes of the abortion, in Germany with two single beds in rooms the size of spindles—wherever they were, they always found a way. Now it was easy. The shabby-chic couch folded out into a bed; its friendly creases made soft curving corners. They slept side-by-side, the *Exercise Book for the Vibraphone* on the table next to them. Yoav's long careful hands touched hers softly, just the way he composed on the piano. At four thirty, there was a phone call from Eve. Long pauses. The sound of sobs. She got up, happy she was still dressed.

Listen, I've had it. I better go.

Yoav didn't answer but stared into space. Just tell me one thing. Did you burn my first book? The one I left?

No. Your stuff is in such a shambles that I could never find it.

And what about those clothes?

No. Not them either.

Well, thanks for coming.

No problem at all. I'm glad to be the patron saint of barfing.

Spare me.

Try thanking me again.

IN THE CAB going home, she wondered why Yoav had called her. It was her empathy, she supposed, an empathy that went beyond spite, an empathy that transcended other moments, like that time she'd taken a razor to his lambskin coat when he went to play a gig the night after her abortion. The early dawn air was thin, drawn out, breathable by just a few stately prostitutes. Traffic lights clicked on and off with the precision of a Mondrian painting, and the cab driver drove a green-light dance, not stopping once until he reached her apartment.

A perfect ride, he said to her as she got out. You get those once in a lifetime.

Silver

I'M ALWAYS IMPALING myself on silver things, things my lover gives me when I'm not looking. He buys me silver rings and puts them on me when I'm asleep. He buckles my waist with a silver belt, drapes me with silver necklaces, fastens anklets under my jeans, puts six earrings in the holes of my ears. Silver and never gold, because silver is the color of the accident one longs for. It's light that slants through rice paper shades, a face on the street that carries you through the solstice.

You can't love someone without hurting them—that's what my brother told me once. We were home from college, washing pots in the sink, and my brother had just gone crazy on LSD. He thought he could climb walls when he was only scaling a chair. He thought he could see the truth when he was staring at a shopping list.

But one thing I knew, he'd said to me then. You can't love someone without hurting them. I saw that when I looked inside my brain and all the cells were singing, You can't love someone without hurting them. They were beautiful, those cells. All of them were made of silver.

My parents were getting divorced, just as I am now. Light was coming through the kitchen, the kind of light that makes you think you're in another century.

Is it fifth-century Greece? I'd asked my brother.

No, he answered. It's the Huang dynasty.

I wanted to hug my brother and say everything would be okay: His brain would stop singing. He wouldn't have to hurt people he loved. In fact, things didn't go well for him until he got a PhD in physiology and discovered that those years of watching his own brain cells had paid off. Now he lives in Rome and writes papers with titles like "The Neurophysiology of Indifferent, Compatible Systems."

SOMETIMES I WAKE up at night, impaled by silver, and think about my brother, far away in Rome. I think how he's found love and hurt a lot of people in the process. I also think of my lover in a small beige room, surrounded by flowering trees. I lie in bed alone, wearing heavy silver.

Why don't you take those off when you go to sleep? my lover asks, touching the scratch marks on my arms and neck. For God's sake, what are you doing to yourself?

I don't answer because then I'd have to tell him about the random silver of his face the day he stepped out to meet me. *Your face was like that,* I would have to say to him. *Don't you remember? It was the day before the solstice, people were racing around to buy presents, and you stepped forward to meet me. A week later you gave me a silver bracelet. A week after that you gave me silver keys. But none of this would have mattered if your face hadn't been an accident.*

Rossetti's Closet

SIX YEARS AFTER Lizzie Siddal died, Rossetti began to pay secret visits to her closet. This was long after he, Swineburne, and Meredith decided they didn't like living together. And it was long after he'd broken ties with most of Lizzie's friends. Except for his housekeeper—a woman named Mrs. Beehawken who had known Lizzie in happier days and didn't like Rossetti much—he was living alone. He wasn't working, either. He'd put his last manuscript of poems in Lizzie's grave.

When he first moved to the house in Chelsea, Rossetti filled it with whatever he found that he thought Lizzie wouldn't like. She'd liked clean surfaces, distance, a sense of space. Rossetti liked bric-a-brac. In Chelsea, he bought old mirrors, crockery, antique spoons, a collection of cut-glass jars. But when it came to Lizzie's closet, he made things just the way she had them in their cottage. He hung her chains and lockets from hooks and put her favorite pen on top of an oak chest that Lizzie had bleached white, using acid. He put her brooches in the chest and filled jewelry boxes with old keys, pebbles, and glass smoothed by the sea. Last he hung up a portrait he'd done of her.

The closet was in his study. Don't let anyone come in here, he told Mrs. Beehawken. Not even the maid. I have the wits to clean it myself.

HE'D NEVER MEANT to make Lizzie a closet in his house in Chelsea. He moved there to forget her. But one day he went to the attic looking for a tiepin he hadn't seen since Lizzie's funeral and for one poem he hadn't sent to her grave with the others. He had the idea they were in pockets of her dresses, which he'd dumped on the attic floor. He held the dresses upside-down and shook them, but nothing fell out but pieces of cream-colored paper with cryptic notes in Lizzie's handwriting. *Rain again. Must delay the roses.* He found himself on the floor, burying his face in the dresses, smelling Lizzie's scent, a mixture of violet and soap.

The closet in his study had a small paned window, which gave off enough north light to paint by. Rossetti spent a lot of time there, arranging Lizzie's clothes, supposedly in preparation for doing her portrait. First he hung her black dresses in a single row. Then he alternated them with crimsons, creams, and whites. For a while he had a sense of entering a secret world, governed by an unknown order. And then he grew tired of the closet. He bought a collection of empty baskets and put them in the downstairs hall. Next he bought a wombat.

A wombat! What would Rossetti think of next? He did think of other things next. First a jacare, which almost gave him a concussion and had to be given away, and then a mandrill, who didn't like English weather and died. He settled for a tropical fish called an isabelita. She needed special food and warm water and had to be protected from the wombat. Then he began to paint portraits of Jane Burden, the wife of

William Morris, and to spend evenings alone, looking at Jane's face. It was calmer than Lizzie's, although not as interesting. Once he visited the closet and compared it with an old portrait he'd hung there. Lizzie also looked calm. He left the closet quickly.

MRS. BEEHAWKEN, THE housekeeper, called the wombat that Australian badger. Otherwise she didn't mention it, until one summer evening when the cook served them both burnt pudding.

I couldn't help it, said the cook, but that animal started making noises. I knew it could smell the pudding and was trying to get out of its cage and I just wasn't going to deal with it.

Mrs. Beehawken smoothed the front of her dress and picked at the pudding's blackened crust. She didn't say a word. But when Rossetti went to the scullery to get apples for the wombat, she followed him and said:

Why do you need these animals? Why do you want to live with these awful beasts?

The scullery was cramped. He could see Mrs. Beehawken's eyes. They looked like currants in the burnt pudding.

Excuse me, Madam, he said. But I live as I please. You knew that when you came.

Mrs. Beehawken bowed, leaving opinions in her trail—opinions about Lizzie's increased intake of laudanum, her poems, her art, her vision, not to mention him and the clutter of their tiny cottage. Mrs. Beehawken hadn't been their housekeeper when Lizzie was alive; she'd been a friend of Lizzie's aunt and paid only a few visits. Stay with me, Rossetti pleaded when Lizzie died. And Mrs. Beehawken had. Even though she didn't like him, and he didn't like her.

After their talk in the scullery, Rossetti went to Lizzie's closet, but not before a sitting with Jane Morris.

You're thinking about something, she said. I can tell. Something about the past.

Not at all. I'm just thinking about your portrait.

They were in a small room off the parlor, and Jane was in a light blue dress. Mrs. Beehawken was knitting in a nearby room. They could hear the clack of needles.

No, said Jane. You're not. She smiled, and her eyes grew full of contained excitement. He hurried her back to her husband in a cab.

THE CLOSET WAS just as he had left it: quiet, and imbued with that secret sense of order. He'd never visited in the evening. By candlelight, the jewelry looked animated. And the dresses seemed obedient and patient, in the simple, quiet way all clothes await their owner. Unlike Jane, Lizzie never thought about style. She looked good in black—a color not thought right for women of her age—but she wore it anyway, and it lined one wall like an eclipse. She also liked subtle, uncomfortable transformations—wetting her clothes to create the impression of draped statuary; or taking sturdy English oak and dousing it with acid until it was almost white. Rossetti preferred natural order. But by candlelight, everything looked sturdy, opaque, even ordinary, and this relieved him.

That night he sat on the closet floor, sipping brandy, thinking about Lizzie; how at night they'd pored over books together, her red hair tumbling against the page; how on sunny afternoons they'd walked down lanes, holding paints and brushes, looking for promising scenery. He remembered less pleasant things, too—but all through a haze of brandy.

The next day when he was getting apples for the wombat, Mrs. Beehawken cornered him in the scullery.

Excuse me sir, she said. But your eyes are looking rheumy. Are you all right?

I'm always all right. And you?

The minute she turned her back, Rossetti raced to a bedroom mirror and looked at his eyes. She was right. They did look rheumy. As well as dreamy and faraway. *Like Lizzie's,* he thought, *or maybe the way I painted her. That viper thinks I'm taking laudanum.*

But Lizzie's eyes in the portrait weren't dreamy at all. They were solemn, astute, as if thinking about what she would need if she returned. The velvet dress. The garnet brooch. And the seed pearls he'd thought of giving to Jane. That night he imagined how Lizzie might walk into the closet, notice the brooch, and think, *I've forgotten about that. Maybe I'll wear it tomorrow.*

Please come back, he said to the portrait. It will be different now. I'll bring the wombat to the zoo. The face looked skeptical. The eyes withdrew. And now he remembered their arguments about their bedroom where his manuscripts were stuffed in jars, or their parlor where envelopes exploded with bills and books sprouted brushes. Everything here is a container for everything else! Lizzie once cried.

One rainy afternoon, a year before she died, Lizzie took the parlor into her own hands. She put papers on bookshelves, crammed books into drawers, stuffed everything else into wooden chests. He came home, dripping wet, hoping for a fire, and found her in a purple chair, drifting on laudanum. Then he saw the spotless parlor.

What *deceptive* order! he said. I'll never find my sealing wax!

Lizzie opened her eyes and got up slowly as if guided by an inner map. She floated across the room and felt along the edge of a bookcase until her hands cradled the mound of wax.

Why can't you live in peace? he asked, angry that she'd found it.

Why can you live in peace in a pigsty? she said, handing him the wax. When she left the room, he threw the wax on the floor. From another part of the house, she called, I've never seen you in a state of calm, Sir. Not once. . . .

Her eyes grew sharp again. Something in the closet annoyed them. *Clutter,* he thought. *It was that nonsense about clutter that did us in.* And now he started to look for his tiepin in earnest, shaking down dresses, opening boxes and drawers. He found a piece of cream-colored paper in a chest, but it was blank.

There were noises at the end of the hall—Mrs. Beehawken shifting in bed, as though she were sleeping on a Catherine wheel. He paused in his search, listened. And now he heard another sound—the wombat escaping its cage. It was a small, stealthy sound, like the rasp of a comb against hair.

It's that animal, Mrs. Beehawken cried out, It's going to come upstairs and befoul the carpets!

I'll take care of it, he said, leaving the closet and going downstairs with a candle. He crawled on his hands and knees until he found the wombat underneath a sink in the scullery. Come back, he said. Be reasonable. But the wombat wouldn't budge until he filled its cage with walnuts. The next day, Mrs. Beehawken said, From now on his cage must have a double-lock. Otherwise I won't go near the scullery.

Then don't, he told her.

THE FIRE IN Lizzie's closet was the wombat's fault: One night, after it escaped, and Mrs. Beehawken was saying something must be done, Rossetti raced downstairs. He'd been working on a portrait of Jane Morris yet felt heady with the notion that Lizzie would return. He ran downstairs in the dark, leaving a burning candle at the edge of her white lace dress. The fire was small, but smoked and crackled as he stomped and coughed, using a greatcoat to smother the flames. Mrs. Beehawken ran in, holding a candelabra, and threw water on everything. Rossetti got drenched. So did Lizzie's clothes.

Mrs. Beehawken didn't ask him what the closet was. She knew it was a shrine, and Rossetti was grateful. He leaned against the closet door and watched her take out all of Lizzie's dresses. He helped her sweep the ashes and put the dresses in the scullery to dry.

It's too dark to put them in the garden, Mrs. Beehawken said. But the next morning she put them outside.

Best to give them a good airing, she said. Best to get them a good airing and give them away.

Then she gave him a look, the look of one who does not believe in shrines, and soon he went upstairs and watched the dresses from an upstairs window. The wind blew them so vigorously, some of the sleeves billowed as though Lizzie's arms were inside them. And that night, when he went upstairs, the closet didn't belong to Lizzie anymore. Mrs. Beehawken had hung up the dresses again, and they smelled of thyme, lavender, verbena, and some other, elusive bargain with the wind. *My tiepin,* he thought. *I'm sure I'll find it now.*

TWO DAYS LATER, Rossetti called Mrs. Beehawken into his study and explained he would no longer be needing her services. He spoke gently, and this startled them both.

It's for the best, she said, even though the dresses weren't under my charge.

Would you like some anyway? As a keepsake?

I'm much too fat to wear them.

Then something to remember her by? Some jewelry?

Maybe those seed pearls, she said.

The seed pearls were in the closet hanging from a pewter hook, and they were covered with light grey ash. He cleaned them in the scullery, using a brush, the way he'd seen Lizzie clean them. When the pearls turned white, they looked fragile. What if Mrs. Beehawken stepped on them with her enormous feet? He put them under her door reluctantly and the next day could see the pearls glinting like eyes beneath her double chin.

TWO NIGHTS AFTER the fire, Rossetti dreamt that Lizzie came to his study holding her dresses. They were blowing in the wind, clamoring for attention. She dumped them on the floor and began to complain about the wombat. And then about Jane Morris and her socialist hypocrite husband. Finally she said, *I know what you're going to do. So do it!*

The house was acrid from the smell of smoke. Rossetti woke in a sweat, rushed to his study, and recorded a different dream. *It was only a closet,* Lizzie told him. *Really, it was only a closet, and I don't need it anymore.* Then she apologized for all the ways she'd made his life difficult—her grief about their stillborn baby, her complaints about the mess in the parlor. She even apologized for appearing in Millais' portrait as the drowning Ophelia because it was more famous than anything Rossetti had ever done. *All those things,* she said. *I understand how you might have hated me.*

It was cold as he wrote. A strong charred odor came from the closet, adding to his sense of chill. He threw a coat over his nightshirt, lit two extra candles, and went back to his desk. *I have lived to regret my actions,* he wrote. *I want to reclaim my poems and continue my life.* He went to the scullery, found crackers and whiskey, and stood by the window, eating, sipping, and listening to the wombat, which, at this moment, he loved more than anyone else. He loved it without recourse, without the sense that it could ever give him anything back. He wanted to hold it, rock it, but he knew that it would bite him.

Lizzie was buried on Hempstead Heath where there were rumors of intact bodies and wild, vampirous ghosts. Rossetti's requests to exhume her grave flowed smoothly. Papers were signed. Gravediggers were hired. People were naturally curious.

When the poems were exhumed, there was a moment in which Rossetti thought he would never see anything but rich black dirt because the gravedigger was drunk and had trouble locating the grave. However, the poems, entangled in Lizzie's red hair, were intact and so was her body—even bystanders agreed about that. She was resplendent in her black mourning dress. Every jet button glistened. Peaceful, someone remarked. Yes, Rossetti agreed.

After the grave was covered, he stayed for several minutes, running his fingers through the grass.

I'm looking for my tiepin, he said to the gravedigger.

Best to let bygones be bygones, the gravedigger answered.

THE CLOSET BECAME a half-ruined hole. Some of Lizzie's clothes were thrown away; others were heaped on the floor. He gave some keepsakes to Jane, and a few more to Mrs. Beehawken, who had ruined the closet forever. Two years later, in 1871, Rossetti, William, and Jane began to live together in a house in Kelmscott Manor. Rossetti did portraits of Jane and made love to her with William's blessing. He wrote a ballad called Rose Mary, which couldn't be traced to anyone he knew. The wombat died. So did the isabelita. And the poems, kept so long in Lizzie's grave, were published to much acclaim. He titled them, quite simply, *Poems*, and only later wrote a book of sonnets called *The House of Life*.

The White Coat

EVERYTHING WAS COLD and white and obvious in the far north of this country. The air achieved unusual clarity in the late afternoon, allowing one to view great distances. Even the snow implied patterns that might be decoded. Ellen Barlow felt no impediments or distractions as her children drank hot chocolate and her husband sipped brandy, nor she was she startled by her failure to miss them. Here, in piles of snow, nothing happened in an ordinary way. People glided by on skis, as if touching the ground would reverse a promise. In cafés and shops, people talked softly—noise might release an avalanche. She remembered almost nothing of her life back home—the cramped little alcove where she did translations, their sprawling city apartment—everything vanished in this air of limitless depth.

Her family didn't share her amnesia. They talked about home as though a walk would buy a newspaper and some imaginary switch would turn on television. The wooden farmhouse they'd rented had no electricity, so her children read books about time-warps and future civilizations, using clever book-flaps equipped with flashlights they'd ordered before they left. Her husband used one too. At night she saw small pools of light where people were reading.

Ellen had wanted a house without electricity. She liked the kerosene lanterns—oddly shaped, with glass so thin they could be an extension of air. Even more, she liked candlelight. When everyone else was in bed and the fire turned to grey smoke, Ellen lit candles and read Montaigne. Montaigne was different by candlelight. She'd read long voluminous essays by Montaigne in college. Yet by this light, just one or two sentences could hold her for an entire night, like a prayer. She didn't remember them in the morning. Except for one. *It is a common enough occurrence to smile upon the misfortune of others.* This sentence trembled in the cold white air. Every night, Ellen opened Montaigne at random and never found that sentence again, or anything else she'd read. By candlelight, Montaigne's essays became a book that never repeated itself.

UNLIKE AIR IN other countries—Hungary, or Russia—the air here had no history: no images of cabals, cafés, cigarette smoke. No sense of perilous adventure. The landscape veiled itself in white like a bride; you had to walk for a long time to find one blemish. Yet it was here, in this neutral country, that people were hauled out of barns and shot during the war. It was here that some of the most fatal raids had been carried out with precision. She knew this from books, and also heard it in the vague way people talked at the café: My grandmother only sewed during the war. She embroidered very carefully, you know. Or, We were traveling most of the time. My father imported coffee.

Alibis were everywhere, as though war were still alive, yet the air was as clean as an abstract proof.

Before she'd left, a friend told her that every winter, he hid icicles in the hay in a farm in Canada, and every summer came back to find them. The hay had hidden the icicles and kept them from the heat. But the icicles had preserved themselves—he was sure of that. Ellen listened carefully, because she knew she was traveling to snow and wanted to immerse herself in another country. She wasn't interested in newly powdered snow, but in snow the country had preserved, ice from other centuries. Instead of skiing with her family, she went to the café at town, taking translations, and also books about the country's past. She intended to leave everything behind and start from the beginning.

Everyone here spoke English and at first ignored her fluency. Eventually they stopped translating, yet nothing much was said. She felt like she was having conversations from a language primer. *Would you like more cream in your coffee? Yes, please. Today it's especially cold. I know—I wore an extra scarf.*

One woman in the café stood out from the others. She had long blond hair, an angular face, and read by herself at a table. Ellen recognized her as another translator, and soon they began to talk shop, using each other's language and laughing when things got jumbled. One day she asked this woman, whose name was Anna, what her parents had done during the war. Anna looked insulted and said, I wasn't born yet.

Of course you weren't. But your parents were alive.

Anna shrugged. Why are you so interested?

I'm not sure. I came here to be distracted.

From what?

From everything at home. Why else would you go on vacation?

Anna looked outside at the fields of snow that could blind you.

This is an easy place to be distracted, she said. You shouldn't have to think about war for that to happen. She smiled and went back to her books.

Ellen supposed that Anna was right. She seemed to have forgotten almost everything, except her children and husband—and even they seemed distant, seen through wavy glass. The only thing she remembered about home was an exhibit of clothes she'd seen in a museum a week before they left. In particular, she remembered a mannequin wearing an ermine coat with white boots and white stockings. The catalogue explained that such coats were worn in Europe over a hundred years ago and were called camouflage coats because whenever women wore them, they faded into the snow. She remembered the coat often, along with the phrase from Montaigne: *It is a common enough occurrence to smile upon the misfortunes of others.* Ellen wondered to what purpose these women had wanted to seem to disappear. Perhaps to surprise. Perhaps on a whim.

While she read in the evenings, her husband snored above her in a quaint wooden loft. They were on a long vacation because they were thinking of divorce, and they once wrote in their marriage contract that if either of them wanted a divorce, they would spend at least three weeks together getting away from it all. When they'd written the contract, they had no children, and imagined getting away from it all would mean going on a trek to Nepal. They also imagined that only one of them would want a divorce: As it turned out, both of them did, so her husband said, We should multiply our doubts by two and go away for six weeks. With the kids.

The fact that he said *doubts* was telling, Ellen thought: It meant that he didn't want a divorce after all and was only matching her feelings to save face. Sometimes, after reading Montaigne, she slipped into the bedroom and lay next to him. In sleep, he forgot he was angry with her. He held her in the dark and pulled her against him, spoon fashion.

DURING THE DAY, her husband and children stayed on the slopes skiing and drinking hot chocolate and warm soup in mountain inns.

Ellen skied for hours on flat country, worked on dull technical translations, and read foreign detective novels that were full of umlauts. One day she saw Anna in the café and said:

I SAW A coat in New York that made me think of a perfect way to cover-up a crime. Anna looked blank. I'm sure you know about them, she continued. Women wore coats like that over a hundred years ago over in Europe. They were called *camouflage coats* because they made these women disappear in the snow. Does it ring a bell?

A lid fell from Anna's eyes. She put her translations aside and stared at the impenetrable white fields. My great-grandmother had the most amazing clothes, she said. And it was the time of the white coats, so she had one, too. The phrase *time of the white coats* made it sound as though the coats were like Leningrad's white nights—an extravagance, an intoxication.

Do you still have it? Ellen asked.

Yes, Anna said. It's been in the family for years. She paused, hesitated, closed her book. Would you like to come over and see it?

Ellen could not believe she would be allowed to come inside this house with a pointed roof and sloping door. People were friendly when they talked but never brought strangers home. The moment she entered the house, she knew why: Outside the air was thin and clear. Inside the air was thick, stale—and redolent with human arguments. Soup brewed on the stove. Books obscured a long pine table.

Forgive the mess, said Anna. I live alone and do more than one translation at a time.

Before Ellen had time to tell her that a mess was no problem, Anna motioned her upstairs.

I turned to translations when my husband left, she said. My family had no money after the war. And my husband lied to me about his. Or—to put it more politely—he used his money for other things. I had to sell everything except this coat.

Anna was speaking English now—fluently, like everybody else—except in her case, it seemed like it was really her own language. Anna led her to the second floor, walking quickly past rooms that once had belonged to children—Ellen saw dressers with decals of wooden shoes, stuffed bears piled on beds. Anna led her up another flight of stairs and opened the door to an attic. The musty smell brought back her grandmother's attic in Indiana, a cavernous room with dampness everywhere. This attic was also large. Eight dormer windows looked out on endless snow.

I've often thought of converting this, Anna said. I like the idea of working under the eaves.

Unlike her grandmother's attic, this room was well ordered. There were trunks of sturdy wood with brass handles and oak bookcases filled with books—some so large they lay on their sides. There was also a pine armoire, which Anna opened with a huge key, trustingly left in its lock. She brought something out that looked like a corpse—something in the shape of a woman wrapped many times over in white linen. Anna unwrapped the cloth and beneath it—improbably, because everything here was archaic—were layers of plastic. She unwrapped those to reveal a white ermine coat more perfect than the coat in the museum. It was made of pure white fur and had matching buttons. The ermine was invisibly stitched, so the skirt fell in folds. The coat looked like snow. Ellen forgot she was repelled by coats made from animals. She wanted to stroke the coat, pet it, see if it would melt.

Anna let her touch the coat briefly. She opened a shallow door that concealed another door, which led to a large, windowless room. This room had a second door that led to a corridor that was narrow and claustrophobic. They walked down the corridor, Anna holding the coat, until they reached a door that led outside to the snow.

My grandparents kept people here during the war, Anna said. It was part of their job. But that isn't the point. This—and she laid the coat carefully on the snow—is the point. Look: You can hardly see it. It belonged to my great-grandmother, and my grandparents used it to smuggle people here. You can't imagine how many people wore this coat when they walked through the woods. Men so large they had to wear white suits underneath because they couldn't button the buttons. Children so short they trailed the coat in the snow and stumbled. My grandparents had to bring everybody one at a time. I was told it was very tedious.

In any case, there was something uncanny about this coat. People wearing it were always concealed. It didn't matter who saw the people accompanying them. It didn't matter who stopped to ask questions. Our family came to believe the coat had magical properties. I promised my mother I'd save it in case of another war.

Anna spoke matter-of-factly. Then she looked around, as if she'd committed a transgression. I've kept this coat outside long enough, she said. We should go in now.

She lifted the coat from the snow and it became visible in her arms. They went in by the back door, and she pulled out a copy of *Mansfield Park* from a kitchen shelf.

You can read this, she said to Ellen. I'll put the coat back in its wrappings.

Ellen picked up *Mansfield Park*, feeling cheated. She wanted to spend more time with the coat.

ANNA WAS UPSTAIRS now. She could hear her trudge on the creaking wood and realized she didn't even know her last name. She looked

on the table for signs, but all she saw was a language she couldn't decipher. Turkish, she supposed. The clock ticked. Soup simmered on the
stove. For a while she heard soft sounds in the attic. Then Anna came
downstairs and offered her tea.

I'd prefer coffee, she said.

So would I, said Anna. Tea just always seems like the right thing to
serve people, doesn't it?

Anna was speaking in many languages at once. Or perhaps it was
no longer possible for Ellen to distinguish her own language from the
language of the country. She didn't know. Her ears felt open, alien. As
Anna made coffee, she heard every sound—the clock, the soup, and an
uzi-sound made by a snow-laden tree. She even imagined she heard the
coat, settling back in its layers, adjusting to a life of hiding beneath white
cloth, a life of *waiting just in case*. She wanted the coat very much. But she
was not a criminal. If just once, she thought, I could borrow the coat. If
just once I could wear it in the snow. She sat while Anna brought strong
coffee in cream-colored bowls, and she drank with her silently. Finally
she heard herself say,

What a coincidence that I mentioned that coat.

What coat? said Anna.

The coat in the museum.

Yes, said Anna, a coincidence indeed. It was clear she didn't think
it was, but found it an accident—and not a very interesting one. Anna's
indifference drove her on.

I've been thinking about that coat, ever since I saw the exhibit: In
fact, besides, Montaigne, it's *all* I think about.

Really? said Anna. And have you been here long?

Four weeks. We're staying for two more.

In that case, said Anna, you won't forget the coat. If you were staying here longer, I'd imagine you might. There's something about this place: people don't remember much.

And yet they talk about the war all the time.

Well, in a sense. But not directly.

Now her desire to wear the coat felt nearly uncontainable. But she wasn't used to asking for things. Like cautious climbers in the Himalayas, she chose indirect, inelegant routes.

How were its properties discovered? she asked.

What properties? said Anna.

What makes it invisible, she answered.

Anna stretched, looked at her translations. Since showing her the coat, she'd assumed the most laconic manner, as if they didn't have anything to talk about.

Well, in one sense, she said, as though she were bored, it only became obvious after the fact. I mean people had worn it and no one had been caught, and pretty soon my grandmother began to wonder why.

Anna looked back at her translations, but Ellen—the seeker of the coat, the believer in totems—waited. She'd learned to be silent in a way that was aggressively loud and used that power now. Outside trees creaked in a rising wind. Soon her husband and children would be coming home from the slopes. She waited.

At last Anna sighed and said with some reluctance: Well, the coat always brought luck to anyone who wore it. But there was one particular time when a man who was very valuable in this . . . in this whole enterprise . . . was in great danger of his life, and had to be hidden here. He was an eccentric man and was also very large. There was another thing, too: He had a strange medical problem, which was that he fell asleep at unpredictable moments. A kind of . . . here she groped, intermittent narcolepsy. Yes. I guess that would be the only way to describe it: *intermittent narcolepsy.* In any case, it was clear he had to be hidden, and since the coat had been lucky for other people, there was no question that he had to wear it. But he was so large! My grandmother found an enormous white suit and decided the man would wear the coat over the suit. And then my grandfather decided not to escort the man himself, but made my aunt—she was sixteen and looked very innocent—be the one to escort him. It was a tradition that whoever went to escort the new fugitive wore the coat for protection on the way, so my aunt wore the coat to the farmhouse where the man was staying. Then she took off the coat and got out the suit and began to try to dress him. This man—as I said, he was very large—kept falling asleep. Two men had to help, and finally my aunt said, I thought he didn't fall asleep that way. I thought he could *make* himself be awake. He's never fallen asleep like this before, said one of the men. Maybe he's nervous. Nervous or not, said my aunt, I'm not sure taking him anywhere is a good idea. One of the men held a gun to her head. The other fell on his knees and began to cry. We have no choice, he said. This man is an expert forger and has connections in the diamond business. My aunt couldn't argue with them, so they set out in the woods through the snow. At first the air revived the man. Maybe you've noticed this about the air here. It has a way of pushing people forward and not letting them lean against it. But halfway to the farmhouse, the man fell asleep. He fell asleep standing up, like a tree. And there was nothing my aunt could do about it.

Anna stopped and poured more coffee for both of them. You have to understand there were spies everywhere. And they also were like trees. They even hid in trees and came out of them. Someone came out of one right then—a farmer named Dirk with connections to the secret police. He had this way about him, so you couldn't even think to mention how odd it seemed that he'd come out of a tree. He and my aunt talked about the weather and the price of beer at a local tavern, and all the time they talked, this enormous man was not only sleeping but snoring loudly. God knows what Dirk thought the sound was, she continued. Maybe he thought my aunt was— Anna stopped, decided upon a word, *farting*. Yes. I guess that's how you'd put it.

She shook her head and continued: I only know that after a while he said good-bye and my aunt brought this man back to the house. Not that it was easy. My grandparents already had five people in that room, and this man was a total boor. Finally they sent him to England. But if Dirk had known about him, he would have turned him in because Dirk turned in everybody, including children and old people. That's when my family decided the coat was extraordinary. Or—who knows?— maybe the coat was just heroic. Maybe certain objects, like people, just did what they had to do in the war. Anna leaned on the table, as if the story exhausted her.

You mean no one has worn the coat since the war?

No. Why would they?

To test the magic.

Oh, our family wasn't like that. The coat worked. That's all that mattered. And when we didn't need it any more, we put it away. Besides, maybe if we tested it, the coat would sense our doubts. Then it would be insulted and deny us protection when we needed it. Or—who knows?— maybe it would be grateful.

Ellen saw her move, and decided to take it. I would love to wear it, she said. Just once. In the snow.

Anna looked startled. Her eyes, clear with memory, became opaque. Really? Why?

Not to be seen!

But you have no reason.

There are lots of reasons not to be seen, she said. Lots of reasons besides wars. She thought of trying to explain—about her husband, Montaigne, candlelight.

Anna held up a hand. I'm sorry, but I can't let you. This coat is for serious service, not for whims. Her voice softened, and her eyes looked sad. I didn't mean you wanted to wear it on a whim, she said. I just meant that this is a coat for emergencies.

Oh, but this is an emergency. I would like, just once, to disappear.

I don't understand.

You wouldn't want to.

Anna reconsidered. How much time do you need?

Only five minutes. I just want to walk outside and stand in the snow near your house. Maybe you could tell me if you could see me. Or—if you didn't want to do that—suddenly she felt accommodating—maybe I could find out for myself.

Anna lit a cigarette and took a long drag on it. What the hell, she said, using a vernacular she'd never used and seeming to address a row of uncles who wagged their fingers, two grandmothers who might faint—as well as a battalion of fugitives.

Wait here, she said, pushing up her hands to keep Ellen from following. No stranger ever took the coat from the attic. That was the family's job.

Anna left the room and began the long walk upstairs. She was gone so long, Ellen wondered if Anna had decided to trick her, then remembered that the coat must be unwrapped from its casing. The fact that she wouldn't see Anna unwrap the coat disappointed her. The unveiling was part of the coat, an essential piece of its history. Eventually she heard footsteps, and Anna came downstairs wearing the coat. She could see her clearly and was disappointed.

Don't worry, said Anna. The camouflage only works outdoors, in the snow.

She then showed her white leather boots, white stockings, white gloves, and a white fur hat. We had all kinds of accessories in different sizes. My family wasn't taking chances. I thought these might fit.

Everything fit perfectly. Ellen felt unremarkable. There was a mirror in the hall, and when Ellen saw herself in it, she thought of the mannequin in the museum. The mannequin's porcelain face looked small and apologetic, just like her face did now.

Don't worry, said Anna. If it works, it's only in the snow. She opened the door and motioned for her to leave. Go for a walk. But not for long. I don't want to take advantage of what this coat has given us.

Ellen went outside, and everything was the same. She'd imagined the air would be a triumphant extension of the coat and therefore an extension of herself. Instead, it was merely cold. There was no memory in the air, yet nothing was concealed. She could hear her own breath, the labor of her footsteps. She walked down a path, hoping that someone would show up and not notice her. No one came. She deviated from that path, hoping to meet someone coming from the slopes, a grandson of Dirk, the farmer, even her husband and children. This path was also deserted, so she had to be content to walk alone, wearing the coat. It was soft, and made her feel at one with the snow, as though she and the snow were a new and singular element. When she returned, Anna answered the door solemnly.

That coat hasn't failed us, she said. I wasn't able to see you.

Are you sure?

Yes. All I could see was snow.

For a moment Ellen felt betrayed and realized she'd wanted Anna to knock loudly at the window and cry with great excitement, Guess what! I can't see you! Anna seemed to guess this. Her face signaled that the coat meant serious disappearance and not a game of hide-and-seek. Ellen thanked Anna profusely, offered to go upstairs and help return the coat to its labyrinthine wrappings.

No thank you, Anna said. It was always a tradition that someone in the family would do that. In fact, and here she looked away, we are very respectful of the coat. We even thank it. She reached out and shook Ellen's hand. I think I should thank you, too. I never got to help anyone with this coat. I only heard about it. In a sense, you helped me understand something.

AFTER ELLEN WORE the coat, everything was the same. She still felt distant from her children and read Montaigne by candlelight. She still ignored her husband in the evenings.

What are we doing here? she asked him once.

Figuring out options, he answered.

What options? she asked. He mumbled something about negotiating, but she'd already opened Montaigne, whom she was no longer reading in French since Anna had loaned her a copy. In this new language, Montaigne's voice had fewer arcs and curlicues. Still, by candlelight, he floated over centuries.

At the corner store, she and Anna sometimes stood close to each other while people ordered sugar, flour, milk. A new intimacy arose between them. She showed Anna a book by a Polish writer she admired. Anna lent her the copy of Montaigne. Sometimes one bought the other coffee or an extra roll. Neither mentioned the coat. Nor did Ellen think about it much. Maybe Anna was right about memory disappearing here. Or maybe camouflage conceals itself—so in a sense, it never happened.

A WEEK BEFORE they were going to leave, she decided to return Anna's copy of Montaigne. Anna was at the kitchen table, working on the same translation. More soup was bubbling on the stove.

Keep it, Anna said, gesturing at the book, I'll never read it again.

Are you sure?

Absolutely, Anna extended her hand. I'll see you in the café, yes? We won't say good-bye.

No, of course not. I still have a week.

Ellen walked out the door, feeling she had no country, no history of her own. She was a citizen of this country, sometime during the war, and on a mission, a mission for someone in trouble. She had guns, cyanide, was prepared to do something reckless. The mission was difficult, and involved bringing secret news. She imagined that she had accomplished her mission and came back to find the small wooden farmhouse in ruins. War had broken out. Her family was gone. Life, as she knew it, was over. As she came towards her farmhouse, she became convinced that what she was imagining was true in spite of the fact that there was no war, and she wasn't on any kind of mission, except to make sense of her marriage and read Montaigne. What relief when she walked up the path to the wooden house, and her children opened the door and raced out to meet her. What relief when they tumbled against her in warm rough sweaters, arguing for attention. They were real, absolute, bony. And they carried with them their own mysterious complications, their own ineffable dreams.

You were out for much too long, her five-year-old scolded. Much longer than you'd ever let *us* be. She stamped her foot in the snow. The powdery dust flew around them.

Sleeping in Velvet

HOW LONG HAD they both been sleeping in velvet? A year? Two? They never told him.

They didn't sleep in the plush velvet of Fifth Avenue stores, but in the ratty, tawdry velvet of vintage outlets. It was velvet where the black looked brown and the fabric was piebald and the brown had a yellow cast. It was velvet on the edge of disappearing.

He'd met them when they came to his art opening. She was draped in dark green velvet and he wore a long brown coat that could have been a bathrobe. Just two weeks ago, he'd ended his marriage, and the two of them—so alike, so in harmony with each other—filled him with longing.

After the opening they went out for wine. He began to visit them in their four-floor walk-up, two rooms cluttered with books and velvet pillows. She often wore a faded black tiered skirt and a crimson blouse with frilled cuffs, open at the neck. He often wore the long brown coat that he'd worn to the art opening—the coat that could have been a bathrobe, perhaps had even been a bathrobe once. They wore other velvet clothes, too—a smoking jacket, a long black dress, hats, scarves, belts, bags. He speculated that they probably wore velvet to bed, but he never asked.

That winter they went to Maine for a week and asked him to feed their cat—a thin marmalade that defied any notions of velvet. Sometimes he lay in their bed, stroking the mangy cat and feeling ordinary in his clothes. He wanted to look through their closet, find the brown velvet robe, maybe even the skirt, and put them on. He restrained himself.

When they came back he never returned the key. And one night, when he felt especially lonely, he let himself in and walked into their bedroom where they were asleep. She wore a black velvet blouse laced around the sleeves and a crimson velvet skirt. He was wearing a green coat. They looked beautiful. He could feel their warmth. They woke up and looked at him calmly, like children looking at a parent.

Do you always sleep in velvet clothes? he asked.

Yes, I guess we do, one of them answered. But it isn't as though we ever thought about it.

She sat up in bed, and touched her soft, crimson sleeve. So opulent. So Edwardian. And when he saw her touch the sleeve, he knew they were lying. Velvet permeated their life.

Soon they were in the kitchen, sitting around a dark round table with a white toaster and salt and peppershakers in the shape of wind-mills. It was a small table. The three of them had to sit close, and she offered him rolls and bitter coffee. *Generous,* he thought as he ate, *they are so generous. . . .*

I'd like to paint you when you're sleeping, he said.

Why not? one of them answered. We don't have to do anything except sleep, do we?

THAT NIGHT HE set up his canvas in their bedroom, and the two of them got into bed.

Don't work too hard, they said.

He promised he wouldn't. But it wasn't easy to paint them: The intricate passageways of cloth. The pockets of velvet he couldn't see. The tawdry feel of fabric between the chasms. And the electric moments when the velvets touched. He used a combination of oil-pastels and charcoal. The more he smudged and worked, the more the whole scene was imprinted in his body.

You've made it all up, they said when they looked at his picture in the morning. All we ever did was sleep.

Yet even as they spoke, they had the self-satisfaction of cats that leap without exercising, cats that are elegantly furred.

You made it all up, they said again. We never look like that.

But it was clear they knew they did. And he knew they liked the picture.

Soon they were in the kitchen again, huddling around the small round table. They made him toast from stale bread—hard ryes, sweet bits of challah, pumpernickel.

We save it all, she said, because we aren't rich.

He sipped the tea and felt morose. He'd spent all night drenching himself in velvet, and all he had was a picture. He was thinking of giving it to them because he knew they wanted it. Yet, out of some perversity, he lugged it from their apartment, bumping it down the four flights of stairs into the freezing cold. It was snowing, not good weather for a freshly painted canvas. He came back, knocking quickly and letting himself in with the same key.

I can't take this out in the snow, he said. You keep it.

Oh no, they said. You can sell it. Wait and see. Really. You'll be surprised.

It was a Sunday morning and they were already back in bed, close in each other's arms, ready to go back to sleep.

Get into bed with us, they said. Not with your clothes. Just you.

He put the picture against the wall, took off his clothes, and got into bed between them. The velvet reached over him and around him like a bridge. He was enclosed in it, encased in it, and knew what it was like to be each one of them separately, and the two of them together. And something else, too—velvet.

That's what velvet does, he thought, it makes you feel like what it is.

Just love me, he said.

We do, they answered.

The Mapmaker

NINEVAH

THE MAP WAS of ancient Asia, purchased by my grandfather in a secondhand bookstore on 4th Avenue in New York. It was part of my grandfather's search for a real, definitive tome, and although the map wasn't a book, it was imposing enough to stand for one. This map was made in the eighteenth century. The countries were inked with dark green, purple—veined as veins would be, if connected to the earth. The map had a compass of the four directions placed in the middle of the ocean. This added to the sense that the terrain might not exist in ordinary time. My grandfather's search for old maps and rare books was fueled by his decision to leave the *stetle* in Rumania and become a doctor in New York. This made him the first son in his family who didn't write commentaries on the Torah, a tradition begun by his ancestors hundreds of years ago. For this reason he searched for documents that were old, books that came from the beginning of history. In addition to the map, he bought had an Assyrian parchment with blurred writing.

The map of Asia was as nomadic as its former inhabitants. First it hung in my grandfather's office in New York. When he remarried and his second wife didn't like it, he gave it to us so it could live in our tiny apartment in Kansas. Sometimes it hung in my father's study, a small, mysterious alcove, where he wrote his books on Renaissance architecture. Sometimes it was in my parents' bedroom, a large, cavernous room where my mother devoted the first part of her day to sleeping. Wherever the map happened to be, I always took time to look at it, particularly at the pictures. There was a nude woman pouring water from a wedge-shaped pitcher and a Christ-like figure offering a cup, a saucer, and a tiny map. I was embarrassed by the woman's nudity but fascinated by her pitcher. Its water spilled in two directions, one right into the sea.

At night when I couldn't sleep, I'd sometimes climb into my parents' bed, and my mother would always tell me the story about the man who had made the map. Her voice was soft in the dark—not harsh the way it often was during the day—and she told me the story as though she'd seen this man from a secret, careful distance. He was already an old man when he decided to make the map, she said, but he was vigorous and strong. He wore a leather jerkin and seven-league boots, and he carried a large staff so he could climb mountains and go down valleys. Mapmakers were rare in those days, my mother told me. Whenever he arrived in villages, people came to greet him. They fed him dark bread with strong crusts, pitchers of wine, and hot, sweet porridge. For this reason, he was nearly eighty by the time he came to Asia, and when he came home, he was almost a hundred. The map we have is the map of Asia, she said. He made it in 1716, and it's one of the oldest in the world.

It wasn't one of the oldest maps of the world. I found this out when

I studied geography in college, but for awhile, I believed my mother and bragged to my classmates.

My mother told me the story as if remembering a past that was real. This was a past that no one left, changed, or entered—yet my mother had been in it, I was sure of that, just as I was sure she had met the mapmaker.

Did you see him? I asked her.

No, she said. I was sure she was lying.

Even though the map was of Asia, I decided that my mother had lived in Europe because that was the part of his journey she talked about the most: Peasants in ruffled blouses danced for the mapmaker. Dark braided bread appeared on tables for him. And Asia—his ultimate destination— was shrouded. If I asked her to tell me about countries he'd visited in Asia, she said they weren't the point. The point was his journey, particularly in his boat, where the four directions were as variable as the winds.

What did he do on the boat?

He wrote letters to people at home. Of course it was a long time before he landed and could find someone who could send them. Sometimes the letters got lost.

I knew—by some ineffable transmission of the air—that in my mother's mind, the mapmaker and my grandfather were the same person. My grandfather—her father—was a doctor with expensive clothes and a penchant for red carnations in his lapel. When he came to visit in Kansas, with his wild woolly hair and heavy woolen coat, he looked like no one else on those long flat streets. He spoke with the oddest accent I'd ever heard, as if he were talking through water, and he had an enormous lump on his nose—the result of being burned when he ran, full-tilt, into a samovar at age three. As my mother talked, it was my grandfather I imagined in the dark. His boots were green and his jerkin purple, just like the colors of the map; however, his coat was black, like the coat he wore when he came to visit us. I saw him with peasants in the mountains, leaning close to their ruffled blouses. His hair was frizzy and white. The lump on his nose was large.

When I became too old to sleep with my mother, I grew more curious about Asia. My mother had referred to the people who migrated across the desert as Yemenites. She said the mapmaker had nothing to do with them, indeed, that he found them crazy because they were part of a religious sect. My parents—one the daughter of a former Hassid, the other the son of a Methodist theologian—were serious, careful Marxists, and it wasn't part of their program to discuss the holy. I looked up *Yemenite* in my World Encyclopedia and saw a picture of someone in dark robes, standing alone on a desert. I went back to the map, looked at it carefully, and saw no signs of Yemenites.

Everything on the map was written in Latin. Its name—*Asia Cum Omnibus Imperious*—and the ancient wonders of the world: *Terra Sancta*, which I later learned was Jerusalem, and *Muro Extra*—China's Great Wall. In the country of Assyria, I noticed a large city surrounded by trees. This city was drawn in gold, its name was Nineveh, and it had a book in its center. I looked at it more closely, saw the words *Lector Benevol* on the book, wrote them down, and took them to my mother who was bending over the stove, taking out a braided bread, much like breads the mapmaker had been given.

My mother looked stern, as though I'd been going through her chest of drawers without permission.

Where did you read those words? she asked.

On the map. The map of Asia.

That means Gentle Reader, said my mother, who had studied Latin in high school.

Did the mapmaker go there?

Where?

To Nineveh. That place with the book.

Of course. He went everywhere. My mother set the bread on top of the table and dusted it with flour. Nineveh was the last place he stopped, she said. And then, after that, he went back home. First he had to go in that awful boat, and then he walked over mountains and down valleys until he came to his village. The children of the village were happy to see him.

It was growing dark, late winter dusk. I saw the mapmaker coming home to a cottage I'd seen in a Grimm's fairy tale book—a cottage with a thatched and sloping roof. Beyond the cottage I saw the vast, limitless outlines of some deeper, urgent darkness.

Where was Ninevah? I asked.

Right where you saw it on the map.

And now?

And now it's nowhere.

At night when I couldn't sleep, I sometimes crept to my father's study and looked at the country of Nineveh. It seemed to be drawn differently from other parts of the map, as if another country were hiding beneath it.

DIME STORE

TWICE A YEAR my grandfather came to visit us in Kansas. Since he needed luxuries we couldn't provide—showers with rough towels, impeccable room service—he always stayed at the glamorous Wilmore Hotel.

My father needs a board in his bed, my mother announced to some invisible person on the phone while she tapped cigarette ashes on the floor. He has a very bad back and needs a good board.

Invariably, someone at the Wilmore told my mother there was no way they would drag an enormous board to the tenth or eleventh floor of their hotel. My mother's voice grew more severe.

A board, she repeated. A good *thick* board. Otherwise he simply won't stay. What? That's ridiculous. Of course you can get someone to find one.

On the day of this particular argument, my mother was in my father's study, sitting on the daybed. I was on the floor, playing with a snowstorm paperweight. *What are you doing?* she mouthed to me.

Nothing, I said. Just playing. In fact, I was thinking that the snow looked like cottage cheese and wishing I could break the paperweight open to find out.

A board, my mother repeated, speaking back to the phone. A very good thick board. I'm sorry. We insist. He's from New York.

My grandfather's picture was on my father's desk. He was reading a book, and I could see his white frizzy hair and the lump on his nose. When he'd first told me about running into the samovar, I imagined a three-year-old with a wreath of frizzy white hair wearing a navy blue, double-breasted suit, decorated with a carnation. I imagined him this way now.

Well that's settled, said my mother, putting down the phone. You'd think they'd never heard of a bad back before. She took a drag on her cigarette and fluffed up the sleeves of her green housecoat. The things that man doesn't do for people, she said. The lengths to which he will go.

I continued to play with the paperweight, and she grew annoyed with my indifference. His generosity, she added testily. Everyone is indebted to him. She meant that as a young doctor, he sometimes made house calls in tenements, delivered children on kitchen tables, helped soldiers get shots for the Spanish Civil War. She also meant he gave us money.

You'll stay with him for a night, she said to me. The Wilmore is marvelous.

What? I shook the paperweight harder. The snowman disappeared.

In the Wilmore. You can stay overnight with him. You'll be his guest.

MY GRANDFATHER ARRIVED at seven o'clock that night, and within hours, I was at the Wilmore, being given a bath that frightened me, as he splashed water and screamed Get down! Get down! Since I wasn't able to go anywhere, I didn't know if he wanted me to dive under the water or lean back against the slippery back of the gleaming white tub. I was much too old to be given a bath, and much too old to be dried, but I'd always been told never to say no.

When he led me to the bedroom, I was relieved that both beds were arranged vertically—mine above his. There was so little space between them, it seemed to me they looked like one big bed that had been folded in half. My bed seemed hard. I wondered if it had a board.

For a long time I lay in my bed, and the darkness smelled thick with the smell of oil my grandfather had used, although I wasn't sure if it was on his body or mine. He was the mapmaker, I knew that for certain— the man who'd walked in seven-league boots and been fed sweet wine and braided bread. He was the mapmaker, taking time off.

The night was not exotic like any of the countries my mother described. Downtown Lawrence was thick and ordinary. I fell asleep to my mother intoning *and so he walked all over the land in his enormous seven-league boots. . . .* I woke up at dawn.

In storybooks, I sometimes read about people who woke up in the morning and couldn't remember where they were. I always longed to have this experience, but that morning, like all others, I remembered where I was. My grandfather was lying in his bed on top of the covers: I could see the froth of his hair like a large white shrub and could even look through it, just as I could look through brambles. Through the tangle, I saw him pull his penis out of his pajamas and push it and pull it until white whale's milk spurted into the air. Afterwards the grey dawn began to push and pull at the walls, like taffy. At last there was no air left in the room at all.

When my first-grade teacher, Mrs. Ryan, found four boys and one girl in a state of disarray behind coats in the cloakroom, she told us that grown-ups do not play with themselves, and indeed, if we wanted to become grown-ups, we would do the same. Of course we didn't want to become grown-ups, and we ignored her. However, in this strange airless room, Mrs. Ryan's words became law: Once more my grandfather became an enormous naked child, running towards a samovar. His penis started to look like the spout of the samovar. I decided he deserved to be burned.

At breakfast, I told my grandfather what I had seen. Perhaps if I'd been able to eat, I wouldn't have bothered to tell him, but the orange juice was viscous, and the toast was as rough as a man's cheek.

You sly little girl, he said, when I finished. You sly, sly little girl.

The dining room of the Wilmore was across the street from the public library. I saw its arched oak doors and wished I could open them, talk to the librarian, and get my quota of four books for the week. Instead, I sat quietly, contemplating what my grandfather meant by *sly*, and finally I said to him,

I want you to buy me a present.

A present?

Yes. A present.

MY GRANDFATHER DIDN'T argue. In fact he nodded, as though responding to an ancient, familiar imperative. Outside, the Midwest became a place the mapmaker couldn't chart, no matter how many peasants he waved to—a land of tired pink houses, plastic bobby pins, dime stores. I guided my grandfather through Woolworth's, past blue binders, strawberry-colored rulers, globes of countries I never wanted to visit. His dark wool coat was larger there—like a topiary I'd seen in a mansion.

He followed me to a glass counter filled with ribbon-candy and plastic wind-up toys. I pointed to a man in a black tuxedo hugging a woman in a flamingo-colored evening dress.

I want that, I said. I want you to buy that for me.

My grandfather nodded. An exceedingly uncomfortable nod. Followed by the phrase, The young lady wants to see that.

The clerk put the man and woman on top of the counter, and they spun around and around. As soon as we got to my parents' apartment, I put them on our mahogany dining room table and made them dance until they fell, since not even a key could unwind them.

SANDRA
GREENAWAY

S ANDRA GREENAWAY'S MOTHER was the head housekeeper
at the Wilmore, and this meant that she and her mother had two
suites to themselves with a kitchen. Sandra was embarrassed that her
mother was the housekeeper at the Wilmore. She was so embarrassed
that twice when I was in second grade, she invited five girls to her private suite for tea, during which she spoke in a fake English accent. My
mother said that maybe Sandra was a relative of Kate Greenaway, the
artist who drew women in empire dresses, but I never mentioned this
to Sandra because I didn't want her to know my mother speculated
about things like that, nor did I want her to know that I romanticized
her surroundings.

The first time Sandra invited us over to tea, I imagined something
exotic was going to happen, even if it was sad. Maybe we would explore
the Wilmore and get locked in an upstairs room. Maybe we'd walk into
the picture of a castle in the lobby and disappear. Nothing happened at
all: Sandra poured bland Earl Grey, served us something called cream

crackers, talked in her fake English accent, and we all went home. This was before I'd gone to the Wilmore with my grandfather, so I wished that I could live there.

ABOUT A MONTH after my grandfather had left, I asked Sandra to come over for tea. I was ashamed that our apartment was small and drab yet felt compelled that she should see it. Since my mother was—according to standards of Kansas—the sort of woman who let things go, we had a green rug that was usually dirty, a brown couch that was flecked with lint, and a kitchen floor that was covered with newspapers. Yet the moment Sandra walked inside, I realized she envied me because my mother didn't have to be a housekeeper so we could live here. It wasn't in what she said. Just a sadness in her eyes, an intake of breath.

Come in, I said, faking an English accent.

My mother let us use her best China teacups, and we drank the same bland Earl Grey. Instead of cream crackers, we ate Mallomars, which Sandra said were Jolly good. We sat at the small white table in my room, facing the ribbon of alley. This was a room of great unhappiness, for me—a place where I hid when my parents fought and where I kept an old attaché case of my father's filled with old draperies, in case I had to run away from home. However, Sandra said, in her English accent:

What a nice desk! I should like to have one.

It's not desk. It's a table.

Well. A table then, said Sandra.

But you have one, don't you?

Yes. But not my own. Sandra looked out at the ribbon of alleys. You're lucky to visit the Wilmore, she said. I have to live there, but you get to eat in the dining room.

I've never eaten in the dining room.

But I saw you. You got to stay with that man—the man with the white hair.

Why didn't you come in and say hi if you saw me?

I'm not allowed to go to the dining room.

I THOUGHT OF the two vertical beds and my grandfather's penis haloed by frizzy white hair—an image that would appear for years, each time I heard a dirty joke, or even considered the word. I wondered if Sandra's mother had cleaned that room and seen his milk on the sheets. I wondered if she and her mother had heard my grandfather giving me a bath.

It was only one night. Besides it wasn't much fun.

Why not? said Sandra in her prim, self-conscious way.

Because. There were boogers in the orange juice.

There hadn't been boogers in the orange juice—but Sandra laughed in a way I'd never seen her laugh, and I told myself that I could fool anybody I wanted to.

Were there *really*? she kept saying. Were there *really*?

Yes, I said. And more. You could hear them blowing their noses in the kitchen.

Oh no, said Sandra.

Oh yes. The whole place was full of people blowing their noses.

On the way out, Sandra stopped at my father's study and looked at the map of Asia.

What's that?

A map, silly.

I know. But of what?

Asia.

But it's *green*. And *purple*. I thought Asia was a desert.

Only part of it. Anyway, that's how they drew them then.

Sandra stood on her toes and looked at the map closely.

Look! They have a book in the middle of a country.

That's not a country, it's a city. It's where my grandfather came from. They have palm trees there. And they don't have boogers in the orange juice.

Sandra looked at me. Actually, she said quietly, I know about that place. It's in the Bible.

You're talking about a different Ninevah.

No. I know from Sunday school. There was war there. They have a library. And now . . . now it's this place you can visit.

We stood there deadlocked. My mother called from the kitchen and asked if we wanted more tea.

No, said Sandra, I have to go.

When she left, I went to my mother in the kitchen and told her what Sandra Greenaway had told me about Ninevah. My mother was taking braided bread out of the oven, and I thought it selfish that she hadn't offered any to us. She took out the bread and began to glaze it with green frosting. The frosting was dark, just like the green on the map. I told her it didn't look like the sort of thing people would want to eat.

It's for Irma Burr, she said. I'm making it for St. Patrick's day. Irma Burr lived upstairs and was Irish.

While my mother frosted the braided bread, I told her that Ninevah existed in the Bible and that people like Sandra Greenaway got to learn about it in Sunday school. I told her it had a library.

My mother didn't answer. She put a towel around the bread and looked away. Then she put the bread on the plate and handed it to me:

Now you bring this up to Irma Burr, she said, and tell her, Top o' the morning.

A HIDDEN CITY

AS RESULT OF the unspoken covenants children make, Sandra Greenaway and I never visited each other's houses again. Now, however, I took great care to study Ninevah on the map, and the more I looked, the more I decided that a real and vital city was right beneath it. I could see this city: outdoor markets with pomegranates, jewelry, enormous bolts of cloth, as well as dark blue bottles that certainly contained genies. I decided the mapmaker had never been to Ninevah but had drawn it from some idea he'd gotten from a book. I told this to my mother, and she said I was talking nonsense.

Later I learned that Ninevah had once been considered a holy city. The library it housed was enormous, and the city was named for a goddess called Eve who helped pregnant women use their ribs to make their children's bones. But we never discussed any of these things in our house. It wasn't part of our life to dwell on this city by the Tigris.

THE JOURNEY
OF THE MAP

WHEN I WAS thirteen, instead of going to school, I spent long tedious hours in my parents' car, which was always parked in back of our apartment building. My father never left for the university until eleven, and I had to crouch low in the car, so he wouldn't see me from the window. It never occurred to me my father might go to the car, and he never did. His movements were always furtive, slow, careful not to wake my mother. I could see his wide moon face framed in the wide sun porch window. Mysterious rituals. Ablutions. My father was unobserved.

My father always did unremarkable things, like drink coffee, straighten the pillows on the sunporch. We were both behind glass, so I always imagined we were living in different elements. The things he did were remarkable only in that he didn't know I was seeing him, although I always imagined that he was going to do something outrageous. Once, when he picked up a piece of paper, I was sure it was the map, which my mother had put away. It wasn't, though. It was a plan of the cathedral of St. Gall for a course my father was teaching.

An hour after my father left for the university by bus, I snuck out of the alley and took a different bus to downtown Lawrence. Two times a week, I saw a leering fifty-one-year-old Spanish tutor who came close, very close, to ravishing me. If I was early, I rode endlessly, getting off at random stops. The air was pale, thin, attenuated. Time disappeared. Tenements rose like pieces of a stage set. Sometimes I read in the green marbled bathroom of Lawrence's best department store, sitting on a wrought iron chair just like the matrons. I was a fugitive. Anybody looking at me should know that. But all the matrons smiled at me: You look so pretty with your hair, and all, dontcha know? This made me feel normal. I always smiled back.

From the department store's enormous windows, Lawrence spread before us like a grey prairie. While the matrons talked, I read important books: Freud, Dostoevsky, Faulkner. The women didn't know these books—they only spoke about my hair. After I left the department store and lay recklessly on a couch with the Spanish tutor, I came home and lied to my parents about school. I told them what I had done, how much volleyball I had played, what I'd learned in Spanish, and the next morning I typed a note, excusing my absence, and stuck it in front of my mother's face. As always, she was asleep. She signed it without reading it.

The map had disappeared: I wondered if my mother had given it back to my grandfather, but when I asked her, she said, I'd never do a thing like that. It's an heirloom. I just got tired of it. You can only look at them for so long.

But the day my father got a new teaching job in Vermont, my mother brought it out and laid it on the dining room table.

Old memories, she said, puffing at a cigarette. She pointed to the map. Is this where you go when you don't go to school?

I always go to school. What do you think?

Never mind, said my mother. She smoked the cigarette and tapped ashes in the ashtray. The ashtray was glass and had an indentation where the cigarette was supposed to go, but my mother never put the cigarette there. Suddenly she said:

We're going to Vermont. My father is very upset.

For a minute I didn't know which father she meant. It was my father, after all, who'd gotten a new teaching job. Then I realized it was her father.

My father, she continued, liked visiting us here. It's different from New York. It gives him a break.

I looked closely at the map: What had once seemed verdant now looked poisonous. Purple and green ink. Who had thought to use those colors anyway? I thought of telling this to my mother then thought the better of it.

We're getting a big house, you know, she said. Lots and lots of rooms.

That's great, Mom, I said. She'd always hated our tiny apartment.

So the map can go anywhere, she said. Anywhere anybody wants it to go.

MY FATHER'S
STUDY

WHEN WE MOVED to Vermont, to a town that did not seem real, I discovered sleeping in the afternoon. In Kansas, I never had slept in the afternoon. Day was omnipresent in that flat, horizontal land. But Vermont gave the promise of eternal night. Its hills dipped and curved. Its houses had attics, window seats, sloping closets. And the town itself was in a valley, surrounded by green mountains.

School began earlier than school in Kansas. As if a switch had flipped, I was going to school now, not hiding in my father's car. I went to pizza parties and found a boyfriend my own age. And in the afternoons, I came home tired.

Before I slept, I always went to my father's study to do my homework. His study was in the basement, half below ground level, with clerestory windows on two sides that were eye-to-eye with rose bushes. There was a sense of order and secrecy in my father's room that didn't permeate the rest of the house, which was open and sprawled like a log cabin. Everything in his study was neat: My father's papers were stacked and labeled like seedlings in a well-tended garden. The air was filled with the soft smell of dark ink and fresh paper. Above me I heard my mother and sister talking, often arguing. Without knowing it, I'd begun to regard them with contempt, and as I listened, I dug deep into my books with a monk-like, masculine virtue. It was an accident that I was a woman, an unlucky one, I thought. I also loved men passionately. That was unlucky, too.

My father was now the overseer of the map's nomadic journey. He'd hung it above a couch in an alcove in his study. The alcove was built into a wall with no windows. This made it feel tucked away, like a trundle bed.

After I did my homework, I went over to the couch, pulled my coat over my legs, and fell asleep. Before I fell asleep, I often looked at the map and imagined I was a traveler in a desert who was given refuge in a tiny village. I was on my way to deliver a dangerous message, something that might cost me my life, but for now I was lying in a whitewashed room, listening to someone bustle in the kitchen. When I finally fell asleep it was always thick, nearly imageless yet imbued with purpose, even speed, as I moved through some unknown country. I ignored towns, landmarks, anything that might stop me, and when I woke up, I knew I'd been traveling. This feeling persisted when I went upstairs.

My father never worked in his study until evening. If he happened to come home early from the university and came downstairs, he didn't wake me but turned on lights, pulled the shades, straightened the furniture, and once, just once, leaned over and kissed me on the cheek. I lay there pretending to sleep—a remote, indifferent princess, my hair arrayed upon the pillow for my father.

My father hadn't always been easy to have as a father. He was punctilious, shy, and kind, except for a terrible temper that emerged without warning. When I was five, in a strange summerhouse, he pulled down my pants, held my legs up in the air, and whipped me again and again. I didn't know why he was doing this and said, many times, as if to make sense of it, You are whipping me. This was the sort of thing that I had to watch out for.

One late afternoon, I woke up late. We were already in the deep brittle dark of a cold Vermont winter. The air was blue-black. A special thin consistency. And outside, next to the clerestories, were the boots and legs of a man I didn't know. The boots were kicking the earth, and I heard him say: She's not going to last the winter. You'll have to do something.

My father's voice answered, but I couldn't hear what he was saying.

No, she won't, said the man, as if he had been contradicted. Mr. Hucksworth wouldn't listen to me when I told him. He said, I don't want the expense.

My father said whatever it was in question had lasted for a long time.

But she won't last now, said the man. You can bet she won't. He kicked the ground again. They walked off, muttering.

I could guess they were talking about a water pipe—something that Mr. Hucksworth, the original builder of the house, hadn't installed properly. But I chose not to know. Instead, I decided, perversely, that they were talking in code——possibly about me, or my mother or my sister. I looked again at the map—the woman spilling water, the words *Lector Benevol.* I fell asleep again, and this time I dreamt that I was in a desert, going to a city like Ninevah, except that it was much older and had no library. My mission was dangerous, obscure. I traveled at night under unfamiliar stars. I looked for the town with the oasis and couldn't find it. *I have to keep going,* I thought.

When I woke, there were familiar sounds upstairs—my mother and father arguing. It was about the pipes, after all: My mother wanted them replaced. My father didn't.

We'll freeze, she said. We'll freeze our goddamn asses off.

We won't, he said. We've never frozen in our lives.

It was usually the case that both of my parents were right. I believed this now, warm from my desert journey. I went upstairs, and soon all of us were traveling. We argued about the water pipes and, when we got tired of that, the conditions of life in China. We traveled full speed, courting unfamiliar gestures.

THE ANTIQUE
WRITING CHEST

THE ANTIQUE WRITING chest came from England and was
the sort of chest gentlemen of means took on journeys in the nineteenth century. It had drawers; boxes for pen, ink, paper, and sealing
wax; and a tiled surface that one could write on. I'd bought the chest in
England when I was seventeen, and my parents and I took a winding
road to the Brontës' house. There we saw the impossibly small buttons
on Charlotte's wedding dress, incompressible books the children had
written in code—and the graveyard beyond their house. The antique
store was at the bottom of the hill, and my mother, who noticed the writing chest, said that I should buy it.

It's not my sort of thing, Mom.

Buy it, said my mother, who had forsaken maps for antiques, You'll
never regret it. It's marvelous.

I didn't want the chest. I wanted to be in seedy French hotels with
shutters like Matisse paintings. I wanted to wake up with my boyfriend
in a tangle of sheets and the smell of sour wine. Nonetheless, I bought

the chest to please her, and she found someone in Vermont to refin-ish it. Soon the mahogany shone and the brass handles were so bright they would have attracted highway robbers. It remained in my room in Vermont as an oddity. Eventually my mother moved herself into my bedroom, which she called her writing room.

The chest is there, she said. Are you sure that you don't want it?

What I really wanted was the map, which I'd come to love again, during those hours of long imageless sleep in my father's study.

No, mother, I told her. The chest should be at home.

A WALK IN
THE SNOW

IT IS NIGHT, deep night, and I am walking up a steep hill to a house I haven't visited in more than twenty years. The driver has let me out at the bottom of the hill, just as he did twenty years ago when I used to take the bus from college. The hill is far too steep for the bus, and in any case the driver, an old Vermont veteran, believes walking in the snow is good for people. As always, I am stricken by the belief that the snow will swallow me up. As always, I am convinced our house has fallen into a precipice. Yet I find the house and walk up the steps, just as I did twenty years ago.

The last time I came home, walking up the same hill, I kept thinking of a particular phrase, and I am thinking of it again: *Here I come in all the fury of my consumption.* I long to tell the phrase to my father, just as I longed to tell it to him twenty years ago, and I want to ask him if he has ever heard it and then say how odd it is that I thought the very same thing the last time I came home. Instead, I sit opposite him at the dining room table drinking sherry, explaining how my husband and son are stuck in a broken-down rented car in Boston. Everything is the same except that my mother is dying.

My mother's death will not be a normal death. It will be ambiguous, wrenching, hard, just like her life. Indeed, the ambiguity looms so large the very thought *my mother is dying* makes me feel like a heretic.

She isn't dying, my father says. She's only refusing to eat. She went to the hospital for a harrowing operation, but now she's refusing to eat. It's all those years of ice cream cones. You know how she would just keep those ice cream cones stacked by the stove and make herself a few every night? Maybe she's gotten used to them.

I can see a huge box of ice cream cones from where I am sitting. They are stacked in a corner, near the kitchen. I can also see the map of Asia, which has moved from my father's study to the mantel: There is the nude woman who used to embarrass me, the Christ-like figure offering a cup and saucer.

Lector Benevol, I say, referring to the words on Ninevah.

Of course, says my father. He knows Latin well.

I won't sleep in my parents' house but will sleep at my brother's who lives in the same Vermont town. The fact that I won't sleep at home is a silent, unspoken code. Our family doesn't talk, though we talk all the time.

It must be a long time since you've seen snow, my father says while he drives through quiet white streets.

I live in the colonies, now, I say, meaning California.

My brother lives on the edge of town. He lives in one half of a house, his girlfriend and her daughter in the other. It's hard to tell if they're having separate, enmeshed, or semi-detached lives, and no one asks them. My father stops outside the house. It's a given that he won't go in.

EATING

WHEN I FIRST see her in the hospital, my mother's breath is sickeningly sweet. She's surrounded in a mist of eerie perfume, shriveled beyond recognition. A crocheted bandage holds the wrist with the IV, and this looks quaint and archaic, like a glove from Mother Goose. She is a puzzle, say the doctors. A medical puzzle.

I don't think my mother is a puzzle. I think she wants to die and no one is letting her. I think she is aware of another woman in my father's life—a large Renaissance scholar, shaped like a Dutch-doll saltshaker. I think she's beset by the false jollity of the nurses (Marla! Are you hungry? Gotta eat your food to get strong!), the denial of my uncle (Her color looks good), and the controlled calm of her Iranian psychiatrist with his almost-perfect English accent (Shock therapy, combined, of course, with other appropriate interventions . . . would, in my opinion . . .).

In the midst of this, I see my mother's dim, struggling presence. The rise and fall of her breath. Small moments of small recognition. Larger moments of self-disgust. (I will start to eat tomorrow. Yes. I promise. But later. You better go.) I have presents for my mother: A small dollhouse I found at the airport. A silver box from Tibet containing messages from my husband, my son, and my daughter, a shawl. She pushes them away.

I have no use for these.

The silver box is useless. You have to keep it.

Later she touches my hair, my eyes, looking for the flaw.

The nurses asked me what you did. I said you were an actress. They were impressed.

Mother! I'm not an actress!

But you are! Don't you remember when you played Hamlet? You were marvelous opposite Ophelia. Tell me something. Are you wearing a bra?

Yes, mother, I'm wearing a sports bra. Look: The straps crisscross in back. In the summer when you wear a low-cut dress, you can see these cool white straps.

This is the Zen of dying. The mystery of a crisscrossed bra. While I talk, my mother tries to breathe. Every breath is a struggle.

Meanwhile, in the next bed, a woman whose cancer has twisted around her lungs and esophagus like a snake is being visited by a handsome, dark-haired cleric in an impeccable wool suit. He is reading from a book about sin and God taking bad lambs back into the fold. This woman does not look like a bad lamb. She looks like a gentle lamb. The cleric looks like a wolf who has never considered that death could happen to him because he has eaten so many lambs and gotten away with it. Perhaps it won't. He probably has his own opinions about Sauerkraut Day in this part of Vermont.

. . . and the Lord returneth all to his flock . . .

Mother, listen. You know all the stuff we went through? The rough times? The hard times? It's all water under the bridge. All that matters is that I love you. Do you understand?

Blank look. Small, dim eyes.

Mother, I love you. It's been a long haul.

I know my mother the way I know the air. I know her the way I know cats who come for an evening and then live on, I know her the way I know a garden in Kansas, over thirty years ago, brimming with lilacs and a rough stone birdbath.

Mother, do you want to die?

No.

Then why aren't you eating?

I can't.

A VISIT TO NINEVAH

THE QUESTION IS, why now? Why isn't your mother eating now?

It is New Year's Eve and I am talking to my mother's psychiatrist on the phone. It's eight o'clock in the evening, and Ari Nafissian has called me at my brother's house. His voice is controlled, concerned: studied solicitude with a hint of the real.

But I understand you want to transfer my mother to a place where she can get shock therapy. . . .

Yes. It is a good idea for her.

He speaks English softly and has cultivated the practice of pausing before speech.

I understand. They say this place has good facilities. Tell me . . . what do you think it will do?

Well. Your mother isn't eating. It may get her started.

A pause between us. Of what? Understanding? I almost tell him about the woman my father has been seeing—a Renaissance scholar who teaches in a nearby town. Instead I concentrate on the children's rhyme: *How many miles to Babylon? / Three score and ten / Will I get there by candlelight? / Yes if your feet are swift and light / There and back again.*

But what do you see as the benefit in my mother's eating?

Well, she'll start to eat again.

I understand. But she's been depressed all her life. What will she go back to once she starts to eat? She can't enjoy food. She doesn't enjoy buying clothes. And my father is almost never home. What will eating for a few months do for her?

Well, of course, we'll have to look for ongoing therapy after the shock treatment. And still appropriate drugs. But why has she stopped eating now? I mean a person can be depressed and want to stop living for three days, and then suddenly feel like living. Our job is to preserve life.

His question *why now?* is a dangerous question, bringing me to the edge of my father's secret. I choose not to answer it and say instead:

She's been depressed for more than three days. More like four thousand. To put it differently, have you ever thought there's a shred of sanity in what she's doing?

How can I regard her behavior as sane?

Our conversation is beginning to sound like a book on conversational English. *Which way to the hospital? Three turns after the light. Do they have any beds there? Oh yes. Care-worn and well-crafted, in the style of the old country.*

Excuse me, I say again. But is there a shred of sense to what my mother is doing?

Ari Nafissian pauses. For a moment we step into another realm, and an erotic, almost sacred current flows between us.

There was a legend about a nomad who fasted for days, he says to me. She went to the desert and became a healer.

It's lovely legend, I say. Was this nomad was a woman?

Yes. It's an old Assyrian legend. Maybe as old as Ninevah.

And so?

And so I never give up hope.

I hear my brother behind me. He's cooking rice with pine nuts, roasted peppers. He's stirring in a way that tells me he doesn't want to hear the conversation.

Well, it's beyond the call of duty to talk on New Year's Eve, I say. So there's only more question, and you don't have to answer it.

Oh no, he says. Please ask.

Well if this were your grandmother. I mean, if this were *your* seventy-four-year-old grandmother, living in Iran, who'd been depressed for years and had very little to live for—is shock-treatment what you would want for her if she stopped eating?

Long pause. Unhappy silence.

I have no way of knowing, he says.

THE NEXT DAY there is a note on my mother's chart: *No shock therapy. Family doesn't want it.*

But of course we do, says my father.

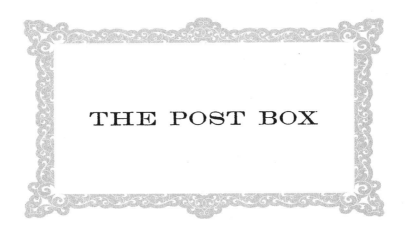

THE POST BOX

BEFORE I LEAVE, my father gives me the antique writing chest—a burden to take home on the plane. When I get home, I open it idly, expecting to find nothing. Instead I find all my mother's writing: letters she has started—often to me—and never finished; notes that toy with suicide; five or six journal entries so close to my sense of her, I'm not sure if they're hers or mine:

The dreamer sleeps and nothing can stop her, she wrote, *because sleep is a consuming possession, a lust that no one can observe. At the same time sleep, the domain of the sleeper, is not comforting. It is cold, solid, burdensome. The eyelid repairs the night. It is morning and the typical day is commenced. Only the seasons change.*

There are also other things in the chest: birthday candleholders from years ago, letters from me, a picture of my mother when she was thirteen, an improbable braided candle—the kind that's used to light the candles on the Sabbath. There is also a single sentence, written on yellow note paper, and it looks quite recent: *When Euridyce knew she was to be chosen she suddenly became afraid even though it was really a very elaborate sojourn that was being prepared for her. . . . There was nothing to go by, not even a map . . .*

I look at everything. The plastic candleholders in the shape of birds. A wooden rattle I played with when I was three. And it occurs to me my mother knew I would find everything in there. Who would know, when we found the chest in England, that it would become a haphazard postal system between a mother and a daughter?

The chest smells like my mother. It's the smell of Ponds Cold Cream—unguents of the fifties and sixties. I put the chest in the living room, and it stays there like a heartbeat.

THE
MAGICIAN'S EYE

AFTER WE LEFT Vermont, my husband flew back to California to be with our six-year-old-daughter, and my son and I went to New York, the city of my mother's childhood. It was a chilling winter. Our tongues stuck to ice, our breath preceded us everywhere. Compared to California, the contrast between the indoors and the outdoors made us both feel safe. We relished the sense of walls, snow, and sky. We took comfort in boundaries close to our skin, cold that was bracing, warmth that could be retrieved.

My son, who was almost eleven, was angry with me for taking him to see my mother. He hadn't liked the presence of death. He hadn't liked seeing someone starve. One night, he did karate kicks in the hotel room until he succeeded in turning the light switch off with his foot.

Why did you take me there? I didn't like the way she smelled.

Because it was the right thing to do, I said. And tomorrow we're going to Ellis Island.

Why?

Because you might find out something there.

Like what?

Like what your grandmother's parents did in order to come here.

IT WAS BITTER cold on the ferry to Ellis Island. Everyone was dressed in layers, like immigrants, except for my son. I cried when we entered the Registry Hall: This was a real passage in my grandfather's journey, before he became a mapmaker, a doctor, a lecher. He had been frightened, bewildered—and amazed that he'd taught himself English on the boat. I astounded them, he told me once. I wrote a compound sentence in English!

The Registry Hall was perfectly, monastically, empty. I wandered among exhibits. My son sat reading in the hall. His face was lit by sun from the enormous domed windows, and he read a book called *The Magician's Eye*. I imagined my grandfather watch his only grandson read the language he'd taught himself on the ship. I imagined my grandfather weeping.

On the ferry going back, my son said he hadn't liked Ellis Island at all.

Angel Island's better, he said, referring to the place where immigrants in California were processed. Here they tried to make it look pretty. At Angel Island they *showed* you the wretched conditions.

My son talked so loudly, a man in a yarmulke smiled at me, and I realized I felt bereft. Back in the hotel, my son did more karate kicks.

Why did you take me to that stupid island? he said.

It wasn't a stupid island, I said. And tomorrow we're going to the Lower East Side so you can see how your relatives really lived.

We didn't go to the Lower East Side after all. Instead, we walked through Greenwich Village, where I bought my son a box decorated with a single eye. This eye reminded him of the third eye that belonged to the magician in the book he read in the Registry Hall and he pronounced it way cool. Afterwards, we went to Washington Square Park, where my son slid down an artificial ice hill again and again. Each time he did, he cried with delight—as though he could reinvent his past in that formidable cold.

THE TIBETAN BOOK
OF THE DEAD

MY MOTHER OUTSMARTED everybody by dying an hour after a well-intentioned nurse's aide painted her nails pink. There was no funeral—she hadn't wanted one—and since Vermont has strict codes about the time lapse between death and embalming, I never saw her again. My father told me her face had a curious dignity in death. I told him she had done the right thing.

For a long time I couldn't believe my mother had died. It was not the same as missing her. We'd rarely been able to talk. It was more like disbelief at the sudden absence of something in nature, as though an enormous gorge had been swallowed up, or the moon was no longer in the sky. To offer some kind of homage, I decided to read to my mother from *The Tibetan Book of the Dead*. This wasn't the first time I'd done this for my atheist, Marxist relatives. Perhaps it was a compensation for never being what they wanted me to be.

Mother. This mind of yours is inseparable luminosity and emptiness in the form of a great mass of light. It will guide you through the bardo. Mother. You are becoming one with the white light.

My mom is being weird, my son said audibly from the kitchen. He and his friend were making snacks. She's reading from a book like my grandmother can hear.

Yeah, the friend said. Well, moms are into weirdness.

That night at dinner my husband made a cruel joke:

Your mother's reading from The Tibetan Book of the Deaf, he said to our son and daughter.

What? they asked, glad to get real information.

This is what it is, said my husband, cupping his hands. GO TOWARD THE WHITE LIGHT. What? I said, GO TOWARD THE WHITE LIGHT.

The children laughed. I didn't. By now it was the forty-ninth day of my mother's death, and, according to Tibetan calculations, she was preparing to be reborn. I couldn't imagine my mother doing such a thing. All I could imagine was how she would be ordering fabrics for a new and interesting living room. Once again I opened the book.

Please choose a loving home, I said to her.

MILDRED

AFTER MY MOTHER died, I was no longer able to write because I realized it had been her, after all, that I'd been writing to all along. My mother had not liked my writing and was disappointed that I didn't write like H. H. Munro or Henry James or any one of a number of people who wrote in what she called good, simple ways. Why don't you write what you know about? she often asked.

It was only when she died that I realized my mother was a confining wall, one I had to scale again and again every time I wrote. I'd always had deep regrets about her sense of emptiness, and the antique writing chest didn't help them, because I knew that the emptiness she felt wasn't the emptiness mystics talk about, but an illusory emptiness that comes when one can't use one's powers.

I asked my father for the map of Asia and put it on a wall near the antique writing chest, thinking I'd invent a story about Ninevah. A day later, though, I took it down and put it in my closet. It was my mother's story, not mine—about what the mapmaker might have done on the deserts of Ninevah, and why he went so far from home. Every time I looked at it, all I could think was that the story was there, hidden in the folds of the map, the way, at night, when I looked up from my desk, I imagined there was a cosmic lining in the sky, and if I could only rip it open, everything that was to be known would tumble out. My husband didn't notice that I'd taken down the map. We had reached a stage of apathy that went far beyond paying attention.

During that time, however, a curious kind of help came, and this was in the form of a pale wraith-like woman, who looked almost exactly like my mother would have looked had she been happy. She was a small woman in her seventies with a hooked nose and tiny, fluttering arms. She wasn't enrolled in the writing program I taught in, but she sat in the back of the room, a grateful wraithlike radiance. I could tell that her only pleasure in life was to be allowed to audit a writing class. I told her she could stay.

My mother had always wanted to be a writer and might have been a good one. But she wasn't able to withstand the occupational hazards of the trade, nor did she have an audacious belief in the powers of her imagination. Her favorite line was from *The Cherry Orchard*, in which a character, whose named eluded her, said, I could have been a Dostoyevsky.

This woman, whose name was Mildred, sat in the back of the room, or, on days when she was bold, in a corner, quite close to me. She had a mole at the end of her nose, and until I looked closely, I could never tell whether this mole was skin or moisture. This added to the impression that Mildred was melting. She always wore a green sweater covered with small woolen balls and dark brown pants. She had glasses like my mother's, but her eyes emanated light. As I fielded competitive remarks from other students, all I saw in her was beatitude.

I have been blessed, I thought, *like a character in a story about Chassidim. My mother has returned to let me teach her.*

I was embarrassed by my belief that Mildred had been sent to me. I was embarrassed, too, that I took to writing paeans to her that I never showed to anybody. I wrote them in longhand in a kind of hieroglyph that even I wasn't meant to decipher, and although I've never tried to translate my handwriting, they were the first things I wrote after my mother died. When a mean-spirited student asked why I was letting a seventy-year-old woman who wasn't in the writing program audit a class that qualified graduate students hadn't been able to get into, I looked at these very notes and said Mildred had once been an accomplished teacher, and I wanted her to critique me. The student didn't believe me, but when she complained, the head of the department looked the other way. Perhaps Mildred had been his lover once. Or maybe he knew I was reeling from my mother's death. The idea of the two of them in bed amused me. She was so frail, he could break her bones.

Mildred gave me just one story. It was about an older woman who took a younger woman in as a boarder in her cavernous apartment. The younger woman who was a cellist spent hours playing Bach Inventions while the older woman served her tea. She met an archaeologist and left to get married.

I found the story lovely—generous, well written, and understanding in a way my mother had never understood me. I waited for Mildred to come back so I could tell her how much I liked it, but she'd vanished. Later I discovered that she'd gone to many classes in the writing program, always submitting the same story.

No doubt she wrote it herself, but a long time ago, a colleague said. Then she laughed a short bitter laugh.

I asked her what the story was about. The colleague said it was about buying a rug in a peasant town in Italy. This convinced me that Mildred wrote about the cellist for me alone. I continue to believe that she was sent. I continue to believe that my mother allowed me to teach her.

ASHES

MY FATHER, WHO did not believe in funerals, could not bury my mother's ashes. He kept the box in a bedroom closet, and when the woman whom he now lived with taught in another town, he sometimes went to the closet and stood close to them. On top of this box he'd put my mother's ring, which the funeral parlor wrapped in a black velvet bag. With it, he also put the miniature oval silver box from Tibet I'd given my mother when I visited her in the hospital. The silver box was used for prayers and contained the written message *dear mother, we send you all our love and here is a mantra which means I am the jewel in the center of the lotus, mother remember, you are also the jewel in the center of the lotus, love , cecelia, nicholas, justin, tanya.*

My daughter Tanya was only six, and it was hard for her to write in the small cramped space, but she'd managed the first three letters of her name. My father thought religions were bunk yet told me that when he looked inside and saw the miniature message, he had an odd sense that all four of us were waving.

The oddest thing, he said to me. The oddest goddamn thing.

We lived over four thousand miles away, so my father told me about the ashes over the phone. It's very comforting, although it bothers me a little, like being close to a shrine. Sometimes I even talk to her.

About the ashes, I had conflicted feelings. I thought it strange, but not out of character, that my father didn't bury my mother's ashes and kept them in a room where he often slept with someone else. On the other hand, I thought it was good that this scholarly man, who didn't believe in shrines and—to his own dismay—missed my mother deeply, should say good-bye in a way that made sense to him.

Do whatever you need to do, I always said to him. It's been a terrible time.

One day my father came to California to see me, and he brought me some of my mother's ashes, as well as her white shawl. The shawl, like the antique writing chest, smelled of Ponds Cold Cream, and also Eau de Vie perfume, which used to make me nauseous when I was trapped in a car with her. I buried my face in her shawl, sickened and moved simultaneously. I opened the ashes, which were wrapped many times over in a plastic bag: They were rough and sandy, and they contained one dark metal circle—part of my mother's artificial hip. It looked like an ancient coin.

Where's that map of Asia? my father asked.

It made me sad, so I put it away.

I want it, said my son boldly. I want it for my own room. He was angry that I hadn't given him the map, as well as the writing chest. He loved old things and was especially drawn to the map.

Someday, I told him. It's not the time.

My father and I stood silently, acknowledging what we didn't want to acknowledge: that objects that meant so much to my mother were now in our own ambivalent archives. I said I'd hang the map on the mantel as soon as I stopped being sad. Both of us knew I never would.

In truth, I wanted to bury my mother in Ninevah. I wanted to visit the ruined city myself, and I also wanted her to be close to Eve, the Goddess of the Rib, who helped pregnant women make their children's bones. I wanted her to wander in the library there, look at fabrics in the open market place. I wanted her to feel the lush verdant green of that ancient Assyrian city.

My mother, however, had always wanted to be buried in the poets' corner of Westminster Abbey, so finally, on a short trip to England, I took my portion of her ashes there. Since Westminster is heavily guarded and I'm an extremely cautious person, I pretended to be looking at Elizabeth Barrett Browning's grave, all the while putting my hands in my pockets, retrieving dust, and touching the stone lovingly. Soon the grave was covered with a rough grey ash. My mother's ash. My mother's bones. I kept the coin-shaped object in the writing chest.

One day my father asked whether I might consider putting my portion of my mother's ashes underneath the stone Buddha in our backyard. I hadn't known he'd seen this Buddha and couldn't tell him the ashes were long gone—picked up by sturdy shoes in England, taken down London streets, dusted off on British carpets. I suddenly felt mean-spirited and said I'd think about it in return for my mother's wedding ring, which she once said she wanted me to have. My father said a decent daughter would never barter for her mother's resting place. I reminded him my mother often liked to barter—was sometimes better at bartering than living.

THE MAP

THE MAP IS still in my closet, close to where I kept my mother's ashes. Sometimes I take it out and travel miles, knowing I won't put it in my house again. This map is nomadic like the Torah, and it has done its job with my mother and her family: Instead of treks on the desert, or days in hiding with a rabbi, it goes from house to house, room to room, neither an heirloom nor something that can be given away. At some point the map will belong to my son: Since he never met the mapmaker or heard my mother's stories, he'll treat it with more dispassion than I did. He'll probably create the map again, and Ninevah will become a bustling modern city, close to its home on the Tigris, a green and mysterious accident.

Henna

I WILL CALL her Ms. Shari, even though she was married. Ms. Shari is how the head of the department and I spoke of her in a tense, unhappy discussion behind closed doors.

I was teaching at a state university—crowded, underfunded, with clocks that never worked, irritable faculty, and windowless rooms that induced fugue states. Still, it was a generous place because it admitted almost everyone: The campus looked like an international mall. There were women in tight jeans and four inch heels, men with beards and turbans, mothers in saris wheeling babies, teenagers in yarmulkes, people in business suits who were ready to tell you they had degrees in physics, anthropology, or phonetics but were getting an MBA to shore things up. The elevators looked as though a sample population on a Manhattan subway had been transported. The school was a strange, cloned miracle: New York had merged with California.

The student in question was a woman who'd enrolled in a course I was teaching called Writing from Life. Ms. Shari sat alone in the back row next to the door, looking at her thick shoes, smoothing her chador or touching her wrists, which were crowded with orange and green flowers as though the henna dots on her fingers had sprouted a garden. My students could write about anything—grocery lists, lovemaking, children, changing tires. Everybody wrote voluminously except for Ms. Shari, who said her culture didn't believe in revealing anything personal, and nothing she wrote could be less than that. When I asked why she'd taken the class, she said she needed credits in English. Then she said:

What do you think? Should a life be open to the public? She left before I could answer. From then on she came to class every third meeting.

DON'T TAKE THAT kind of thing, said Nicole. Tell her to drop because she's flunking.

Nicole, who wore large shaded glasses and designer suits, was the department secretary and ran the English department. She knew the curriculum and figured out whose turn it was to teach freshman comp. She decided who should share offices. Nicole had given me a cherished key to the Xerox machine and made sure I never taught eight o'clocks so I could drive my fifteen-year-old to school. I wondered if telling Ms. Shari to drop the course was extreme. Extreme? said Nicole. No one takes shit like that.

I've never had to take shit like this before, I said.

You've never had to teach here before, said Nicole. This isn't a school. It's a certificate factory.

I didn't like to think about this anymore than I wanted to think about a lot of things around my divorce. I nodded.

Well don't let her push you around, Nicole said.

I'll think about it, I answered.

THE NEXT TIME Ms. Shari was in class, I leaned by her desk and told her she should drop the class because she was flunking. The cloth of her chador exuded a faint aroma of spice, making me think of alien weather, deserts vast as oceans. She picked up her books and left.

That day we talked about the journals of Sylvia Plath. Most of the students thought they were a microcosmic view of an unhappy, roiling life. Some worried that writing about that life reified the pain responsible for Sylvia Plath's suicide. But Gabriel Gonzalez pointed out that Virginia Woolf's journals were macrocosmic sweeps of an outer world, and she'd committed suicide too. So it might not matter how you wrote about your life, he said. Or even if you wrote at all. Gabriel was twenty-two, and his eyes were failing: To focus, he used a rolled-up newspaper. It looked like a spyglass, confirming my impression that the windowless room was a ship and we were all in a hold underwater.

Actually, said Ms. Tapali, who was from the Philippines, If you're already crazy, a journal won't make you crazier.

Everyone laughed except Gabriel Gonzalez: He approached almost everything with melancholy. After the class, he stuffed the newspaper in his pocket and said he didn't see a problem with being crazy. I said I agreed as long as you could manage the world.

I was about to tell Gabriel—not for the first time—that he should try to get his work published. He knew I would say this and left before I had the chance. All at once, I heard a noise and saw Ms. Shari and another woman looming in the florescence at the door. The other woman was so tall I thought she might be a man wearing a chador. I felt a sudden, boundless fear and knew I mustn't be alone with them. I walked into the hall.

I am a representative, the taller woman said, and we are accusing you of racism. You have asked Ms. Shari to write things that are against our beliefs. You leaned down to talk to her in a condescending way. You never were clear about the assignments.

This school is for everybody, she continued. You can't ask people to do things against their religions. You are a racist, intolerant person.

Her voice rose, and the international throng in the hall began to look at us. I said I couldn't change the way I taught. The representative said they would take the case to the dean, or, worse, to the president. She made her orange and blue hands into fists, pushing them close to my face, and said I would have to pay for my lack of understanding. Ms. Shari raised her fists, too, and my heart began to race. Their twenty painted fingers became tiny people endowed with magic, malevolent powers.

Nicole's office was at the end of the hall. From her open door she saw everything through her shaded glasses. When the women left, I went to her office and began to cry. I hadn't cried in school since kindergarten, when I'd been sent back from the playground for walking across fresh tanbark. Nicole closed the door and gave me chocolates filled with brandy.

They're just crazy is all, she said. You're not a racist. I know about that.

Of course she did. Nicole was black and was raised in the South.

That night I surfaced from sleep and saw women's fists morph into fabulous artifacts—puppets with frightening powers. I was sure they wanted to hurt me.

TWO DAYS LATER the head of the English department called me to his office. When I passed Nicole, she shook her head and said, I'm sorry.

The head of the department, who came from a distinguished line of Asian scholars, looked at me sternly through rimless glasses. There had been a complaint about me, he said, a serious complaint, and it was ill advised of me to take Nicole's advice. Perhaps, he continued, I wasn't used to teaching. Perhaps, he said delicately, I was the artistic type and never had written a syllabus. I knew it would be umbrage to tell him I taught in graduate programs: Instead I showed him the syllabus, which he looked at carefully. When he found nothing wrong, he got more upset.

Then the issue is racism, he said, and racism is serious. Ms. Shari says you're asking her to do something against her religion.

I said maybe I was, but she'd taken the course. I tried to focus on his bookcase—*Semiotics Applied to Keats, Reader Response,* and volumes of Henry James.

She can't flunk, he said. She absolutely can't. We're here to give people degrees. Everybody is entitled to a degree. He explained what would be involved if this were taken to the dean, and then to the president: a disgrace to all of us.

Again I felt a boundless fear. I offered to meet with Ms. Shari privately to find out what felt right for her. This was the humility the head of the department wanted to hear.

Oh no, he said. No one expects you to spend that kind of time with a student. I'm going to tell Ms. Shari she has to turn in the assignments you ask for. He stood up. The meeting was over.

THE NEXT DAY Ms. Shari came to class and sat in the back the way she always did. She began to hand in work. Her pieces were so precise they reminded me of mosaics, but I never told her because I was afraid she'd say I was thinking about her culture in stereotypes.

Because I must keep her writing confidential, there's only one piece I can paint in broad strokes: It was about Ms. Shari and her husband celebrating their wedding anniversary on an early spring evening. They came home from work, ate lamb stew on a red and golden cloth upon the floor. They opened presents from their families and then, because working overtime was essential, both went back to their jobs. This is how we live our lives, Ms. Shari wrote. It's very simple.

I was in the middle of an acrimonious divorce. The piece made me think about my almost-former husband—the gifts we'd gotten, the gifts we'd lost. The pages felt like a door to her house—prayer rug, pillows, lamb. For a moment I walked inside.

At the end of class, people read their work aloud: Ms.Tapali about training to be a law enforcement officer, Gabriel Gonzalez about meeting himself at every second of his life—an infinite number of Gabriel Gonzalezes with anxiety about future ones or grudges against previous ones. Ms. Shari, the last to volunteer, wrote about visiting her country for a relative's wedding. She wouldn't read her piece aloud, but agreed to answer questions if she could sit in the back. Everyone was curious:

What about men and women being segregated during a wedding?

If our whole life consisted of going to weddings, she said, It wouldn't be worth being married!

People laughed and asked more questions: Has your history been recorded?

At least as well as yours, Ms. Shari said.

Even Gabriel Gonzalez fixed upon Ms. Shari with his newspaper spyglass. When she finished talking, people applauded. She left without picking up her papers. I gave her an A.

LATER, MUCH LATER, when the university and its twilit rooms became an underwater dream, I found Ms. Shari's piece about her anniversary. I'd put it unthinkingly in a cabinet with rubber bands and stamps. Once more the pages became a door: the lamb, the blessing, the opening of gifts. I'd never forgotten her work, although I'd forgotten all the others except the extraordinary writing of Gabriel Gonzalez. Was it because of the difficulties I'd had with Ms. Shari? My unhappiness about my divorce? Or was there an aura of intimacy to her writing that belied her reluctance to write in the first place? The word *beloved* rose inside my heart. It was the beloved of old walled cities, hanging gardens. I discarded it as a romantic notion.

I found her piece in winter. Rain was beating on the skylights of my study—steady, endless rain that's poured on wooden roofs in Japan and mud huts in India and passes again and again through this northwestern sky. It drummed on the glass above my head. I wondered whether Ms. Shari's country also had rain.

Yes, it did, an atlas said. Deep, steady rain, except not nearly as frequent as rain in northern California. I remembered Ms. Shari's hands and wondered what it would be like to have my own hands decorated with henna. Was this a whim from a catalogue dreamt by a liquid metal bracelet by Sergio? Or did I want my hands to look like Ms. Shari's? I discarded the idea as another romantic notion.

I remembered her sarcastic wit, her dark eyes, her thick shoes. I re-read everything she wrote and was obsessed with the idea that I had to tell her how much her journal meant to me.

I didn't believe I would do this, but the idea morphed into an image of Ms. Shari and me—once adversaries, now friends. And one day, without knowing what I'd do, I went back to the school of broken clocks to see if I could find her. The head of the department was on sabbatical. Nicole had left to direct admissions at a private school. The registrar, speaking through an assistant in a sari, said it was a policy not to release addresses: I was on my own.

From something Ms. Shari wrote, I guessed she lived in a part of the city called the spice streets because it was inhabited largely by Indians and Muslims. I went to this section, which was crowded with women in chadors, men wearing business suits, and stands filled with fruit and vegetables. The more I walked there, the more I understood the chances of finding Ms. Shari were slim to impossible. So when I did see her, carrying a briefcase with one hand, holding a two-year-old with the other, I felt tongue-tied, shy, surprised. Ms. Shari gave me a direct look, clear as rainwater. Then she walked away. The look signaled something irrevocable: I imagined seeing me was something she thought might happen. It was minor, but satisfying, the way it feels when a horizontal letter in a crossword puzzle jibes with a vertical word.

I kept walking in the opposite direction, passing meat shops, tea parlors, walking without purpose, until I remembered the night when I thought about decorating my hands with henna. At first it was a memory. Then it became a desire. Women I asked about henna shook their heads. A man unloading a crate of apples overheard me.

It's private, he said. Women do it together here. But someone from Turkey has a parlor for women who aren't Muslims. They call her the henna artist.

The parlor was around the corner from the winding street. It was dark with red pillows—the sort of pillows I'd imagined in Ms. Shari's house, except the room was filled with western teenagers. The henna artist wore modern slacks and crescent earrings.

Do you want a traditional design or a modern one? she asked.

Traditional, I said.

She worked with terse efficiency, using wet clay and a thin brush. At one point she told me about a woman in her village whose husband left her for a month.

This woman gathered eleven friends and read the Koran back-wards by the light of a full moon. As soon as they'd finished reading, her husband came home.

I wondered if she knew I wasn't happy about my divorce and was giving me advice. But she looked at me sharply and said, It was a coin-cidence, in my opinion.

The henna artist put my hand under a dryer used in nail parlors. And when the clay had dried, my hands looked like those of Ms. Shari and the representative, as well as the hands of many other women on the spice streets. The dots on my fingers were fertile, sprouting innu-merable gardens: There were garlands around my wrists, flowers on my forearms. These hands could hold a pen, drive a car, make a meal. They could morph into deities of anger and protection. Indeed, if you only looked at my hands, you'd never guess who I was or where I came from. And then, with surprise beyond fear, I saw Ms. Shari and her child walking to catch a bus a block from the parlor. It was an accident outside of a puzzle. The collision made both of us smile. Ms. Shari told me the name of her son. I showed her the patterns on my hands.

Stories We Began to Tell

A FEW MONTHS before he said he was moving out, my husband began to tell me bedtime stories. His habit had always been to fall asleep as soon as he got into bed, but one night, without ceremony, he began:

Once there was a woman who was so large, her dimensions were measured in longitude and latitude instead of inches. Her measurements, or degrees, were known only to her, but once she took a lover who set about measuring her secretly in the dark. To his amazement he found out that she had the same longitude and latitude as the city of Thebes—a discovery which excited him, although he couldn't say why.

At this point he stopped, as if surprised by what he was saying. I leaned forward and said:

What happened? Did he tell her?

No, he said. He never told this to the woman but kept on making love as if nothing had changed. For awhile she seemed to notice nothing, but one night she said: It's the oddest thing, but whenever we make love

I keep feeling like you're exploring ancient ruins. Tell me, has anything changed? The man could have lied, but he felt impelled not to, and so he confessed everything, and the woman ended up feeling miserable because it wasn't her he loved after all. He tried to explain that it *was* her, but she didn't believe him, and she made him leave, right in the middle of the night, and they never saw each other again.

It was quiet when he finished. In the dim light, his eyes looked deep and large. He took off his glasses and sighed, as if telling the story had required tremendous effort.

Is that the end? I asked.

Yes, that's the end, he said.

How did you think that up?

I don't know. It just came to me.

EVERY NIGHT OTHER stories followed: There was a story about a man who fell in love with a tree and set up his computer in a forest, and story about a woman whose lover was a sheepdog she'd known as a human in a previous life. There was a story about a man whose body was illuminated and a story about a child whose mother became a dinosaur. He told me these stories in a driven, abstracted way, as if recounting information from the air. I sat next to him listening.

Much later I realized the stories were codes, urgent messages about his own condition—but I didn't think about this at the time. At night when we got into bed, I couldn't wait for him to start; and though I'd never liked our bedroom—it was small and full of old furniture—whenever he told stories, it transformed into a crowded, intimate theater.

Since the stories were so unusual, I always asked where they came from, and he always said, I really don't know. They just came to me. My question and his answer became a ritual, an exchange that marked the story's end. But one night after an unusually complicated story, he said:

You told me that one—remember? About a year ago, at that hotel in Bangkok when we couldn't sleep.

I remembered the hotel—a small two-story building with filigreed banisters that we'd stayed at on our way back from Bali. It had no air conditioning, not even in the lobby, and the bedroom contained an old-fashioned pitcher that smelled of mothballs.

I never told you that story, I said. I couldn't have. I've never heard it.

But you did, he said. It was that night when we opened all the windows and drank iced tea and talked about what we wanted to do to the house when we got back home. We got to talking about the roof, and the plumbing system, and then you told me that story.

He said this as though he meant it. But there was no way I could have told him the story. First, because I'd spent most of that night in the hotel lobby, trying to cool off before its massive, half-open door. And second, because it was completely beyond my imagination—so much so, I could hardly remember the details, and didn't even want to.

The story had been about a thirty-five-year-old man whose heart, lungs, and liver had turned into the plumbing system of an old house. The clangings and groanings kept his wife awake all night until she put a wrench down the man's throat and turned him off. Quiet ensued, and she got some sleep, but the next morning when she put the wrench down his throat to turn him back on, he was dead. Her explanation to the police was so improbable, they held her on bail until they performed an autopsy. Finally they released her, and she returned home grief-stricken—imagining she could hear groaning in the plumbing of their own house. She sold their property and moved to Florida.

While he was telling me this story, I had been feeling unbearably sad, almost to the point of asking him to stop. Every time I thought about the wife listening to this old and terrible plumbing inside her husband, it took some effort not to cry, and when she finally guessed what was happening and stuck a wrench down the man's throat, I felt a curious relief—the same I'd felt when our senile dog had died.

I knew I couldn't have told him this story, but the more he kept insisting he'd heard it from me, the more I began to think I'd told it to him after all. It was as though the truth became a path I was too exhausted to follow, and I could even see myself in that hotel room, wrapped in a white bedspread with dirty fringes, sitting on the edge of the bed, telling him about that man. The more I saw this, the more I grew furious that he should tell me this story again.

That story was for you, I said, getting on top of him and holding him by the shoulders, and I asked you never repeat it—not to anybody, least of all to me.

No you didn't.

Oh, yes I did. And even if I hadn't, I'd think you could figure it out.

The light was on, so I could look into his eyes; they were incredulous, with a certain softness, and for a moment we were brought to a delicate, almost loving tension. I even thought we might make love, but suddenly he shook me off and said:

I am that man and you can never deny it. His life is my life. How can you expect me not to talk about him?

He said this in a whisper, almost like a curse, and I knew that it was true, and any more stories would have to come from me. Thrown to my side of the bed, not knowing how to begin, I waited until a story appeared—it was small and somewhat tremulous. But before I'd even taken a breath, he touched my arm and said:

Please don't tell me that story. Please don't tell me anything.

The Mole

HE NOTICED THE mole the only time they ever made love, a light blue mole, nestled on the inside of her thigh. It was delicate, translucent, and when he touched it, it felt fragile, like a mushroom. He was an ear, nose, and throat specialist, and he hadn't thought about moles in many years, but later, when they were sitting on his bed talking, it occurred to him that it might be cancerous. The mole was blue, and, from medical school, he remembered that blue moles were often malignant. And so he looked at Sharon, sitting opposite him on his bed, wrapped in his shirt, her hair falling over to one side, and he wondered how to broach the subject. She was a medical technician—certainly she knew about such things, and surely she'd be angry if he presumed she didn't. Also he had a feeling she didn't like him very much: She was a tall, restrained woman of about twenty-eight with a sense of smoldering inner heat he'd been unable to release, even for an instant.

This is my kid, he said, by way of entering into a certain soft-ness with her, a softness that might allow him to mention the mole. He reached over to his bedside table and showed her a photograph of his son in his Little League outfit. I'm divorced, he said, as he handed her the picture. My kid is eight.

Oh, she said, lifting the picture, and looking at it without much interest. I guess I already knew that.

After a while, she left, pausing by his collection of geodes, the only bright thing in his sparse apartment, and refusing his offer of a taxi. He was glad he hadn't mentioned the mole, but later, around midnight, he began to worry again. He had never been interested in diseases of the skin—he preferred what was hidden, accessed through apertures and tunnels—but now he pulled out his old medical-school textbooks and looked at photographs of moles. None of them looked like her mole: they seemed darker, larger, less fragile. He went to bed reassured, yet the moment he woke up, he remembered. The mole was dark in his memory, almost black.

FOR GOD'S SAKE, said a dermatologist friend, whom he'd cornered at the hospital, she's probably had it for ages, and if she's a medical technician, she knows all about it. They were in the doctor's lounge and he'd told her the entire story.

How old did you say she was? Twenty-eight?

I don't know, I didn't bother to ask.

You don't know how old she was, but you noticed her mole—Dennis, you're distraught. I bet you've been sleeping around too much. The friend laughed, and added, It's your divorce. You should stay out of circulation for awhile.

The conversation relieved him, but later that day, he went to the medical library. *Moles are like hieroglyphs,* he thought, walking through the stacks like a sleuth—hard to decipher, crudely beautiful. As soon as he opened the books (he did so secretly, with the sense of seeking forbidden knowledge) he felt sucked into a universe of moles. Horribly, a small purple mole on the thigh of a young woman had turned out to be fatal, but eleven black moles on the back of a middle-aged man were benign. The more he looked at the pictures, the more Sharon's mole changed shape and color in his memory.

DID HER MOLE have a hair on it? his dermatologist friend asked, when, for a second time, he cornered her at the hospital. They were at the cafeteria, having coffee, and she looked at him with concern.

I don't remember. Why?

Because moles that have hairs on them are almost always benign.

He closed his eyes. I can't remember. It's just a blur.

Why don't you call her then?

She'd think I was stupid.

I think you'd live. She reached over and patted his hand. He noticed that she was wearing an indigo scarf that looked lovely against her blond hair. Also, she had a mole on the right side of her nose, a small brown mole he hadn't remembered seeing.

Is that new? he asked, touching it.

No, I've always had it. Anyway, almost everyone in the world has a mole somewhere on their body. You, too, Dennis. And she touched a small brown spot on his wrist in a way that moved him. He asked her to dinner, but she shook her head. You've just gotten divorced. Give it some time.

It was too cold to walk home, so he took the subway, and as he stood there, being jostled with the others, he began to see moles everywhere—erupting on faces and on hands that weren't wearing gloves. Their owners seemed calm, impervious, yet as he looked at the moles, he began to wonder if he had a moral obligation to speak to these people. His small amount of knowledge felt like a burden, and that night he dreamt about Sharon's eyes staring past him towards a fixed and finite point—just like the eyes of certain terminally-ill patients who are able to see ahead to their very last moment in time. He woke in a sweat and decided to call her, but the next day he changed his mind and wrote her a letter instead. He signed his full name—Dennis Gaviola—and he used plain white paper, not his doctor's stationery:

Dear Sharon: I hope you won't think me untoward if I mention to you that the other night I happened to notice a mole on the inside of your thigh. It was a small blue mole, and I only bother to write because I know that blue moles can sometimes be dangerous. Although I'm sure you probably already know about it, I couldn't walk around in good conscience without mentioning it to you. By the way, I really enjoyed meeting you and I hope we'll see each other again. Sincerely, Dennis Gaviola.

He wasn't sure about the phrase *I hope you won't think me untoward.* It had an oddly formal quality, and he decided to consult an old friend, an editor, who lived in Boston.

I think it's ridiculous, the friend said, when he read him the letter on the phone. For God's sake, don't ever send it.

But what if I took out *untoward?*

It would still be ridiculous.

Why?

Because. There's nothing wrong with her.

His friend sounded remote, safe in a happy marriage. Terrible things can happen, he continued, but they're never the things you worry about in advance.

He didn't mail the letter, but kept it by his bed, in its envelope, reading it over and over, trying to imagine that he was Sharon at the exact moment of opening it. He always saw her reading the letter fully clothed, except for once, when she was wearing his shirt, and her reaction was always the same—contempt. The letter became creased, began to look like a map, and twice he had to snatch it from his eight-year-old son. Finally he stuck it in his dresser drawer and read it only occasionally. He never could decide about the phrase *I hope you won't think me untoward.*

LATER THAT SPRING he met, and had an affair with, a woman who had no moles. Her name was Corazon Martinez, and she was from Argentina and an interpreter for the State Department. He had vowed he would never mention moles in her presence, but one day, to his own amazement, he said to her, You have no moles! and she answered, solemnly, I know. I am completely unmarked. They were lying on her bed, and Corazon sat up and looked at her skin as if trying to see it from a distance.

Do you think moles are important? he asked.

Oh yes, she said. Very. They're like keys to unknown cities. I've always wanted one.

That night he came home and tore up his letter to Sharon, bit by bit, piece by piece. It was like tearing up a love letter, written to him by someone else. When the letter was shredded, he burned it on the stove, and finally, mercifully, Sharon receded in his mind. He forgot about her, forgot about her mole, and was surprised when he saw her on the subway, about eight months later near Christmastime. It hadn't occurred to him that she would still exist, living an ordinary life, yet here she was opposite him, holding packages, wearing a dark blue coat—still with that smoldering sense of unavailable inner heat. She was staring into space and looked abstractedly, quietly happy.

The instant he saw her, he remembered her mole. Indeed he had a graphic image of it, nestled on the inside of her thigh, a hidden eye, a secret pearl, surprising other lovers or—maybe she was married now— her husband. Sharon didn't notice him, didn't even look his way, and when she came to her stop, he waited for her to disappear. But as soon as the doors opened, he found himself racing to catch up with her. He reached her at the top of the stairs.

Are you okay? he said, when she turned to face him. I've been meaning to call. I've been thinking about you.

Oh, I'm okay, she said, smiling. Even though I've been to hell and back.

Was it your mole? he blurted out. Was there anything wrong with it? He looked at her eyes and noticed, to his relief, that they didn't look like the eyes of a terminally-ill person at all. They were relaxed, some- what dreamy, and seemed to stare ahead towards an indefinite, unde- fined point on the horizon. Now they turned to him, puzzled.

My mole? she said. Is that all you can ask me about after all these months? Jesus. No. I mean I've finally gotten my divorce.

I didn't know you were married.

You didn't ask.

But you didn't tell me!

She smiled again, wryly, that heat still locked inside of her, and then she walked away, leaving him over twenty blocks from home. He began to walk—quickly, fiercely, with the sense of some new and unnamed burden having nothing to do with her mole, or with anything else he would ever be able to decipher.

The New Thieves

ONE NIGHT MY husband said: You must learn to be like one of the new thieves—they never steal, they add. They enter rooms without force and leave hairpins, envelopes, roses. Later they leave larger things like pianos; no one ever notices. You must learn to be like that woman in the bar who dropped her glove so softly that I put it on. Or that man who offered me his wife so carefully, I thought we'd been married for seventeen years. You must learn to fill me with riches—so quietly I'll never notice. After saying this he draped himself in all my scarves and lay back in bed.

What do you really want? I said.

Nothing I can tell you about, he answered.

THE NEXT DAY I brought home a woman in camouflage and placed her on top of our bed. She looked just like me and talked just like me, and that night while I pretended to sleep, the woman made love to my husband. I thought I'd accomplished her mission, but as soon as she left, he said to me: I knew she wasn't you. I knew by the way she kissed.

I tried other things, but nothing worked—new shoes just like his old ones, scuffed in the same places; keepsakes from his mother; books he'd already read. He recognized everything and threw it away.

One rainy fall afternoon when I couldn't think of anything else to give him, I went into an elegant bar, the kind with leather chairs and soft lights. I ordered a glass of chilled white wine, and suddenly, without guile, the bartender smiled at me and I smiled back. That night while my husband slept next to us, we made love, and the next morning he hung up his clothes in my husband's closet. Soon after, he moved in with us, walking like a cat, filling the house with his books. My husband never noticed, and now at night he lies next to us, thinking that he's the bartender. He breathes his air, dreams his dreams, and in the morning when we all wake up, he tells me that he's happy.

Using the Car
for Business

WHEN ALEXIS SAW a stranger get into her car, she didn't race to the phone and call the police. It all seemed so natural—like the time she'd been living in New York and a burglar came to her window and she thought he was going to wash it. It had taken a minute to realize who he was, and by the time she had, the man had run up the fire escape, and she could hear his footsteps pounding on the roof. This time she had the same delayed reaction, only when she came to her senses, the car was gone. A bald-headed man in a shiny grey suit just opened the unlocked door of her station wagon, revved up the engine, and drove it down the street. The maneuver was deft, dexterous, executed with grace. Where the car had been, the air now shimmered in darkness.

Alexis was a therapist. She was having a session with a client. And while the car was being stolen, she was listening to a long and complicated dream about a wind tunnel. For about thirty seconds after the car was gone, she stayed quite still, amazed and strangely fascinated. When the client paused, she righted herself and said:

Excuse me, Jeremy, but my car's just been stolen. I just happened to look out the window, and I saw this guy get into it and drive away. So I think I ought to do something. Like call the police.

Sure, said Jeremy, looking irritated and vaguely startled. Go ahead. He looked away from Alexis and at his feet, which were long and shapely: Jeremy was a dancer and always took off his shoes during sessions. Go ahead and call, he said again.

My car's just been stolen, said Alexis, when she reached her precinct. Some bald-headed man's just driven it down the street. It was all so natural. Maybe he made a mistake.

Don't you wish he had, said the policeman. Those guys with skeleton keys act so cool, like the car's just theirs and they're using it for business. Did you say you had your car keys?

Yes, they're in my pocket.

Then there's no way the guy thought the car belonged to him.

Alexis hung up and saw Jeremy looking at her searchingly. The look was unusual. Mostly Jeremy stared at his feet.

Jeremy, are you having any feelings about being interrupted? she asked.

No. I was feeling sad about your car. It's a very strange feeling. Right in the middle of my stomach.

Maybe it's about some loss of your own.

No. It's about your car. It's strange, but I feel sad about it. He touched his stomach lightly, and Alexis noticed that a pervasive grey veil that always hovered around Jeremy's eyes was replaced by a steely gaze. He turned, looked out the window. Alexis looked too. Where her dark blue station wagon had been, there was now an ancient yellow VW bug. Jeremy frowned and sighed. Suddenly he asked:

Are you feeling sad about it, too?

No. Actually I'm not.

How come? Didn't you like it? Wasn't there stuff in it you needed?

I don't know. I'll have to think.

Alexis thought. So many things were in the car's back seat: Her red silk scarf, a bag of roasted chestnuts, her daughter's favorite bear, a book on the emergence of the ego, plastic diapers, a bottle of wine. But all she felt was a strange, light-hearted curiosity, as though the car belonged to someone else.

No, Jeremy, I guess I'm not really feeling sad, she said. I mean, it's not that I don't want them to find the car. But somehow I don't feel sad. Maybe I'm still surprised. Maybe I'll feel sad later.

I know what you mean, said Jeremy. I always feel that way with lovers. When it's over there's a kind of relief, and then later I miss them and I like that. What would you call that? Poignancy?

Poignancy's a very good word for it.

Jeremy nodded slowly, and the veil rose around his eyes again like mist.

The tunnel was very dark, he said, and it was like I was just about to meet someone. He paused abruptly and stared into space. I was wearing this brown silk scarf and an olive-green trench coat I would die for. I liked the way I was dressed.

After Jeremy left, Alexis called her insurance company and told them about her car. Then she called her husband Caleb who taught musical history at the university. He was listening to a recording of Grieg's Nocturne, and the music made her sad.

Caleb, she said—hoping her voice would match the sadness—something terrible has happened. My car's been stolen.

My God, said Caleb. How?

I don't know. Some bald-headed guy just got into it and drove it away. I saw it from my window. I was with a client.

Caleb turned off Greig.

My God, I had a musical score in there! A flute concerto that someone sent me from England! For God's sake! It's in that car!

You mean you just left it in my car?

Sure. I thought it was safe. How come you didn't you run to the phone when you saw him? How come you didn't call the police?

The truth is, it took me a minute or so. I only get a dollar and forty cents a minute for being a tabula rasa—it's not like I can just snap out of it. Anyway, my client was telling me a dream. I waited until he stopped.

What do you mean you waited? Weren't you upset?

Yes. I was upset. And I waited.

Caleb poured himself more coffee—Alexis could hear gurgling over the phone.

Aren't you supposed to set an example for your clients? he asked. Aren't you supposed to teach them about passion? What is this jerk going to think if he's telling you a dream and you just watch someone steal your car?

I'm not supposed to teach people anything, said Alexis, feeling a protective rush. I allow them to be themselves.

Well I'm myself and I'm pissed, said Caleb. He gulped more coffee and then hung up. Alexis stayed at her desk, holding the phone to her ear. Since she'd made the call herself, there was no dial tone, just an uneasy silence, broken by scratches and squeaks.

After she hung up, Alexis remembered the musical score. It was in the back seat of her car, mingling with the chestnuts, and she knew exactly what it looked like because Caleb brought so much old music home—yellow, delicate paper, with frail spidery notes. She could imagine the bald-headed man regarding it curiously then throwing it away. She could also imagine that for a while Caleb would bring home no more precious things—no rotting viola da gambas, no torn opera programs from London pawnshops. The house would become less cluttered, and Caleb might even agree there were too many things in the world and having one of them disappear, even if it happened to be a car, could only be cause for relief. As Alexis imagined this, she began to confuse Caleb with Jeremy, as though Caleb were sitting in her office in his stocking feet, a veil lifted from his eyes. In fact he never visited her office, hated going without shoes, and his veil—for of course he had one—was around his ears. Sometimes she talked to him about it, but whenever she did, he said that he had perfect pitch.

While Alexis was thinking these things, a stern voice rose from the phone and told her to hang up. She did as she was told, and soon a policeman called with news that they'd found her car. It was by a warehouse near the bay, he said, with the door unlocked and the key under the driver's seat. There must have been a foul-up with the rendezvous.

Alexis caught her breath. For a moment the car seemed too close, too fragile, precariously near the water.

Was there an old piece of music in it? Something on very old paper?

Yes, as a matter of fact there was, said the policeman. It looks like an antique.

IN THE FOLLOWING months, Alexis was called to inspect several police lineups. She liked being ushered to a darkened room where bald-headed men were assembled on an empty stage. The men lined up impassively, looking detached, surreal, daring Alexis to discover them. No, she always said to the policemen. None of them come even close.

What's the scoop? Caleb would ask when she came home. Did you find him? Did you turn him in?

He was writing an article linking the musical score to chamber music, and he looked safe, intelligent, close to the eighteenth century. He had forgiven her about Jeremy's dream, and Alexis smiled vaguely when he asked about the bald-headed men.

I'm sure the real one went to Mexico, she'd say. I mean . . . wouldn't you if you stole a car?

After one visit to the police station, Alexis went to a burrito parlor, sat at a table in the back, nursed a glass of cheap wine, and watched punk kids, bag ladies, close-knit Mexican families. One day the door opened and the bald-headed man who'd stolen her car walked in, tentatively, then briskly, heading straight for the bar. He wore a rumpled tie and a rumpled suit and had the seedy elegance of certain deteriorating buildings. Alexis looked at him, he looked back, and for a moment she felt a curious collapse of space, as though she could reach out and touch him from where she was. Not that she would. The way he was smiling, with his mouth stretched wide—just the way dogs stretch their mouths when they seem to be smiling. She drank the last of her wine, drove home without any headlights.

You could have killed yourself, said Caleb, when she came into the house.

The Second Husband

MY SECOND HUSBAND, Aaron, is wedged somewhere between my first husband, Dan, and my third husband, Walker. Those two men are clear and distinct, and whenever I think of them, I can always imagine what they are doing—Dan asleep, his hairy shoulders rising above the blankets like epaulets, Walker, ever wakeful, looking at maps. These two men are obedient to the commands of time, as is my fourth husband, Malcolm, who is in our living room, reading. But as for Aaron, I can never imagine what he is doing, or even where he is: He remains in my past like a segue, a half note, and if I imagine him at all, he is walking in thin air, looking at nothing in particular.

Aaron had a singular appeal: He always seemed awe-struck. He was blond, delicate, and once spent a long hot summer putting a floor in his slum apartment, board by board. I watched him put in that floor yet often confuse him with other men who were also good carpenters. His face is fused with other faces, faces that are more distinct—and indeed, for a long time after we were divorced, I forgot that we were ever married. The memory came back after Malcolm and I had returned from a two-day honeymoon in the high Sierras. I was thinking about the wedding—how Malcolm had insisted on having friends throw rice, how my six-year-old son, Walker's son too, had stood by, looking bewildered—when suddenly I remembered being in Manhattan City Hall, next to an unknown man. . . . And then I was remembering dragging huge bags of groceries up to the fourth floor of a narrow walk-up apartment in Greenwich Village, near the Hudson River; and then Aaron's flat, with its wonderful hardwood floor, part of which was a false floor concealing bundles of marijuana. It was then that I remembered Aaron (I could see him clearly, smoking a joint in the bedloft) and I realized I had been married to a drug dealer for all of three months. *My God*, I thought, sitting up in bed.

I looked around our book-strewn bedroom. My previously-third (but now, I realized, fourth) husband was lying next to me. Moonlight fell across our bed and illuminated his face, which looked peaceful. For minute I couldn't remember his name. When I did, I shook him gently. Have you ever been married before?

Don't wake me, he said from the depths of sleep.

I FORGOT ABOUT Aaron, consigned him to the past. He lived in those archives for a month, and then a friend told me that one night she also woke up with the memory of having been previously married. Details came back slowly, and the features of the other husband were indistinct. Still, she was able to remember that he had a childlike charm, talked his way into deals, and then got out of him.

Was his name Aaron? I asked.

No, she said. His name was Henry.

After we talked, I wrote Aaron a letter (which I'll never mail) thanking him for everything he gave me, which was, among other things, a sense of mystery about my life. But this wasn't the end of the matter: A few days later I was walking down the street, and a man looked at me strangely. It wasn't a leer, it was a look of distinct recognition, and I nodded and hurried past him. The moment I got home, I called my friend.

Listen, I said, are you sure Henry is the only one you forgot about marrying?

Oh no, she said. I'm not sure at all.

Doesn't it bother you?

Of course it does. In fact, whenever I meet someone for what I think is the first time, I panic. Like: Have I seen his dirty socks? Does he know what I look like naked? That sort of thing. The friend coughed nervously, as though she were remembering other things.

And how about children? I persisted. Do you think you've ever had any others besides the ones you have?

There was a pause. No. I don't think so. Somehow I think you'd remember children. Don't you?

I wasn't so sure. There's a kind of generic child that could easily be forgotten or confused with other children, a child like mine with a round face and a smooth, unworried expression over a glass of milk.

No, I don't think you necessarily would, I said. In some ways kids are pretty much the same.

While we talked I could hear Marge moving about her kitchen. She was making lentil soup for dinner, celebrating a settled life. Suddenly she said to me,

Listen, don't ever tell anyone this, but once I think I slept with a man I'd forgotten.

What do you mean?

I mean I ran into him in the supermarket and we ended up in a motel. We didn't spend much time together. It was as though we didn't need any introductions. It wasn't exactly like a one-night stand. There was this . . . feeling of familiarity.

She laughed and sounded nervous.

How could you know? I said. I mean if you've forgotten him, then how could you remember?

I don't know. There was this strange sort of pull. Like gravity.

And did he remember you?

God. I don't know. She sounded tired. Hey, please don't tell.

As soon as I hung up, my husband came into the kitchen and began to poke around the refrigerator, bringing out carrots, onions, and peppers. What were you talking about? he asked.

Oh, nothing. Just the ways of the world.

Really? I don't think so. His eyes had a piercing quality. I think you were talking about your other husbands.

Oh no. I really don't think about Walker or Dan.

I don't mean that, he said, waving me away with his hand, which held a Chinese cleaver. I mean the other ones. Those guys you don't remember. Don't worry, it's not a big deal, I've had other wives and I think of them in my sleep. But I never remember their names. He smiled in a generous way. I figure I've been married about fifteen times.

In a sense I wasn't surprised. Angry. Jealous. But not surprised. What were they like, your wives? I asked.

Honestly, I don't remember. The most vivid one was an advice nurse named Dodie who worked at St. Vincent's when I was an intern, and she knew everything. Like what time it was in Tokyo. Or whether Chaucer had ever had children. Finally she left nursing and went into filmmaking. Anyway, don't worry. You're the best. He came over and put his arms around me. The best, he said again.

I wanted to tell him that he was the best. I wanted to tell him how my heart had surged when everyone had thrown rice, as though I were a newborn bride. But Aaron was in my heart, his face enclosed in light.

Were you *really* married all those times? I asked.

Oh, that's just an estimate. Like I said, I don't remember their names or where we lived or anything about them. It's only a guess. He found some yogurt, took a couple of bites, and began to chop vegetables for dinner. He looked strong, inscrutable, and a little sad, as if all his marriages had worn him out. How many times were you married that *you* forgot? he asked. Come on, tell the truth.

Only once. You're really the fourth.

And who's the one you forgot? Do you remember?

Oh, soft of. . . . A semi-criminal drug dealer. Very charming. It's kind of a blur.

What did he look like? he had stopped chopping vegetables and set the cleaver down carefully.

I don't remember. Blond, I guess.

Cute?

Sort of.

Very cute. This was a statement.

No, really, he's all in a blur. Like I said: a semi-criminal type. Before I had limits.

I was spared having to say anything more because my son came in the kitchen with a toy I'd never seen—a green plastic monster with a red mask and a menacing spear: I was appalled.

Where did you get that? I asked him.

You gave it to me.

No, I didn't! I'd never let something like that in our house. What is it?

A Ninja Turtle.

What's that?

Well, it's this dude, he said. And then he told us how the turtle had been living in a sewer with his friends when some bad guy poured slime all over them and they mutated into five-foot-tall adolescents with ninja fighting skills. He was still holding the turtle, who carried several spears. As he spoke, he gestured, and I noticed that the turtle was carrying not one spear, but seven. Seven for luck, my son explained.

Why did you buy him this thing? I said, turning to my husband. It's a violent toy. I don't want it in the house.

I didn't buy it, he said, I thought *you* did.

We looked at each other, thinking the same thing.

Who bought that for you? I asked my child.

He looked puzzled, genuinely puzzled, and his eyes traveled deep into mine as if trying to retrieve something. I realized then that he easily had a hundred mothers, all of whom he loved, none of whom he remembered. I leaned over and gathered him up in my arms.

Hyperventilation

ALMOST AS SOON as the pasta was brought to the table, one of the guests began to hyperventilate and asked to be excused. He was a tall, high-strung man in his middle thirties, and it wasn't the first time he had hyperventilated at the house of this particular couple. The hostess sent him an ill-willed glare. The host, however, was sympathetic.

Poor Jonathon, he said after he disappeared. He's so exhausted and the kids are driving him crazy.

He was referring to the students in the art school where Jonathon and he both taught.

Just the other day this woman came up to him in the hall and asked if he would please mind strangling her. He thought she was crazy and then all these people began to clap and he realized it was a performance piece. The terrible thing was he didn't *get* it. You know Jonathon, he has this terrific sense of irony, but he didn't get it.

Do you really think that happened? said one of the guests. Do you really think those kids would be so cruel?

The guest was trying not to look at the fusilli, steaming in a blue and white bowl. The hostess had cooked it *al dente*, and soon it would have the consistency of cold rubber.

Of course, said the host. To those kids everything's an event. Except me: I'm the dean. He laughed and gestured toward the fusilli. Should we serve it? he asked, raising an eyebrow.

No, said the hostess in the silent language of couples. *This time I want Jonathon to eat my food.*

Jonathon's girlfriend, Ashley, a spindly-legged woman who looked like Orphan Annie, saw the signal in an instant.

Excuse me, she said, I must see to Jonathon.

She bolted from her seat and raced down the zigzag hall filled with photographs of construction sites. Jonathon was sitting on the toilet with his pants on and his eyes closed, breathing deeply, furtively, as though the air were meant for someone else. Ashley knelt by the toilet and put her hands on Jonathon's knees.

What in God's name are you doing? she asked. Are you stoned? Did you take something before we left?

Jonathon opened his eyes. They were wide, like someone else was holding them open.

No. I just forget to breathe, that's all. Or I breathe too much. I'm not sure which. Jonathon looked around the bathroom, inhaling the sea green tiles, the towels staggered artfully on a rack. Why can't we live this way? he asked. They do it in such good taste.

Because we have different values, that's why. We buy books. We like to travel. Anyway, do you really like it? Ashley picked up a brass spyglass on the edge of the sink and looked through it to see a sea green wastebasket, a sea green rubber duck, and a plastic shower curtain with a map of the world on it.

Yes. I mean I think I like it. But probably I don't. Jonathon was breathing normally now. Ashley touched his arm.

Are you ready to come out?

No, it's not like I'm breathing automatically or anything. It's like I have to think about it. He looked at Ashley sternly. I'm not like other people. I don't have automatic functions. I have to think.

Well let's go out anyway. It must seem really odd to them, our going to the bathroom at every party. They probably think we pee together. Or make love. Or do coke.

Who cares?

I do, said Ashley. Anyway, how come you can't breathe here? How come you always breathe at other people's parties?

I *don't* breathe at other people's parties.

Sure you do. You breathe at Bob and Joanna's parties. And at the Motlers'. You breathe at them just fine.

Okay, you're right. I do breathe there. It's all this hi-tech crap around this damned loft. Fiberglass aggravates my asthma.

Ashley looked unimpressed. You don't have asthma. You went to the doctor, and he said you don't.

Jonathon shook his head, and Ashley held him by the shoulders.

Jonathon, she said. You're fine.

No, I'm not fine. There's a rare kind that's hard to diagnose. I read about it in *The Merck Manual.* It's called *apernative asthma.* That why I can't have sex.

But we just did! It was great.

No. I mean in the morning. I can't breathe.

Jonathon, for Godssake. You won't even talk to me in the morning. It doesn't have anything to do with asthma. Ashley picked up a piece of jade and held it to the light. We're living out of boxes, she said, and they have all this crap in their bathroom.

The other reason my asthma is worse, Jonathon continued as if Ashley hadn't spoken is because of what happened with that student in the hall. I was freaked: And there's more to it than people know.

What do you mean?

I mean I avenged her, that's what I mean.

Ashley looked quickly at her watch—a black watch with a globe where four o'clock should be. What do you mean avenged? she said. The word sounded dark. She picked up another piece of jade that was lying on the sink. Smooth and green. It could have been soap.

Don't you want the details? They're pretty ugly.

No, I really don't. I just want to get through this evening. Ashley looked in the mirror and saw that her eyes looked frightened. There was a cake of Cynthia's eye shadow on the sink, and she smudged some over her lids—silver-gold, the shadow of Egyptian queens.

Listen, I'm going out, will you be okay?

Without waiting for an answer she opened the door and stepped into the hall. It was dark, except for one downlight, and she paused. In the dining room one of the guests was saying, What I don't understand is why he comes to these things at all. I mean if he's not the social type, then why does he bother? Ashley turned and knocked loudly on the door, commanding silence from the people at the table.

Are you coming out now? she asked. Her voice sounded flat and far away. Jonathon! she cried. Are you coming out?

There were footsteps in the hall. It was Mark, the host. Is there a problem? he asked, putting a hand on Ashley's arm, pressing softly. He stared at her with concern, and she was forced to look at his eyes and remember the student that Jonathon had avenged. Mark was eight years older than Ashley and handled his lust by being avuncular. His regard was pensive, kind. Ashley made another show of knocking on the door.

Jonathon! she cried. Jonathon! She opened the door a crack and squeezed inside. Jonathon was sitting on the edge of the bathtub looking serene. He, too, had put on some of Cynthia's eye makeup, and was reading an art flyer.

Well it's passed, he said. I can breathe now without having to think about it.

Good, said Ashley. Because they're wondering. She noticed the silver-gold shadow up on his lids. For Godssake. Will you take that off?

Wait. I'm getting my bearings. Jonathon stood up slowly, eased his feet to the floor, and patted the shower curtain with the map of the world.

How would you like to see Guatemala every time you took a shit? he asked.

Ashley didn't laugh. She took some Kleenex, and made Jonathon hold still while she wiped off the shadow.

Listen, she said. I want to know something. How did you avenge that student?

I didn't. I thought about coming after her with a rope and pretending I was going to strangle her. But I decided not to. In the interests of higher art.

You mean you made it up?

Yes. You wanted a reason.

Then go to hell.

Oh for Godssake, Ashley. The truth is, I don't have a reason. I don't even know if I have apernative asthma. This is just one of those places where I can't seem to breathe, that's all. Jonathon paused, looked around the bathroom. You know what I discovered? he said. I discovered they have a false floor. Look! Those tiles are uneven. I bet they keep coke down there.

I don't give a damn, said Ashley, who never wanted to spend another minute in the bathroom. She picked up the sea green rubber duck and made it squeak.

How fucked, she said. They have a duck, but they don't have kids.

Yes, Jonathon agreed, it's crazy.

They smiled in sudden agreement. Ashley opened the door, Jonathon offered her his arm, and together they walked to the center of the loft. The fusilli was being served. Jonathon slid into his seat.

To breath, he said, raising his glass.

Buying a Rug
in Esquares

A T SEVEN-THIRTY IN the morning, a man named Arthur Moldera from the United States knocked on the door of a rug weaver in Esquares, Mexico. Her name was Senora Martinez, and Arthur had seen her once before on a visit to Esquares several years ago. He had been with his wife then, and the two of them had argued so violently about the kind of rug they wanted that Senora Martinez sent them away, saying, I can't deal with the two of you, come back when you agree.

Those Americans, she'd thought, watching them disappear down the street. *They put these rugs on their walls, not their floors or their backs—they don't know enough about them to disagree.* She'd made herself a brew of strong black tea and gone back to her loom.

TO ARTHUR'S RELIEF, Senora Martinez didn't recognize him. After sizing him up, she led him into her small interior workroom, piled with rugs, pottery, milagors, crucifixes. Arthur sat quite still, with his elbows close, but when he took out the design of the rug he wanted—the same design he and his wife fought over five years ago—he managed to knock over a wooden bird perched on the shelf right next to him. Senora Martinez waved away his apologies, then looked at the design.

Pretend folk art, she said, pointing to the stylized black flower and a shoe in the upper right hand corner. She looked at the shoe more closely. It was a light blue stiletto. This is blasphemous. Do you really want it in the rug?

Yes, said Arthur, nodding. He was an architect and had thought of the design himself, although he didn't mention this to Senora Martinez. She looked at his sketch again, carefully, clearly not remembering it, and then quoted Arthur a price, which he knew to be outrageous.

A month, she said. I'll finish in a month.

AS SOON AS the deal was made, Arthur felt a wave of relief. He had a roll and a chocolate at a café, and he checked his messages. There was one from his girlfriend, who hadn't liked the idea that he was leaving. There was also a message from Leah, his ex-wife, who sensed his departures like radar.

Hello, I'm in town, thought I might see you, the message said.

Her voice was indifferent, curious. Arthur texted his girlfriend a quick *xox* and then wrote Leah: *Guess what? I'm finally getting the rug.*

Writing the message gave him a vicious guilty pleasure. After Leah left, he'd knocked about in their old, empty Victorian for nearly a year, moving his sleeping bag from room to room, until one night, in the living room, he'd had a vision of the rug where it always belonged, above the fireplace. Arthur had never had a vision before. It had been Leah who ran to psychics, conferring about auras, past lives, future prospects. Yet here was the rug—*his* rug—hovering over the fireplace with numinous authority. It was about midnight when he'd had this vision. Arthur could hear two people arguing on the street and shut the window, savoring the absolute nature of his vision. Without remembering that most of his things were in boxes, he began to look for the design of the rug in an empty desk. When it wasn't there, he progressed to orange crates. At three in the morning, he found the design in a box labeled *Trips*. It was wedged between a brochure on Puerto Vallarta and a picture of Leah on the beach. The picture was face up, inviting him to look. He didn't, but he saw her anyway.

Leah had moved to a town on the coast, a port. She'd started an interior decorating business and sounded happy; but he knew she'd be upset about the rug, which had been an object of contention. He sipped his chocolate, looked at the stone streets and the yellow houses with ornate railings, and couldn't remember anything else they argued about.

He also saw a white donkey nibbling on rose petals as though they were lettuce. Leah had worried about the animals in Esquares eating flowers. Do they get anything else? she'd asked. Do you think they're hungry? Arthur had said they ate the flowers because there were so many of them, He told her that animals were lucky in this town.

THAT NIGHT, IN the courtyard of his hotel, Arthur met a man named Estevan with the same last name as his—Moldera. It was a friendly, comradely meeting fueled by a shared name: Arthur's family had come to the States from Spain. Estevan's family had been in Mexico for three generations. Moldera was a common name; there was little chance that they were related. Nonetheless, over wine, in the lush, sweet courtyard, hung with bougainvillea, they told each other stories. First of childhood, then of marriage—three in Estevan's case, one in Arthur's. Arthur also told Estevan about his vision of the rug—the same rug he and Leah had fought over five years ago, in front of Asunta Martinez, who sent them away, shouting after them, I'm not a priest! I don't settle disputes!

Arthur was a restrained man. Yet as he talked, he became emotional, as if his voice were molded from the hot, thick night. His Spanish waxed eloquent, he formed poetic phrases, and soon told Estevan what he'd barely dreamed: that getting this rug felt like a redemption, the beginning of a new life. When he was finished talking, Estevan Moldera sighed, wished him well, and then—as if he knew he were treading on something delicate— said:

Just one thing. Maybe you should be careful about this Asunta Martinez. A friend of mine came all the way from Vera Cruz to get her to make a rug, and he got taken for a ride. At least that's what he said.

How?

Well, of course, I don't know. But this is what he said: He said she wove in pornographic figures but they looked so much like flowers he never noticed until he put the rug up on his wall. You can't imagine what he saw. Or said he saw. The most obscene stuff. Animals and children. Women and birds. He's not naive, but he was so upset he wrapped the rug around two stones and threw it in a pond.

Do you believe him?

Oh, yes! Otherwise I wouldn't be telling you. Anyway, Oaxaca is famous for rugs. Why don't you go there to get what you want?

After Estevan left, Arthur remained in the courtyard, smelling the night-blooming jasmine, looking for signs, talismans. The exchange of the two stories dissolved the apparition of the rug over his fireplace. It was only a thought, had never been a vision. *I should never have talked,* Arthur thought, and this thought—his first thought that evening in plain English—felt cold and real. There was still wine in his glass, and he drank it, hoping to get the vision back.

Early in the morning, he walked all the way to the edge of town and looked in the window of the rug weaver's workroom. Everything was quiet on the street. Only another donkey nibbling roses—a grey donkey. In the strong light of the moon, Arthur saw all kinds of rugs, rugs he hadn't seen yesterday on his single-minded mission—stacked on the floor, the walls, spilling out of sturdy wooden shelves. He tried to imagine men and women tangled in strange poses, children and animals copulating. But he couldn't see them. And suddenly he regretted the whimsical high-heeled shoe he'd wanted in the upper-right-hand corner. He would write the rug weaver note and ask her not to use it.

Asunta was rumored to have a lover—maybe two—and now a mound stirred in the little alcove off the workroom. Someone sat up in bed. Asunta? No. A man! Arthur backed away and was walking down the street when he felt a tap on the shoulder.

What are you doing in front of my grandmother's house? Don't you know you can't come here except by appointment?

I was just about to make one. I need to discuss a rug. I want to change part of the design.

The man, who had the dashing good looks of a matador, looked blank. Arthur took a pad from his shirt pocket and wrote his name on it, adding *cliente*.

Will you give this to Senora Martinez? he asked. Tell her I'll come by again later in the morning.

The man shrugged, took the paper, walked away, but then he turned around and shouted:

Voyeur! Pervert! I won't be your messenger at all!

Shutters opened, doors slammed, and Asunta Martinez walked down the street, looking regal in a maroon flannel bathrobe and enormous slippers. When she came to Arthur, she spoke to him in perfect English.

I remember you, she said. You're the gentleman with the very loud wife. And here you are, arguing again! You wanted a rug with a shoe in the corner? Okay, you'll get a rug with a shoe in the corner. But you're still arguing, aren't you? You and your shitty rug.

More shutters had opened. Arthur waited, expecting an official banishment. But all she said was:

The rug will be ready tomorrow. Is that good enough? If it's ready tomorrow will you leave?

Yes, Arthur said, forgetting to mention the shoe.

How wonderful, said his girlfriend, when Arthur told her he was coming back the next evening. You'll be home. You won't have to wait. And you'll get your rug! She was performing some cosmetic ritual while they talked—he could hear a scraping sound over the phone.

What are you doing?

I won't tell you! Getting to have secrets is the only benefit I get from your not wanting to live with me.

When he hung up, he texted Leah. It was a long message about the subtle dissonance of the shoe, the fight they'd had outside the weaver's. The message went on and on. He decided not to send it.

THAT NIGHT ARTHUR found Estevan Moldera in the courtyard drinking wine. Guess what? he said. She's making me the rug in a hurry. Like tomorrow.

Really?

Yes. She wants me out of town.

Good.

Good?

Yes, said Estevan. Good. He seemed to have forgotten what Arthur had told him and looked like he wanted to be alone. Nonetheless, Arthur sat down.

Was that story true? he asked, leaning close to him.

What story?

The story about the pornographic rug.

Yes, it was true. You think I would lie?

Maybe. Is this a habit with her?

I don't know. I just know it happened to my friend. Like I told you.

Yesterday Estevan had mentioned to Arthur that he'd come to Esquares to talk to his former wife about some shared property. He spoke as if this were commonplace, something he did often, adding that she lived in a villa with another man but he was always welcome. Now Arthur looked at Estevan and imagined an enormous wooden door being slammed in his face, the large carved kind one might call a portal. The interior of the house contained mysteries, the rejuvenation of love.

Can I do anything? he said.

No. Nothing, said Estevan.

Arthur guessed they'd fought, could imagine his wife's face behind the door, in a sense envied Estevan his drama, when he was having sham battles on the street with a contemptuous rug weaver.

I'm getting that rug made with the shoe, he said, by way of sounding interesting.

What? said Estevan.

The shoe, said Arthur, the light blue stiletto shoe in the upper-right-hand-corner. She's weaving it for me, after all.

Good, said Estevan, as though Arthur had clarified something important. Arthur realized that Estevan was drunk.

Arthur went to his room and began to pack. Socks. Stamps. Guidebook. A piece of silver jewelry for his girlfriend. At one in the morning, he peered out into the courtyard and saw Estevan still sitting at the wrought iron table. He was in shadow. It was impossible to tell whether his wine glass was empty or full.

Would you like to go see Asunta? he called. Would you like to see her weaving my rug?

Are you nuts? Estevan answered.

No, I'm not nuts.

He went down to the courtyard, sat down at Estevan's table. Estevan poured him a stingy amount of wine and told him the entire story: Indeed his ex-wife had been outraged when Estevan appeared and indeed she had slammed a large wooden door right in his face. The fact that the truth corresponded so perfectly with what Arthur had imagined made him ecstatic, elevated his vision of the rug, reinstated his belief in amazing one-to-one correspondences.

Come, he said, tugging at Estevan's sleeve. Come, let's go see Asunta. At first Estevan was stubborn.

I won't creep through this god-awful town to see some silly old lady weaving a rug. I've already been a supplicant once today.

You're not a supplicant. You're my witness!

Estevan grumbled and the two men crept through the town, past the square, through the ever-widening streets, until they came to the rug weaver's house, where a light was on. She was alone, by herself, in half-light, head bent, fingers flying, weaving the rug, working quickly, rapidly, alone. Arthur looked. The rug was half-done and was perfect, not one optical illusion. She had already woven the shoe, and it didn't look blasphemous at all, but was delicate, sacred—a pale blue, almost white, just as he'd imagined it.

How does she do it? he asked, to Estevan, who had fallen asleep. How does she do it? he said to himself.

He shook Estevan, and they prepared to walk home, but not

before he paused before a white donkey eating roses. My wife loved this animal, he said, although he had no idea whether it was the same donkey Leah had seen five years ago. She always worried whether he got enough to eat.

Estevan nodded, the way people nod when they are drunk.

Postcards

L ONG BEFORE YOU died you told me you planned to send your
friends postcards from beyond the grave that said: *Having a wonderful time, wish you were here.* You said you would choose a conventional
photograph of American scenic grandeur—and you would pre-address
and stamp the postcards yourself.

This was in the early stages of your illness. I appreciated the sharp-
ness of your mind, and your quote, from Johnson, that there's nothing
like the anticipation of the noose to strengthen a man's wit. I laughed,
and felt hopeful, and said you wouldn't need to send the postcards for a
long time. But after you told me, I worried that you would to ask me to
mail them, and whenever you came to visit, I thought you were bringing the postcards. I could imagine scenes in which you asked me to mail
them, and I said I wouldn't, and you got angry, and eventually I said I
would. But this never happened: All we ever did was sit around, make
jokes, and drink tea. Once you came over wearing a black top hat, black
jeans, and a black shirt and told me that your illness was about to get

worse. I asked how you knew, and you said that always, before entering a new stage, you had an impulse to change your hair, grow a moustache, buy offbeat clothes, use a cane—as though death might know your name but not your face.

AS IT TURNED out, the only thing you ever wanted from me was supreme restraint in leaving you alone when you began to die. You told most of your friends to go away and they did, and you also said no one could cry at your funeral, and we obeyed. You liked junk food, so your family served macaroni salad and salami and popcorn, and we all stood around pretending to have fun. I assumed you'd been too sick to remember the postcards, but a month after you died, I got one that said: *Having a wonderful time, wish you were here.* It was in your small, slanted writing, and the words transmitted your voice. For a moment I could hear you speaking.

The postcard was a color photograph of American grandeur with mountains, sky, sea, and a meadow of flowers. When I look at it now, I remember what I used to imagine when I'd see you coming to my door: You asking me to mail the postcards. My saying no. A terrible explosion of anger. And then my saying yes. You offer me hundreds of postcards. They float from the palm of your hand.

Soulmates

THE FIRST TIME I heard that it was impossible to live with a soulmate was from my friend Marge who was three years older than me. She was sitting on her bed painting her toenails, and I was sitting in a rocking chair watching her. Suddenly out of the blue, Marge said:

You can never live with a soulmate, it doesn't work. I've lived with three guys and I had too much in common with all of them. Believe me, the next guy I meet isn't going to like poetry, or Bach, or rainy mornings. We're going to meet pragmatically and discuss what food we're going to buy and how we're going to raise the kids. Marriage isn't communication. It's living.

I'd never lived with a man, and I couldn't stand what she was saying. I decided that she was being bitter because she'd lived with three guys and none of them had worked. She's deluded, I thought, and trying to spoil things for me. I reached for the polish and painted my toes. An extravagant earth-colored bronze.

THEN IT WAS three years later and I was living with a tall reedy man named Harlan Green. Harlan and I were soulmates: We had met in Paris, at a summer course for Americans at the Sorbonne. Eventually Harlan was going to go to medical school, but then he was twenty–one and it turned out that we liked Yeats and a French poet called Supervielle. (We were always quoting a certain poem that began O! old house of the light and rose!) We also agreed that beverages influenced one's sense of time: Tea, for example, created a sense of leisure, while coffee created a sense of urgency. And over espresso on the boulevard St. Michelle, we agreed that the reason people got so crazy around Christmas was that they ignored the solstice, and just when they should be allowing themselves to be pulled into that primal sense of darkness, they spaced out at the peak of consumerism. After we came back to the States and decided to live together, the first thing we did was get a dog that we named after Kafka's favorite sister. There had never been one doubt between us about the dog's name. We just looked at her when we saw her at the pound and thought: Ottla.

Fortunately, I had the restraint and presence of mind not to brag to Marge that I'd found a soulmate I could live with. She'd kept her word and was married to a lawyer with an excellent sense of humor. Every week they planned their menus in advance and he had already taught her how to rock climb. It isn't Yeats, she wrote, but it's a hell of a lot better than what I was getting.

One night, near Christmas, Harlan and I were in bed, talking. The bedroom was furnished according to our superb and singular tastes: one simple oak dresser from the Salvation Army, an orange plant by the window, a blue and white patchwork quilt, and a bedside table with a pitcher and a dark wooden bowl of winter pears. We were talking about the Crusades, when suddenly a great wind began to rattle the trees. It was a wild, unruly wind, and it seemed to be blowing in a perilous direction. I said this phrase, *perilous direction*, to Harlan, and he said, almost for the first time, I don't know what you mean.

You don't know what I mean? I said.

No, he said, I really don't know what you mean.

I paused and took a deep breath. And then I told Harlan something I'd never told anybody: Namely, that ever since I've been a kid, I've always felt that the wind created a kind of time-warp so you could see things from other centuries. If you listen, I said, you can really see things beyond this time.. You can literally be transported in some astral way.

How can someone be transported by listening to the wind? said Harlan.

I remember the room very vividly then. Everything poised, wrapped inside the wind, the perfect furniture, the orange tree, all attuned to some higher frequency.

This feeling about the wind is important to me, I said, something I've never told anybody.

For a moment, Harlan looked blank. Then he said, Well, for me the wind is connected to the most awful night of my life, which is the night when my father walked out on my mother. Then he told me that one windy night in August, he and his brother had to sit in his room listening to a violent argument between his father and mother until his father slammed the front door and drove off. The next day he'd come back, bringing the boys a bunch of soap from the YMCA where he'd slept, but that night he and his brother didn't know if he was ever coming back, and they had to listen to the wind and think that maybe their father had drowned, like the father of a classmate who had come home, stood outside the door, whistled his characteristic whistle, and then disappeared. The next day they'd found him in the river.

I listened to Harlan carefully. I knew I should care about what he was saying, yet I felt a distinct sense of claustrophobia. And finally, I told him that I couldn't listen, that I just wanted the wind to blow through my bones, and I went out to our porch and stood there in my bathrobe. It was a violent wind. It was making garbage cans rattle and blowing paper boxes and newspapers, sweeping them out of the world. I stood on the porch in my bathrobe, assuming a pose of enjoyment, but in truth I couldn't, because Harlan had made the wind sinister. Instead of messages from far-off places and esoteric times, it was full of fathers sleeping at the Y or drowning. I went back inside, feeling cheated, and meanwhile Harlan, in just a T-shirt with his hairy legs sticking out, was making tea. He looked sad, and drank his tea quickly, as though he really wanted it to be coffee.

I wish you hadn't brought it up, he said. This whole business about the wind. . . . It's really gotten to me. That was the most terrible night of my life.

I'm sorry, Harlan. I was only talking about what the wind meant to— It's been very influential.

Harlan got up and put the teacup in the sink. He took the tea bag from the cup and swung it like a pendulum.

Isn't that a little grandiose? he said. Pinning a major influence on one of the four elements? You're making yourself out like Black Elk or something.

Well isn't it the same for you? I asked. Doesn't the wind have to do with the night your dad left?

That's different, he said. It was just connected by accident to something that happened to me. But I'm not making out like it's special, or I have some transcendental connection to it.

Harlan said this peaceably, yet suddenly he looked quite ornery in his T-shirt, with the hair on his legs like spikes.

Screw you, I said. You've really spoiled something. Then I went back to bed and listened to the wind, feeling hurt and even guilty, but thrilledby its wildness. It was a dangerous wind. A perilous wind. I didn't care what Harlan felt about it.

AS IT TURNED out, it was one of the most violent winds that ever hit Northern California. It reached a velocity close to that of a tornado and tore open the roof of a downtown department store called Hinks (which has since gone defunct and been made into seven movie theaters) and lifted up a lot of merchandise, which landed on people's lawns. Our neighbor got a pinball machine and the family down the block got fifteen extension cords, and a widower a block away got Christmas tree ornaments. The next morning, which happened to be the morning of the solstice, everybody was running around looking for things, and right on our front lawn, Harlan and I saw two gnome-like figurines, an imitation crystal candle-holder, a pocket dictionary, and a can of tennis balls. We were feeling angry and greedy, so we ran like mad, and each of us got what the other didn't get his hands on. Then we looked at each other and knew we wouldn't be living together anymore.

Afterwards, there was the nagging question of whether I should tell Marge that she was right—it wasn't possible to live with a soulmate after all. She was divorced from the lawyer and living in Oregon and the whole thing probably wouldn't have mattered to her, but somehow I felt that telling her would make her theory official. So I didn't. I kept it to myself.

Harlan moved from the apartment, leaving me with everything but the orange tree and the wooden bowl. Eventually I decided I needed more furniture, and I got an oversized couch and a desk, which made the place look like a student's apartment instead of a farmhouse in the south of France. That was seven years ago, and Harlan and I have remained friends. We don't see each other often, but always when we break up with someone, we call each other with a gloomy Hello, and there's a feeling of being a soldier called back into the reserves. Just the other day, I got such a call from Harlan.

Can I come over? he said. I'm really depressed.

He had just broken up with a blond anesthesiologist who liked to windsurf—definitely not a soulmate.

Sure, I said, and he came right over from the hospital where he's doing his residency in internal medicine. His melancholy made him look vulnerable, and when I noticed his stethoscope dangling from the pocket of his jeans, I felt jealous at the thought of him putting it close to other hearts. To make us both feel better, I told him Marge's theory about soulmates, and he looked startled and a little angry.

For Godssake, why didn't you ever tell me before? he said. Think about the time we'd have saved.

Do you think it was wasted time? I said.

Sure, in a way.

But it was wonderful being with you.

Really?

Oh yes. I wouldn't have not done it for the world.

Harlan was getting sleepy in a way that was familiar. We sat on my overstuffed couch, not quite touching, and it seemed, for a moment, that we were still the people who'd met in Paris, walking down cobblestoned streets. I pressed my hand in his palm, he pressed back, and then his eyes seized on the figurine gnomes, and the candlestick I've kept on the mantelpiece since I found them the day of the solstice. You still have those? he asked.

Why yes, I said, Didn't you keep the dictionary and the tennis balls?

God, no. I lost the tennis balls and the dictionary was useless.

Really? I'm surprised. They were kind of significant to me.

The pleasant, sleepy atmosphere turned to silence. I could see nubbly pieces of fabric on the couch, some of which were darker than the original beige. I picked one off and began to roll it in my hands.

It's that wind, Harlan said. Now whenever there's a wind, I don't just remember my father—I remember that lousy night. Do you?

No. I love the wind. It reminds me of other centuries.

Even after what happened?

Yes.

We looked at each other with the ill will we'd discovered that night.

Your friend Marge is right, Harlan said. Soulmates can't live together, after all. I think we should write some kind of confession and save other people time.

For Godssake, Harlan. Let's not!

Why? Let the whole thing out in the open. He reached for a pencil on the coffee table and scribbled on the back of an envelope *forget all about shared sensibilities.* Then he began to write numbers.

I'm going to make a list of all the crazy assumptions I've ever had about love, he said, and then I'm going to refute them.

You're just angry, I said. You're angry about breaking up with that blond. I went into the kitchen, poured myself some wine, and called Marge in Oregon.

I hadn't spoken to Marge in ages, not since her divorce. When I called she was alone, working on a software project. She sounded gentle, sad, and far away. I'm sorry, she said after I told her. I didn't want to be right, and the opposite didn't work either. There's not any kind of theory about what kind of person you can live with.

What about publishing some kind of confession? That's what Harlan wants to do.

Oh, I don't know. At the very least people should find out for themselves. I mean the way adventures have to play themselves out. Anyway, who knows? Maybe you can live with a soulmate.

We talked for a long while, said we'd try to see each other at Thanksgiving. When we hung up, I went back to the living room and looked at the figurine gnomes. They were glazed a bright green, and I could see parts of the room in them. Behind me, on the couch, Harlan was staring into space, the abandoned list on his lap. I turned around and told him what Marge had said.

What do you think? I asked. Could soulmates live together?

Who knows? said Harlan. Maybe they could. And for a moment there was a flicker of static between us, like matches being struck.

A Brief History
of Camouflage

S HE DIDN'T REMEMBER when she decided to make a dress that matched the colors of her favorite living room chair. Maybe one night, when she was sitting in it reading, watching her husband from the other end of the room. Or maybe on a different night, when she was sitting opposite that chair, looking at it. The chair was covered in muted greens and golds, not the purples and blues she usually wore. She sat there looking at it and decided she would look nice in a dress with the same colors.

The next day she left work early and went to a dry-goods store. She almost never sewed, and it felt strange to enter a world where women murmured over patterns and fingered fabrics. She spent a long time choosing material and finally bought some green and gold semi-transparent silk. She also bought a pattern for a chair from an upholstery book. The next night she wore what she had made and sat in the chair that matched its colors. Her husband stared in her direction for a long time. Finally he said: You blend with those colors almost perfectly. She smiled and said she knew that.

She enjoyed resembling the chair, but at some point, she discovered a stronger force inside her—a force that wanted to look exactly like it: She added sleeves that looked like the arm rests and made a green and gold hat with a matching veil. That night she sat in the chair watching her husband stare into space, and he didn't notice her at all. Clearly he thought he was alone, and at some point she felt guilty for spying and cried out:

Where am I? He jumped up and looked around the room, but he couldn't find her. Where are you? he kept asking.

Over here, she answered.

Finally she got up, and he thought the chair was walking: He only believed it was her when she took off the veil. She felt vaguely guilty about what she'd done, but she was curious about what he was like when he was alone. So she began to wear the matching outfit and sit in the chair without telling him. She discovered that his private face was sad and his eyes seemed more transparent. Usually he read, but sometimes he spoke out loud, saying things like: What? or: I didn't want to do that. Once he delivered an angry monologue about a bar of soap she'd allowed to disintegrate in the sink. I can't live this way, he said. You never do what I ask. She decided she would try to be more careful.

She enjoyed being the chair, but she wanted to be other things too: She made a dress that matched the living room blinds, with cords and slats that could be opened and shut, and a jumpsuit that looked like their couch, with bolsters on the shoulders. These clothes were uncomfortable, but comfort wasn't the point: They allowed her to get to know her husband. Over time, he got used to seeing less of her and talked out loud more often. Mostly he talked about things that annoyed him, but one night he had an imaginary conversation with a woman who lived down the street: I really can't come over, he said, because I'm married. Then, imitating the woman's voice, he answered: But I know how you really feel about me. I've seen you watch my legs when I get into my car.

She listened quietly, disguised as any number of things. He talked about his favorite movies and his track record in college and things that happened at his office. He talked about a pie-eating contest he'd won in high school and a Maserati he intended to buy. One night while she was sitting on the couch wearing the outfit with the bolsters, he said:

I have to think things over, so I'm going to go to the mountains. That's right, I really have to think.

He said this a couple of times, then went to the attic and got a duffel bag. She rushed to the bedroom, put on a robe that matched their curtains, and stood by the window. Soon he came in with the suitcase, pulled clothes out of their closet, and began to pack. He packed a lot of familiar clothes, mostly sweaters and jeans, but he also packed some clothes she'd never seen and that didn't seem like anything he'd wear in the mountains: a striped vintage suit that looked like it had belonged to a gangster, and the kind of sweater-vest he always said he'd never be caught dead in. He stuffed the familiar clothes carelessly in the duffel bag, but packed the new things carefully as though they might be fragile. He also packed books and shaving cream and toothpaste, and a carton of after-dinner mints, which she'd never known him to eat. The whole procedure took over half an hour.

She watched without saying a word. When he was through, he zipped up the duffel bag and said:

Well, that does it. I'm going to go to the mountains, now. Then he left the house, and she heard his car revving up in the driveway. As soon as it drove away, sounding like a dangerous muzzled beast, she took off the curtains and drank some wine and then put on the outfit that matched the chair. Perhaps because he wasn't there she didn't feel like herself at all—she simply blended with the chair and knew what it felt like to be it. The same was true of all her other disguises, and she found this restful.

During the day, she had to go to work and run errands, but as soon as she came home, she put on whatever she wanted to become and sat down with a glass of wine. Over time she began to experience the house as though she were inanimate: She got to know its changing gradients of light and special sounds, especially at night, when it seemed to sigh and shift on its foundation. From this vantage point, she sometimes stared out the window and saw the woman her husband liked walking down the street. She felt a sense of pity for her, pity mixed with dispassion.

One day her husband called and said he wanted to come back. He had thought things over and he really missed her. She told him she'd prefer that he didn't because she'd entered another realm. He asked what she meant, and she answered: The realm of the inanimate. He persisted, saying that life wasn't the same without her, and finally she told him that of course he could come home, but he would hardly ever see her. He said that was okay, certainly better than nothing.

He called on a Tuesday and came back over the weekend. She was waiting for him in the chair, wearing the fabric that matched it, and as soon as he opened the door he walked over to the chair, kissed her, and said that she couldn't fool him, he could see her. She looked into his eyes and knew, from the reflection in his pupils, he wasn't seeing her, but was seeing the entire house, crystalline in detail, glittering, complete. Under the circumstances it was fine to kiss him, too, and she did, again and again, loving as only inanimate objects can love—mutely, impartially, without wanting anything back.

Night Visits

AN AFTERNOON
IN KANSAS

WHEN I WAS three years old, long after we'd moved from the east and old enough to understand, my mother tried to strangle me. It was late afternoon, the time of raw nerves, hard for her in the middle of Kansas. I was in my crib, crying. She came in the room, looked over me. Then, from the ceiling of my bedroom, I saw my own eyes as her hand twisted my head, pressed her thumb against my throat, pushed my chin into my neck. My doll caved against my ribs, an ally of sorts, with hard, plastic fingers.

This was a time of intense silence: Bits of air, meant for me, fanned around my mother's throat. Her eyes, framed in slanted glasses, were dark, electric, furious. Maybe I made a deep appeal, asking her to let me live. Or maybe we met in some mysterious, ineffable harmony. In any case, the phone rang, and her hands loosened.

Later my father walked me around the living room. He wanted to see if I could move my neck. I could.

Afterwards, I only remembered I'd swallowed a bubble of air that kept me from breathing. I felt it when I was at the movies, or on long walks through Kansas fields—or in a flash, when I saw dead animals. Years later, I looked in the mirror, saw my mother's face above my own, remembered the deep vitality of her eyes in that moment above my crib. For an instant her face became my face, her eyes became my eyes. And then she separated out, became miraculously herself. Never again have I seen another person more clearly.

MY FACE

WINTERS WERE BLEAK in the Midwest. There were days when the furniture lost its edges early, and the world had darkened by four. Then, until the lamps could do their work, everything was obscure, and my mother often sat in the living room staring into space. She didn't like winter, she said, because it was confining.

What is confining? I asked.

Too small. The kind of small that makes you nervous.

I was small. And I knew that I made her nervous. Therefore I deduced that I, too, was confining, and I tried to make myself scarce. I sat on the other side of the dark room watching her, wondering what else was going on behind her vacant, darting eyes. It seemed that she looked ahead to places she would never reach and back to places she had never been. I could imagine a world in front of her eyes, but I didn't want to enter it. Like the day, it was dark and barren.

Outside, the old French peasant who kept chickens in the heart of suburban Illinois came out to gather her five o'clock eggs. I could see her kerchiefed head bobbing up and down while her chickens flocked around her. I could never be sure whether she actually gathered eggs or performed some act of obeisance as she bent toward the ground. With something, or perhaps nothing, in her basket, she hobbled back to the house. My mother looked out the window and sighed.

Meanwhile, men returning from work began to walk down the avenue opposite the alley. It was a promenade, I thought, a promenade of hats and newspapers—and I watched them, hoping to see my father. But my mother didn't notice: Her gaze went somewhere beyond the window—to an opera house, where women in tiered gowns fanned themselves, or to a London street, where Pears soap was displayed in shop windows. Her century wasn't this one: She bought cheap earrings that duplicated the patterns of chandeliers and liked glass that looked like crystal.

Sometimes my mother slipped into evening without a trace. Then she was gathered up by the walls and couldn't be distinguished from the faded green brocade of the couch. Her near-disappearance was accompanied by listlessness and a sense of abstract grief. Her eyes, which actually were small, grew large, and I was never sure whether this was a theatrical expression or sadness. As for my father, when he came home to find her in these states, he would always appear bewildered. As though her revival were imminent, he would pad around the kitchen opening cans of soup, ferreting out boxes of stale crackers.

Would you like some soup, Marlie dear?

No.

A little bouillon?

Maybe later.

My father's voice was tense and cheerful—an affront to the tragedies my mother witnessed. Had there been a fireplace, he and I would have sat in front of it looking at the flames and further denying her grief. But instead we had to sit in the small kitchen, painfully aware of her presence on the couch.

Sometimes it seemed to me that the beginning of night, where the moon rose over the chicken coop and my father and I ate our soup, was only a convenience—something to create the illusion that my mother actually existed. In truth, the real night was somewhere else, and my mother—on the couch under the wedding scene by Brueghel—was an imperious ward of the night with unusual privileges. Once I saw her staring at the chicken coop across the alley, and as she stared, it seemed that the pattern of the moonlight changed directions on the rug. I wondered if my mother's imperious voice continued to speak inside her head, invoking the night, asking it to protect her.

But there were other times when the approach of evening didn't quiet her. The furniture refused to absorb her, and the walls didn't let her fade. As if the night wanted to expel her, her hawk nose became sharper, her eyes became brighter, and her thick hands became unbearably distinct. Having lost control over the night, she turned her attention to her surroundings. She called our apartment a slum and denounced my father—who was absent—for not finding us a better house.

Once, after a frightening oral inventory of everything in the room, during which the furniture seemed to stiffen and the ashtrays looked polite, she wrung her hands and looked at the ceiling as if invoking a family of bats. In the hall, invisible neighbors paused—discreetly, for the boards creaked.

I wanted a place to hide. I knew that soon my mother's voice would blow in my direction, like a monsoon that happened with the seasons. In spite of her cluttered closets, my mother's memory was neat. Nothing I had ever done, or not done, eluded her:

I begged you to leave the house, but you insisted on trying on those gloves. Those crummy dime-store gloves. Pieces of cheap felt! I begged you and begged you and begged you but you tried them on. Hours while I waited in the hall. Hours! We missed the bus! We missed the bus! You tried on those gloves and we missed the bus!

Sometimes in the heat of her tirade she would decide I wasn't clean. Then she would fly at me, undress me, and put me in the tub, invading me with soap and language. But these scenes were reserved for the greatest miseries, the nameless, wrenching kind that could only be relieved by an assault on another body. More often, she dismissed me, and turned her attention to the smaller objects in the house, all of who witnessed her like frightened rabbits.

Look at this! she would say, picking up a clock and throwing it against the wall. Everything cluttered in this goddamn room! Everything in a heap!

The clock would fall to the floor—still, apparently itself, only now with a hairline of glass across its face. Obediently, it kept on ticking.

Books! she would then say. Books and magazines everywhere!

The books were in the bookcase, their embossed titles looking at her like eyes. She would glare back at them, pick up a magazine and rattle it: This thing! This goddamned thing! she would say, holding it in front of her and shaking the pages as though it were a head of hair.

USUALLY I FOUND myself in the same position as the objects: motionless, mute, enduring with a sense of apology. But one afternoon, around four o'clock, as my mother hovered between absorption and exile, I went to her room and sat in front of her dressing table. All of her makeup was laid out in front of me—her mascaras, her eyeliners, her powder. There was also a small cut-glass pot of rouge—a rouge so red, so dark, so fragrant, it promised unholy forms of transformation. Without ceremony, I opened it and began to rub it on my face. The effect was fascinating. Like an etching becoming visible, I saw myself all radiant and red and strange, flying under the flag of another country.

The night had refused to absorb my mother. When I came back to the living room, she'd just assaulted one of her black high-heeled shoes (those shoes that embarrassed me whenever I saw them) and was about to attack another one.

This life! she cried. How I loathe and despise this life!

She didn't see me, and I stood as still as the shoe waiting to be thrown. Red radiated from my face to my feet, riveting me to the ground. As my mother turned to pick up the shoe, she saw me.

Get that red off your face! she cried. Go inside and wash that red off!

I didn't move. Inhabited by a power I didn't understand, I stayed still, compressed and hard as stone. I felt small, yet billions of years old, like an alien and stubborn star. My mother stood poised, holding the shoe, and I stood in front of her, radiating.

Suddenly my mother started to laugh. It was an amazing laugh, as though her skin were about to crack open and lay bare her bones, as though something deep inside of her had burst. I stared at her, and she laughed and laughed and laughed, as though night were pouring out of her, from her bones to mine.

ORIGINS

WHEN I WAS a child, I thought our family had no origins. Not in the sense that we had no ancestors, but in the sense that nothing of the past assured the present. Other families, it seemed, had something behind them, something that said to them: This is us! But for my family, the sun rose every morning by accident. Days began from scratch. Living was imbued with a perilous sense of adventure.

On mornings when my mother happened to get up, she always surveyed the house as though it were an enormous jigsaw puzzle—the kind that took months, even years, to finish. Rummaging through my dresser drawers, she would despair of finding what I needed for my day at school.

Your shoes! she would cry. Your socks! This room is like a bird's nest.

And indeed the whole house felt like a nest. Not a cozy, down-filled robin's nest, but the nest of a chaotic bird. Yet the cry of Nest! had curious powers: Clothes would be found, a pair of matching socks would be produced. And borne by the grace of these rituals, I would be out the door walking to school. Miraculously, my shoes enclosed my feet, my clothes surrounded my body. And by the time I got to school, any memory of my mother and the house (now cool and dark, my mother back in bed) was a dream, a half-life.

On mornings when my mother didn't get up, I had to invoke the day alone. While she slept (and it was a deep, amazing sleep that elongated the ceilings and stretched the walls) I opened drawers and weeded my way through a maze of clothes. Bit by bit, as though it were forbidden, I invented myself from whatever I happened to find. I never invoked the terrible cry of Nest! but used an incantation of my own, whispering about what I was doing.

BREAKFAST WAS NEVER possible in this process of reconstruction. If my mother happened to be up, it was an affront to her notion of what people were supposed to be doing at that hour. I was alone; the morning was too real and too lonely to feed myself. The only times I ever encountered breakfast were the rare mornings when my father was home. His offerings consisted of real food, but the breakfasts struck me as being only memories of breakfasts from his own childhood, which I knew (by some osmotic sense) had approached normalcy. My father would set out grapefruit, orange juice, and cornflakes (the latter he called breakfast food), start to eat, and urge me to do the same. But I couldn't because the food struck me as being simply representational—that is, as standing for food, rather than being it.

Eat, my father would urge, appealing to his origins.

Daddy, I'm not hungry, I can't.

My father and I sat in the kitchen with a sense of apologetic conspiracy, for tucked away in the northeast corner of the house, my mother slept in a darkened room. This room had the feeling of a chapel, and there was the sense that something more important than sleep was going on in there. It was both glorious and terrifying to me, the way my mother transcended ordinary notions of time and space and wrested her portion of the night, from the night, and hauled it back into the day. Often when I was at school—singing songs, doing arithmetic, copying sketches of animals—I'd think of her at home in bed. It seemed remarkable to me that while all this life was going on she slept, and I worried that she would become confused, wake up, and appear at school in her transparent rose-colored nightgown. This image of her blooming in the classroom like a transparent rose persisted for many years. I never could decide whether I would claim her as my mother.

MY FRIEND, KATHY Montague, had origins. I knew this not just from the pictures in her hall: brown and yellowing ancestors, women from Ohio with mouths like mail slots. It was something else, something in the air around her. Her mother's name was Margaret. She made melted-cheese sandwiches with strips of cut-up bacon on them, and she bought Kathy ruffled dresses, which she ironed, carefully, diligently, while Kathy and I played. I have a persistent image of Margaret weaving the iron in and out of hills of cotton. I also see her making pancakes in such a way that the edges appeared ruffled.

Why do you want to be like her? my mother asked, catching on to my desires when I asked for a dress with ruffles. Kathy Montague is a very dull, precise little girl. She counts when she does ballet, and she always colors inside the lines.

I decided that I, too, would be dull and precise. I began to count when I did ballet, and I got a coloring book and colored inside the lines. I made everything red, even the trees—and shockingly, startlingly neat.

My life as Kathy Montague was only the beginning of a long career in which I assumed strange names and wore impossible disguises. But my mother remained the master of reversals: She could perform the same sleight-of-hand trick with the night as she did with the day, and when everyone else in Kansas had gone to bed and the sun was assaulting the Indian Ocean, she came to life. From my little bedroom (an alcove with a blanket tacked over it to shield the light), I could hear her only three feet away. She read Dickens, Austen, Thackeray, Agatha Christie. She cracked walnuts and disappeared into the kitchen. There was rustling, crunching, coughing. Sometimes my mother would laugh.

Mother, what are you eating now? I would cry.

Go to sleep, she would answer.

But what are you eating? I can hear you!

Walnuts. Now go to sleep.

But I couldn't sleep. It seemed incumbent to stay up with her while she celebrated life. I lay in bed, surrounded by a dozen stuffed animals, listening to her, being with her, imagining what she was doing. At midnight a certain Tchaikovsky waltz came on the radio, and I could feel her winding down. The pages turned more slowly. The chewing stopped. I felt her veer towards sleep, I'd get sleepy, too.

ONE NIGHT MY mother came into my room, sat on my bed, and looked at me. My stuffed animals left almost no room for her. She sat way on the edge of the bed.

Why don't you sleep at night? she asked. Why do you stay up? What's wrong with you?

The Tchaikovsky waltz came on. Lovely, delicate, from an earlier time. And all I felt I could give my mother was my eyes. We looked at each other for awhile, and then she said, You're tired in the morning.

You are, too, I answered.

Oh, well . . . that, said my mother, as though her tiredness were to be expected. But I can sleep. You have to go to school.

It was the first time, and maybe the only time, that she acknowledged how different our lives were. I nodded. She stood up and stayed poised in the arched alcove, looking at me. Then she went back to the living room. Suddenly I called out:

But I want to be with you!

There was a pause, a turned page, an intake of breath. And then my mother's voice, softer, less far away.

Children need their sleep. But grown-ups can do what they want to.

But I wish you would make me sandwiches, I said.

Sandwiches? said my mother. You want me to make you sandwiches?

I want you to make me sandwiches.

Without saying anything more, my mother went to the kitchen and made a radish sandwich.

I shouldn't be doing this, she said, setting it by my bed.

Why not? I said. It's just like breakfast.

Yes, she said. I suppose it is.

One morning, a few weeks later, I heard noises in the kitchen and found my mother making me breakfast. It wasn't my father's sort of breakfast. It was hard rolls with jam, butter, and cheese—like the European breakfasts that her mother had given her. She sat in front of me fully dressed, drinking coffee.

What happened? I asked.

Nothing, she said, appearing to be somewhat insulted.

That morning when I went to school, I had origins. Not the shadowy origins of our ancestors—strange Jews with beards on my mother's side, rigid Presbyterians on my father's side—but tangible roots in a house not far away. My mother was up doing chores. She was ironing, cleaning, mending, baking. She would shop and greet other mothers at the store, maybe even learn to drive. I envisioned the beginning of a very different life and was surprised when I came home and found her asleep. It was noon, and she had taken a piece of the night back to bed with her. I stood there, watching her, realizing that she had some covenant with the night she couldn't break, a bargain she had made, while the rest of us were trapped in daylight.

THE KISS

WHENEVER I THINK of my first kiss, I think of the lie I told my mother, and whenever I think of the lie, I always think that I didn't grow up in this country at all, but in some barren, eastern-European country, like pictures of countries after WWII. I see dingy curtains, dim lights. Lace curtains in the kitchen and a hunk of black bread on a wooden table. I also see the meager gestures of children who have no toys, inventing games in the snow. My mother is in a chair, part of her in our house, the other part in a house she never lived in.

The country first appeared when I was seven and kissed, without warning, a boy named Jerry in the hall of our apartment building. The night before, I had seen a naked, half-paralyzed man being bathed by his elderly mother in a wide-open window while hiding in the bushes with my friend. And the next day, I found Jerry in the hall and kissed him.

Jerry was nine years old. His breath smelled of mint gum and he had slanted, lizard eyes. He wore a leather jacket and claimed he came from Baghdad, which I knew to exist from *The Arabian Nights*. When I kissed him I thought I could feel a rim of extra teeth inside his mouth, although I never looked too closely: The extra teeth suggested a second person, hidden deep inside him.

What's your phone number? he asked as soon as I'd kissed him.

I don't know.

Go upstairs and ask your mom.

Why do you want to know? my mother asked when I went upstairs. She was leafing through a copy of the *Ladies' Home Journal* and looking mildly depressed.

I need it for a library card.

She told me our phone number, and I ran downstairs, panted the number to Jerry. He said he'd call me and never did.

As soon as I came upstairs, the other country appeared, altering our house, particularly our kitchen. Lace curtains at the window. Oilcloth on the table. Children playing in the snow. I sat in the living room looking at the picture of Brueghel that stayed the same, but when I looked at the rest of the house, this country was there. For a year it came and went like something in a flipbook. Anything could bring it on. The faintest glimmer of a lie. A tone of voice with an edge—hers or mine.

In second grade, I knew an underling name Karen, a child who was very small, who had dark plaited hair and a hesitant way of speaking. She could easily have been an orphan from a war torn country. But she lived in America, like us. One day, while two of my friends hit Karen with her own umbrella, I watched, not trying to stop them. She ran off, in her green jacket, crying in the snow.

I was sure she was running off to that other country, but it was to this country that her mother wrote a note to the teacher, naming everyone who had been involved in the incident, including me. My friends, who were more cunning, lied and said I had hit Karen with the umbrella. The teacher believed them, I was powerless to say no, and I came home and told my mother what was true. She wrote the teacher a note, which I delivered, too frightened to read. I never knew if the note released me from my friend's lie or bound me to it.

After this, the other country receded. Perhaps I had been redeemed, my lie exchanged for someone else's. Or perhaps I had entered a third country where lies were as commonplace as Kansas. In any case, our kitchen became our kitchen again: an ordinary Midwestern kitchen, with white pre-sliced bread, linoleum on the floor, venetian blinds at the windows. Our windows looked out on a flat Midwestern street. No war orphans played in the snow. Sometimes I looked at the wedding picture by Brueghel, thinking that if I looked back at our house, the country might appear. But I wasn't to see it again until high school, when more lies came between my mother and me. Then I began to reenter that unnamed country, walking with more certainty, sure of where I was—and I still can go there. In that country my mother sits by a window looking at a landscape she's never seen. She sews for me, cooks for me, gives credence to my lies. Her bread is bitter and always dark.

THE
ENCHANTED MAN

A T THE END of the block of my childhood, like a ship forever
sailing toward the avenue, was the stately Victorian house of the
antique dealer, Adrienne Glass. She didn't use this house for her antique
store—that was at the other end of town. But she did use it for storing
four-poster beds from every corner of the world. Through the bay window of her living room, I often saw such a bed, covered with brocade,
near a stand with a vase of flowers that matched the color of the spread.
These flowers were made of glass, like Adrienne's last name.

I was six years old, too little to speculate if the beds had any visi-
tors. But one day, Danny Johnson, who was twelve, made up a song that
everybody sang:

Old lady Glass has five hundred beds
Eighty for her fingers
Eighty for her head
Eighty for her toes

Eighty for her feet
And the rest for her bum
When she walks it down the street

This song wasn't right on a couple of counts. First, Adrienne Glass wasn't old; she was young. And second, she was lean and beautiful and self-sufficient and needing no help transporting any part of her person anywhere. Half the year she'd spend in Europe shopping for antiques, and once, according to my mother, she'd gotten involved with a German art dealer, just so she could buy his bed, and when the roads outside his villa were snowed-in, she'd hired three students from Heidelberg to portage the bed through a forest.

Mostly, Adrienne Glass kept to herself. But from time to time she visited another house on our block—a house that was notable in suburban Kansas because its backyard was used for keeping live chickens. The few times she visited, she always came out with something old: once an enormous oak umbrella stand, once a large gilt mirror which reflected, briefly, the flat Midwestern sky. After she left, the owner of the house, a Mrs. D'Agnelli, stood in the doorway, looking after her. She came from Bordeaux, and she addressed her chickens every morning in a stream of French. My mother explained that Adrienne Glass was buying Mrs. D'Agnelli's antiques, and she said this with a darkness that we children seized upon. For Mrs. D'Agnelli was an object of interest quite apart from her chickens: She was said to keep a man who was enchanted. This man was young. His name was Armand. And all day long, he sat in a silver chair with wheels the size of spinning wheels. My mother said this chair was a wheelchair, and if Mrs. D'Agnelli would only get a chair-lift, Armand could mingle in the neighborhood. But the French are very closed, she said, and that's the problem.

It was my girlfriend Christine Haag who got the notion that Armand was enchanted. And this was because a nun at her school gave a talk about entering the age of reason. Christine, who was eight, had entered that age a year ago, and I, at six, had a year to wait. This nun had said that when one entered the age of reason, a kind of grace was bestowed, a grace that allowed you to know what you really wanted, but that sometimes people lost this grace and then they floated around like someone who was enchanted. This information impressed Christine, and soon she applied it to Armand.

Armand can't think, she said to me one day. He does everything Mrs. D'Agnelli says. She gives him pears, he eats the pears, she gives him glue, he eats the glue. Just you watch. Armand is a zombie.

I had never seen Armand eat glue, but I felt obliged to believe Christine. My status as a non-Catholic frightened me: With the blessing of her priest, Christine gave me a plastic cross that glowed in the dark. I kept the cross under my bed, and at night, when I was sure my mother wouldn't see me, I would crouch on the floor and look at it.

FOR CHRISTMAS THAT year, I'd been given a little castle, which was set up in such a way that you could tell the weather. When it was about to rain, a white-haired woman emerged from the door, and when it was sunny, two dark-haired children appeared. Whenever I thought of Armand and Mrs. D'Agnelli, I thought of this castle—as though each were opposite ends of the weather. Mrs. D'Angelli had a beautiful face with snow-white hair, and Armand was handsome and dark, like the children. Be he also looked like the prince in my picture book who kissed Snow White awake, and this gave me the idea that enchanted people could be two different ages at once, as well as free other people from a spell. Armand was impeccably dressed, as though he were about to leave for work. Christine was sure he was sitting on the porch, waiting for us to free him.

In the dark place beneath Christine's back porch—a place where we showed each other our underwear and whispered secrets—Christine told me stories about Armand. She discounted the rumor that Armand was Mrs. D'Agnelli's oldest son and had once been a public accountant, in favor of the idea that Armand was Mrs. D'Agnelli's nephew. He had been rich, she said, and Mrs. D'Agnelli had bewitched him for his money. The story was embellished with Christine's notions of France— old stone castles, people with pointed hats. Christine said that whenever she passed Armand, he looked at her, and she knew by his eyes he was waiting for us to free him.

He has a special way of saying things. He talks in a secret code . . .

We never went up to talk to Armand. He seemed happy on the porch, by himself, dreaming his private dream, and it was enough to know that Christine and I shared a secret. Of course, in addition to this secret, I had a secret of my own, which was that I sometimes thought of going to live with Armand after I had saved him.

IT WAS ADRIENNE Glass who provided us with absolute evidence that Armand was enchanted. One winter afternoon, she drove to the D'Agnelli house in her black antique-store truck with gold letters on the side and came out with an amazing-looking chair, which she carried downstairs by herself. After shoving the chair into the truck, she removed a large porcelain pitcher, went back up the stairs, and handed it to Mrs. D'Agnelli. My mother said that the chair was a valuable nineteenth century privy chair, and the pitcher was a gift because Adrienne Glass felt sorry that Mrs. D'Agnelli had to sell her last heirloom—for Armand she said, who needed oxygen.

It was clear to Christine that one instrument of enchantment had merely been exchanged for another:

People always make their spells in special chairs, she said, and later they use some water, a little like holy water, except the priest would never bless it.

We were sitting beneath her porch, shelling peas and eating most of them. I looked at Christine and thought that she looked like the saint above her bed. Curly blond hair, a few freckles, blue eyes that gave the impression of informed intelligence.

My mother says the chair was for a chamber pot, I said. People used to use it for going to the bathroom.

That's because the bathroom is where they do their spells, said Christine. She dropped a pea-pod on the ground and looked at me.

Never let anyone come to the bathroom with you, she said, even when you're sick. Just pray and pray to God that you're not going to vomip.

Ever since I'd known her, Christine had pronounced *vomit* as vomip. But I was at a loss to correct her because somehow, when pronounced that way, the word became unspeakable.

One day, in late spring, something made me decide to visit Armand by myself. He was sitting on the porch, and I stood below the stairs until he noticed me. The he nodded his head—rigidly, the way a bird would nod. I took this as an invitation to come up.

The stairs to the D'Agnelli house were steep, with space between them like a ladder. As I walked up, I was afraid I might fall through one of the holes. When I got to the top, I discovered how small the porch was—about the size of the chair-lift that would have let Armand mingle in the neighborhood. I also saw that his view of the block was the same view I had from my bedroom window.

Hello there, said Armand.

Hello, I answered.

Indeed Armand was handsome. But up close, his face looked less like the face of a prince and more like the face of a handyman who sometimes came to help my mother. He was wearing a clean white shirt and a brown sweater-vest, and the brown of the vest was the same color as his hair. From where I stood, I could see tiny flecks of dandruff—waxy, white, arranged upon the vest like snow. I thought I shouldn't see this, so I turned to face him more directly.

Do you come here often? said Armand, pronouncing *often* with a *t*.

Yes, I said, I live across the alley.

That's nice, said Armand. And in that moment I realized that for all we talked about him, he never noticed us.

I turned my head again so I could take another look at Armand's view—the same view I had when I looked out my bedroom window. There was the large white house facing the avenue, the houses facing that house, and beyond those houses the lake. It was the first time I'd realized that someone else could see my world.

Do you go to school? Armand asked.

Yes, I said.

Where? he asked.

At Noyes Street, near the bakery. As soon as I said this, I felt chagrined because Armand has never been to the bakery and didn't know where Noyes Street was. So I pointed in the direction of Noyes Street, and Armand looked. It was impossible to see Noyes Street—we could only see the underpass to the railroad. I told him it was beyond the tracks, and described the route.

Suddenly Mrs. D'Agnelli opened the door without a sound, startling me with the whiteness of her hair. She nodded to me, almost bowing, and wheeled Armand into the house. After the door was closed I stood quite still, until suddenly I remembered two things: first that Armand was supposed to be talking in secret code, and second that Mrs. D'Agnelli slaughtered old hens. I ran down the stairs, terrified, and met Christine who had been watching me.

What happened? she cried.

Nothing!

But she knows. She suspicions you and she knows.

Suspicions sounded dreadful—like it was made of scissors and knives. I decided I would never talk to Armand again.

That was the summer I turned seven, and all the rest of that year, Armand sat on the porch with his dreamy eyes, and twice I forgot my vow and went upstairs to talk to him. We talked about commonplace things—a tree, a truck, a passing bird. Unlike other adults, whenever Armand talked, he seemed to be talking about *just that thing,* and for this reason, I was at a loss to decipher a secret code. Our conversations never lasted long, because Mrs. D'Agnelli always wheeled Armand away. Through the open door I could see a sliver of their narrow hall— dark, with a huge porcelain vase filled with lavender.

In late spring, Armand began to appear on the porch less often—he was weak, my mother said, and needed oxygen. Christine and I turned our interest to trading cards—we especially liked pictures of dogs—and we might have forgotten him completely except for one summer evening when Mrs. D'Agnelli forgot to draw the curtains on her kitchen window. It was a warm, milky dusk, a time when everything was comingling and bursting with light, and Christine and I were playing hopscotch across the street. I had just reached the four and was about to throw my skate key on the five when I looked up and saw Armand lying naked on a table. He was on his back and his legs, which were covered with dark black hair, were drawn up like a baby about to be diapered. Christine and I crept to the hedge outside the D'Agnelli's garden, with a delicious illicit feeling that didn't prepare us for what we saw: Mrs. D'Agnelli was washing Armand with her hands. She dipped one hand in Adrienne Glass's porcelain pitcher and the other in a clear glass bowl, filled with water. She alternated hands, smoothing them over his body, washing, rinsing, while Armand lay quietly, looking at a point on the ceiling as though he weren't in the room at all. After Mrs. D'Agnelli was done washing him, she dried him with a towel, paying special attention to his legs as if she meant to dry every hair. And then she gave Armand a toothbrush, which he used to brush his teeth. Twice he took water from a cup, which he spat into another cup. When he was done, Mrs. D'Agnelli turned off the overhead light.

All this time, Christine and I had been crouched by the hedge. But when the light went off, we came closer to the house by way of the path. In the near dark, we saw Mrs. D'Agnelli wheeling Armand away. The table seemed to float, and as I watched him disappear, I knew that Armand wasn't enchanted, only ill, and that his body wasn't being used and never would be used in a way that I sensed, even at seven, he wanted to use it. While Christine and I stood in the darkness giggling, I experienced a terrible shaken feeling, as if it had been me, not Armand, lying on the table. That night I pushed Christine's cross to a far corner under my bed, and the next day, impelled by a force I didn't understand, I kissed a boy three years older than me in the hall of my apartment building. It was a heady, passionate kiss, and he received it with aplomb and pleasure. Then he asked me for my phone number, which I didn't know. Afterwards I felt relieved, as though the secret of Armand had been crowded out of my mind, and I regaled Christine with stories about the boy. It was the first time I had ever been able to engage Christine, and over time, the stories grew bolder. Armand never appeared on the porch again—or if he did, I never saw him—but the boy I'd kissed grew larger and more amazing in my mind, dark, exotic, always smelling of his leather jacket. Christine listened to me enraptured, and it was only later that year, when Armand died, that I was able to remember that night without any sense of betraying him. Then I could talk about it, dwell on it, and even admit how beautiful I thought Armand was. And after a while my belief in his enchantment returned, and Adrienne Glass's water pitcher was restored, once more, to the realm of mysterious objects.

THE STORE

THERE WAS ONE place in Lawrence where no grown-up ever followed: This was a store at the end of a black gravel alley whose air was soft and quiet, like a library. This store, the only dark refuge in our bright Midwestern summer, had a sweet, stale smell that repelled grown-ups, and everything sensible, like soap, was on a dark, inaccessible shelf. Only the candies were lit, faintly, in the glass cases: There were bottles filled with green liquid, red wax lips that one could chew, and small dark babies, called by a name I'd been told never to say. There were sugar cigarettes and glass jars filled with hearts.

A man named Sabbey owned the store. As he was, in fact, very shabby, I gave some credulity to his name. I never talked when I came into his store: I pointed. Whatever I pointed to, Sabbey reached for with his long white hands and put in a paper bag. His eyes were watery, like a fish's, and his face was so long it didn't stop at his chin but faded into his neck below his tie. I paid him with my allowance.

Thank you, he would say, as though he were swallowing candy. His lips were moist.

Outside, in the sun, the candies were still illuminated. But their edges were defined, and so were their sharp, sweet tastes. The green liquid exploded in my mouth, and round bits of sugar clung to their white papers like barnacles. Alone, or with Christine Haag, I walked home feeling the grit of asphalt on my sneakers. The asphalt looked like broken coal and made us walk in a rhythm that matched our chewing.

One day an unthinkable event occurred: My mother went into Sabbey's store. It was late in the day, and she needed soap. While I stood in the door, wanting to hide, she entered it as she would any store— bustling, announcing herself in the dark.

Hello, Mr. Sabbey, she said. I would like to buy some soap.

Soap? said a voice from the back of the store.

Soap, said my mother.

A curious waiting silence. Sabbey shuffled from the back of the store, got a stepladder and a stick, and reached to an unknown cavern in the precarious dark. From it he retrieved a bar of soap.

Thank you, he said, swallowing to my mother. Thank you very much.

While we were walking home through the alley, I instructed my mother that no one called Sabbey Mr.

His name is Sabbey, I said.

Sabbey? said my mother. Why that's very rude. You should always call him Mr. Sabbey. That's his name.

That night at dinner, I thought about my mother going into Sabbey's store. The whole scene—viewed from a distance, as though I were in the movies—was extremely vivid. I saw my mother going into the store, standing in front of the sacred candies. And I heard her voice encircling him like a wreath. The next day, I took a dollar from her purse, went to Sabbey's store, and bought a whole jar of cinnamon hearts, which were absolutely forbidden. Sabbey handed me the jar—not knowing that he was an accomplice in crime—and suddenly he became mine again: fish-like, tall, with his watery way of saying things.

MY MOTHER'S VOICE

I DIDN'T TELL you to take off the hat in the store, my mother said quite loudly. I told you to put it in your pocket once we got inside. I knew you would take it off and lose it. But did you listen to me? No, you did not. And now you've lost your hat. She peered at me from the rows of vegetables and then went on, magnificent and launched. Kathy Montague listens to her mother. Molly Perone listens to her mother. Chickie Messick . . . Christine Haag . . .

The list went on. Names of various children were invoked. All these children listened.

But do you listen? No! You do not! You do not!

My mother wore long dangling earrings, bright red lipstick, and rouge kept in a crystal pot from her days at drama school—all of which enhanced her enormous nose, which communicated whatever her voice failed to convey. While she talked, her nose sniffed, snorted, and bobbed, and her small eyes blinked rapidly, as if overwhelmed by the nose, possibly propelled by it. In a moment the hat would be found, but the hat wasn't the point.

From the other side of the vegetable bin appeared the thin, unhappy face of Mr. Hummerford. Mr. Hummerford was from England and had impeccable manners, which meant, in this case, that he looked at us as though we were space aliens.

Is this the hat? he asked, pulling a blue beret with a crest of ice from some broccoli.

Why yes, my mother said. It is.

I think it fell out of your coat, said Mr. Hummerford.

He meant my mother's coat.

How is your wife? asked my mother, putting the hat in her shopping bag as though it were an onion.

Quite excellent, said Mr. Hummerford.

Give her my best, said my mother.

Mr. Hummerford wore glasses without sides and had never finished shingling his house or his store, both which he owned. But my mother owned Mr. Hummerford, and when we left, I was sure he would disappear—only to reappear when she said his name.

A very fine man! she said after we left. A most unusual man from England. She paused to peer in her shopping bag, saw the hat, and looked away. A very fine man but actually very peculiar, she continued. He will never finish shingling his house. We turned the corner, and her voice claimed a neighbor in an orange-red coat. Oh, Mrs. Grever! Mrs. Grever! A sale on beans today. Ten cents a pound. Green. You must go.

Mrs. Grever went.

Mr. Hummerford never did finish shingling his house, something that didn't surprise me—for what my mother's voice decreed often happened. At its black, strident command, Mr. Hummerford appeared, disappeared, my hat vanished, Mrs. Grever went off to buy beans, and my father wrote an entire book on the architecture of Italian Renaissance churches and owed that book to the extraordinary volume of her voice. According to my mother, he should have finished this book long before I was born, but instead he spent days in the bathroom playing solitaire: Savagely, restlessly, on weekends when he wasn't teaching, my father sat on the closed lid of the toilet seat and used the laundry hamper as a table. Everyone who passed could hear the slap-slap-slap of cards on the plastic hamper. Tiring of the sound of cards, my mother would periodically scream:

The book! The book! The goddamned book! When are you going to finish the book?

Silence would emanate from my father, an exquisite, waiting silence, the compressed silence of a desert. Soon he would emerge from the bathroom, go to his desk, and begin a frightened, staccato-like typing. One felt that her voice controlled a switch in his brain, turned on some hidden interior light, a light too bright, too cold, too white for one human being to sustain. Ignited by her voice, my father wrote his book in seven years.

TWO YEARS AFTER my father finished his book, my mother lost her voice. By virtue of sheer volume, she'd developed a polyp on one of her vocal cords and was condemned to surgery and silence. Who knew, the surgeon said, why a woman with such a quiet life would have an affliction common to circus barkers? My mother, too, drew a blank.

For six weeks, whatever my mother wanted to say would have to be conveyed through writing. To this purpose she purchased chalk and a slate. There were two virtues to this situation: First, it took her longer to write than to speak, so concision was forced upon her. Second, the house was silent.

HOWEVER, TWO DAYS after her surgery, I was summoned to the slate, where she wrote: *I do not feel comfortable using this goddamned thing with anyone but my family, I will not walk around the streets like a deaf-mute. You have to come with me to Marlowe's when I return these ripped stockings.*

I came with her to Marlowe's, walking through the flat streets piled with snow. My mother wrote a message about the stockings. I consulted the slate. And all the while the saleswoman looked on curiously. The ripped stockings were returned without a hitch. But on other days there were arguments: about a frozen chicken potpie, which my mother was trying to return because she claimed it had a dent in the crust. Or a pair of gloves she'd purchased with lipstick stains.

My mother says this chicken potpie had a dent in its crust. (Me, to Mr. Hummerford.)

Our pies are in perfect condition. (Mr. Hummerford.)

IT HAD A DENT. (From my mother, on the slate.)

My mother says the pie had a dent in it.

These episodes were mortifying. Not only because I was twelve and pretended, with the rest of my friends, that mothers didn't exist. And not only because the mother I had neither drove a car nor believed in God nor wore cloche hats and tiny earrings. They were mortifying because, in my own way and for my own reasons, I couldn't speak either and was terrified of being found out. It wasn't that my voice was gone, or that I couldn't think of what to say. It was that certain words wouldn't come out of my mouth, and speech was like walking through a minefield. This had begun to happen insidiously and was getting worse like a slow and terrible plague. I never knew what words I couldn't say: One day it would be words that started with *d*, another day words that started with *s*. Another day it would be my name, or a country we were studying in school. I had developed a lexicon of substitutes in my head,

so people couldn't guess what was going on (except when I had to intro-
duce myself, in which case I simply declined). But now, with my mother
writing things down and expecting me to repeat them, I was afraid it
would catch up with me.

She always changes what I say, my mother scribbled to my father. *She
never just says what I write.*

For Godssake, said my father—weakly, as if obligated to come to
my defense. She's doing you a favor.

Why do you always say my mother says? she continued (now writing at
me). *They already know it's me.* Her hooked nose came close, digging for
an answer.

It's just my way, I said.

Your way? she wrote.

Yes, I said. How could I tell her that if I disowned whatever I was
about to say, it was easier to say it.

AT THE END of our block, in an apartment so full of ferns it looked
like a rain forest, lived an elderly lady called Mrs. Dean, whose name I
could never utter. Her husband had once taught Greek on the Princeton
faculty, and it was never clear why she had come to a university town
in Kansas after her husband died. Mrs. Dean was unusually thin, her
face was lined like a palm, and her hands had big brown spots on them
as though she had been playing with grasshoppers. Her life was con-
siderably more orderly than my mother's, and this meant that during
the time that my mother had no voice, Mrs. Dean, unable to comprehend that my mother's infirmity affected her voice, not her feet, would
knock on the door at around five o'clock to ask if she wanted anything
from the store. Whenever she knocked, my mother would make me
speak for her.

My mother says hello, I'd always have to say. And also that she'd like you to come in. Mrs. Dean would then stand at the threshold considering. Sometimes she would decide not to come in, and then all I had to do was give her a shopping list. But more often she would say, Yes, I believe I will . . .

Our apartment stretched out like a snake from east to west. In the west was our living room, and here, so they could watch the sunset, Mrs. Dean and my mother always had "tea," even though my mother drank coffee and Mrs. Dean drank sherry. I would sit near my mother on a high stool, so I would be able to look over her shoulder and read whatever she wrote.

Mrs. Dean had a curious effect on me. In her presence, it became difficult to think of substitutes for words I couldn't say. It was as though her piercing eyes became lodged in my brain and made it almost impossible to look backwards inside myself. For this reason, whenever Mrs. Dean visited, my speech was characterized by long pauses while I pretended not to be able to read my mother's handwriting. Cat's got her tongue, hasn't it missy? Mrs. Dean would say, while my mother would erase the slate and begin to print. Eventually I would retrieve my secret lexicon. But I came to loathe her visits.

One day Mrs. Dean came over with an interesting piece of news. A neighbor boy named Larry Hegenberger had been operated on for appendicitis and now was in a coma at the hospital. The operation had gone without complications, and nobody had a clue as to what was wrong.

They are beside themselves, said Mrs. Dean, referring to Larry's parents. He has tubes stuck in every opening in his body. Believe me, every opening. While she talked, the wrinkles on her face creased and uncreased like a palm when it's being closed and opened. My mother leaned forward, and wrote, *Oh my!* on her magic slate. After I conveyed this, she then wrote, *What is the prognosis?*

Terrible, said Mrs Dean. Even with all those tubes it's touch and go.

I knew Larry Hegenberger. He was good-looking in a way that made me shy, and once he had stolen my eraser. It seemed horrible to me that while he was lying in the hospital, sick, with all those tube, these two women should be talking about him as though he were a freak. And the more they talked, the more the words my mother wrote became impossible to say, until finally she wrote a sentence that had nothing in it I could utter. There was no word in that sentence that didn't stick in my throat, and there were no words I could think of to substitute. So all three of us sat there in silence.

Cat got your tongue, missy? said Mrs. Dean. And at that moment, when she looked at me, her eyes bored a hole in my head. It was a strange hole in that it penetrated the very barrier she had previously created. There were no words at all inside, just a series of fiery shapes. And then suddenly a single sentence rose from my throat, unbidden.

I think it's terrible that you're talking about Larry like that, as though he's some kind of creature.

My mother gasped—fighting not to speak. And Mrs. Dean looked at me through her glasses like a grasshopper. The phrase old biddies flew into my head, but before it came out of my mouth, I left the room.

One day after visiting the doctor, my mother came home and said, I can talk now.

But what came from her mouth wasn't her voice: It was a croak, a sound a bird would make. Her face crumpled, and she started to cry.

My voice is gone, she whispered. My voice is goddamned shot.

With time, however, her voice returned—still a glorious instrument, able to stiffen clothes, command things from afar, and announce items of interest from newspapers (her nose pointed straight into it like a diver). It was the voice of gossip, the voice of daily speech, and a voice whose capacities far exceeded my powers. (A marvelous woman! A stunning opera cape!) Her amazement always heralded by disbelief (Can you imagine? I can't get over it, her eyes shuttering rapidly like a camera). And, as though a balance existed between the two of us, as my mother talked more, I talked less. Relieved of being her interpreter, I became encased in a world of silence so deep, it surrounded me like snow. And since it now turned out that there were more and more words I couldn't say, I began to find it convenient to claim that I'd lost my voice. Nobody seemed to notice or care that I had a permanent case of laryngitis. And as I sat in Mr. Bridge's Latin class, relieved of having to recite the dreadful words of Caesar, I would let my eyes rest on Larry Hegenberger, who had recovered from his coma and sat three seats ahead of me. Whenever I looked at him, I felt something very close to love—not just because he was handsome but because he was my last vital link with living speech. Sometimes he would smile at me, and always, I'd smile back.

DOOR INTO DARK

BATHS, MY MOTHER said. We must all go to a good hotel in Lawrence and get baths with decent towels. It was early evening, and we were leaving Kansas for good. A scion of Renaissance architecture had died, and my father had been offered a job in Vermont. The movers had come and gone. My parents' friends were drinking wine in an empty apartment.

Stay with us, a friend said. It's too late to leave. We'll have another party.

I can't sleep in other people's houses, my mother said. No. Really. I can never move my bowels. Everybody laughed. We should stop at the Willmore, she continued. They have the nicest rooms. That lady professor from France stayed, and she loved it.

I went to say good-bye to my room, imagining I felt nothing. I had been having what came close to an affair with a fifty-one-year-old doctor who was supposed to help me talk, recite again in Latin class. I couldn't call him to say good-bye, and none of my friends mattered to me. I looked at my plaid wallpaper, which I hated, and my mother leaned into the room. Are you ready? It was clear that we were leaving.

We left Lawrence, Kansas, at nine o'clock, the air still soft in early summer. There was a large round moon in the sky, a moon that didn't look real. My parents' friends gathered around the car expressing general disbelief that we were leaving at this hour. Come take a bath at our house! said Morla Horton, who wore long modern earrings she had baked in her own kiln. We'll leave you alone! You can use the bathroom in peace! My father shrugged. My mother said no. More expressions of disbelief. Kissing. Hugging. We drove through downtown Lawrence with barely a nod to the remote, white, porticoed Willmore Hotel, all lit up like the moon. My mother kept saying how we would stop, take baths, relax. Nearly two hours later, we reached the industrial steel town of Port Feyre, Kansas, and she realized that we hadn't stopped at the Willmore.

There are no vacancies, my mother announced as we drove through motels hidden in the yellow smoke of the steel mills.

This was true: Even though Port Feyre was a hellhole, the *No Vacancy* signs were lit like neon samplers. I thought we would all take baths, my mother said again.

My father agreed that there weren't any vacancies. He drove to a milkshake stand, got us milkshakes, looking awkward in his baggy suit. I knew Port Feyre well from other trips east: It was the denouement of my father's no-vacancy cliff-hangers—the town where we always realized that all the motels in Kansas were filled.

Baths, my mother said, sucking the straw of her milkshake. I said we should all take baths. With towels. In a lovely hotel. I said that.

My father didn't answer. The back of his neck bristled with the force of someone who intends drive all night.

Didn't you hear me? my mother said.

Yes, he said grudgingly, I heard you.

At the outskirts of town, my father picked up speed. He drove past fiery furnaces whose smoke obscured the moon. He drove past another motel with an orange *No Vacancy* sign. My mother rummaged in her purse, looked at her face in the mirror. Then she asked:

Who do the hell do you think I am? No, really. Who the hell do you think I am?

Silence from my father. She answered for him: I'm a middle-aged woman who needs my respite, that's who I am. For once we could have stopped at the Willmore and all had baths. After this lousy day. But no, not you! Drive on and on all night.

No motel was in sight. We were over the appointed edge, into the chill of being homeless. With sudden dispatch, my mother opened the door to her side of the car and announced, I'm getting out! I have nothing more to live for, and I'm getting out!

My father stepped on the brake slowly, reached over to close her door. They wrestled, he lost, my mother toyed with the door like an accordion. She opened it to the frontage road—houses, steel mills, apocalyptic smoke. Then she closed it, and Port Feyre disappeared. I said I had nothing to live for, too. My father told me to shut up.

My mother then shouted that she was really leaving and opened the door so wide I could see the whole Midwest—ordinary, frightening, far too real. My father ground to the side of the road, leaned over, closed the door, then picked up speed. We drove until morning, when we slept in the shelter of a truck stop. The night contained us, somehow.

COUNTRY BOY

I LEFT SOMETHING behind in Kansas—something dreadful, nameless, having to with Ivan Suronovsky, the fifty-one-year-old lay analyst who had ravished me and made me happy. In Vermont, Ivan Suronovsky seemed unreal. I could barely remember his office, or the picture of his wife, or his enormous glittering glasses, or his repertoire of clichés. He was part of the flat, paralyzed Midwestern landscape.

While I commenced a normal life—making friends, suddenly able to recite in class—my parents discussed Ivan in low voices. What had we really done, he and I? Who in hell did he think he was? Ivan had been my mother's analyst before he became mine, and I heard her tell my father she felt guilty for taking me to see him. My father was impatient: Nothing could be done, he said. Leave it alone, for God's sake.

One night in late autumn, my parents' voices rose in the living room.

What do you know about it anyway? my mother said. I was the one who saw him first!

I know quite enough, my father answered. Believe me. Quite enough! This answer made me tremble because one day, as if guided by radar, I'd walked to my father's closet, reached into the pocket of a certain suit jacket, and pulled out a page from my diary: *How interesting,* I'd written, *when a fifty-one-year-old man kisses a fourteen-year-old girl for a solid fifteen minutes and licks her legs like a puppy dog. . . .*

Not wanting to hear anymore, I put on my tall rubber boots and went outside. Vermont nights weren't like nights in the Midwest, where the dark was thin, equidistant, spread out against the horizon. Here the dark was dense, thick, complex, shaped by winding roads. I walked through this darkness down a road that wound all the way to the edge of town, where I found a small carnival setting up. I saw crates, animals in cages, stilts that looked like crutches. Near one booth, I saw a boy about my age with long hair tacking a roulette wheel to a piece of board. It was dark and had begun to rain, but his face loomed up at me, strangely light. *He's a country boy,* I thought, *someone different than me.*

I stood at a distance, watching him hammer. He noticed me and smiled. Hi there, he said.

Hi, I answered back.

Suddenly there was a sense of elevation in the air, some wild feeling of exhilaration, as though the carnival had already started. He left the booth, and we fell into step. You have to see something, he said, bringing me over to a cage. I looked inside and saw an animal that could have been a black domestic cat. This is a panther, he said, just a baby.

It looks just like a cat to me, I said. He threw back his head and laughed.

In Vermont I had acquired a respectable boyfriend—a boy who excelled in math, wore black sweaters, and carried an umbrella. I thought I saw him now from a distance—amused, abstracted, looking at another booth. Let's go for a walk, I said to the country boy.

We walked farther down the road, came upon a cluster of trees and a stone bench. I looked at the country boy, we both smiled, and then we sat down on the bench and kissed—a long, full kiss, pulling us close, making me remember Ivan. In that dark, I saw Ivan's small cluttered office, his desk, his artifacts from Russia: a leather-bound book from his childhood, a nesting doll in peasant clothes, a silver candlestick, a glass paperweight. . . . Things I could touch but never bring home.

I wanted to tell the country boy about Ivan, but instead I told him something that was only half-true, about going for a walk at two in the morning to an all-night diner and meeting a linguist from France. Only the part about the walk was true. The country boy listened, then kissed me again. When it was time to go, he said:

We should give each other something—for memory.

I thought for a moment, reached into my pocket, and gave him a pencil. He reached into his pocket and handed me a photograph of the panther. You'll see! he said, laughing. It isn't a cat at all! I took the picture and went home through the beribboned night.

My mother was reading in the living room. Where have you been? she asked.

At the carnival, at the edge of town.

What did you do there?

Nothing. Just wandered around.

For God's sake, she said. Hold yourself dear. If you don't, nobody else will.

She came into the kitchen, began fixing herself a sandwich—briskly, somewhat angrily. The unspoken name *Ivan* hung in the air between us. It was Russian, dark, connoting wolves, forests, ice maidens.

It's not that I begrudge you anything, my mother continued, slapping some mayonnaise onto the sandwich. But for God's sake, you must have some sense. She sat down and began to eat.

I pointed out that I did have sense, since coming to Vermont I had become miraculously normal, made friends, recited in class. What else did she want from me? She shook her head.

Suddenly there was a knock on the door. It was the country boy, dripping rain. You forgot something, he said, handing me the picture of the panther. You dropped this when you left.

I took the picture, held it to the light. No question. A baby panther. I grinned. He grinned back. From the kitchen, my mother gave me a stern look. The look, usually reserved for magazine salesmen, meant *get him out of here.*

The country boy showed no signs of leaving. My mother stood up.

Who are you? she said to him, in a low, theatrical voice.

Bill Baise, Ma'am. I'm with the carnival.

My mother looked at me fiercely, pulled the skin below her left eye. Another signal. It meant *this person is peculiar.* What business have you following my daughter home? she asked.

None, Ma'am. Just wanted to give her the picture.

He didn't move from the threshold. My mother walked over, and we all stood together. From where I was, I could see our kitchen shift slightly, become the dark, post–World War II European kitchen that used to invade our kitchen in the Midwest: flowered wallpaper, a yellow cast of light, a certain thick dimension to the furniture. My mother frowned.

Where are you from? she asked Bill Baise.

Florida. Near the Everglades. I went to school in Boston, but then I quit.

I don't believe you, said my mother. But she smiled at him.

When he left, she said to me, Who in God's name was that?

A country boy, I answered.

For heavens sake, don't dramatize! He was a hick.

I didn't argue. My mother returned to her sandwich. Suddenly she said, Ivan Suronovsky. That lousy charlatan!

I froze. She had not mentioned his name to me since we'd left Kansas. He wasn't all that bad, Mom.

Oh yes he was. He was awful. There was a mirror in the hall, visible from the kitchen, and my mother looked into it sharply. Outside it was raining hard, with sudden swells, pauses, as if the sky were opening to let more rain in. Such a pause occurred now, and the room seemed to expand. My mother hesitated. Then she said, You know I was seeing Ivan before you were. You knew that, didn't you?

Another swell. The house began to rock, unfurling into darkness. Yes, Mom. I knew, I said.

I thought he was a very sympathetic man. Very good to talk to. But then one day after you started seeing him, he said me, 'I can't see you and your daughter at the same time. It simply isn't done.' So what could I do? I stopped! A mother's sacrifice!

Mom, if you wanted to keep on seeing him . . .

No. I didn't. I got what I needed. Her voice was mildly ironic.

She didn't say what she'd needed, and I didn't ask. The house swelled again, accommodating our silence.

Goodnight, Mom, I said.

Goodnight, sweetie, she answered

A look passed between us—neither forgiveness nor understanding, simply a meeting of the eyes. I went to my room and thought about the country boy, walking back to the carnival, through that complex darkness.

Hearfelt thanks to:

Dan Smetanka - creative editor

Diana Finch - super-smart agent

Jack Shoemaker, Charlie Winton &
all the people at Counterpoint Press

David Young - poet and teacher

Karen Kevorkian & Dennis Phillips
-poets, fiction writers & fellow travelers

Kelly Winton - impeccable production manager

Barrett Baise - creative proofreader

Michele Hunevan - fiction writer and critic

And my beloved university: Sylvia Brownrigg, Harriet Chessman,
Ron Nyren , Elizabeth Rosner, and Sarah Stone.

Courtesy of Loic Nicolas

About the Author

THAISA FRANK IS the author of three previous collections of short fiction and the novel *Heidegger's Glasses,*which sold to ten foreign countries before publication. She is also the co-author of *Finding Your Writer's Voice: A Guide to Creative Fiction*. Her essays have been anthologized, and she contributed the Afterword to the Signet Classics edition of *Voltaire: Candide, Zadig and Selected Stories*. She is the recipient of two PEN awards, has been Visiting Associate Professor in the Honors program in Creative Writing at UC Berkeley and teaches writing in MFA programs in San Francisco. A native of the Bronx, NY, she lives in Berkeley, California. Her website is www.thaisafrank.com